Thomas Arthur Nash

The life of Richard lord Westbury, formerly lord high chancellor,

with selections from his correspondence

Vol. 2

Thomas Arthur Nash

The life of Richard lord Westbury, formerly lord high chancellor, with selections from his correspondence
Vol. 2

ISBN/EAN: 9783337157012

Printed in Europe, USA, Canada, Australia, Japan

Cover: Foto ©Raphael Reischuk / pixelio.de

More available books at **www.hansebooks.com**

THE LIFE

OF

RICHARD LORD WESTBURY

Formerly Lord High Chancellor

WITH SELECTIONS FROM HIS CORRESPONDENCE

BY

THOMAS ARTHUR NASH, B.A.

BARRISTER-AT-LAW

WITH TWO PORTRAITS

IN TWO VOLUMES—VOL. II

LONDON

RICHARD BENTLEY AND SON

Publishers in Ordinary to Her Majesty the Queen

1888

CONTENTS OF THE SECOND VOLUME

CHAPTER IV

1865

CHAPTER V

1865

CHAPTER VI

1865

CHAPTER VII

1866-1868

CHAPTER XII

LIFE OF LORD WESTBURY

CHAPTER I

1861–1862

Fresh Bankruptcy Bill—Letters to Lord Palmerston—Opposition in the Lords—Bethell becomes Lord Chancellor—His own views on his appointment—Bankruptcy Bill passes—Scheme of Church patronage—Responsibilities of office—Death of the Prince Consort—Land Transfer—Registration of Title Act—Causes of its failure—Judicial qualities and decisions.

SIR RICHARD BETHELL was now in his sixty-first year, and his powers had reached their full maturity. Though he sometimes spoke of retiring from public life, the sense of what was due to his party and of his own ability to carry into effect reforms which had been too long delayed prevented his taking such a final step. The crowning triumph of his career was near at hand.

He had strictly pledged himself to renew the attempt to amend the bankruptcy and insolvency law in the Session of 1861. Profiting by the experience of the previous year, he reluctantly abandoned the idea of consolidation, and framed an

amending measure of less ponderous dimensions
than its predecessor. The question had become
troublesome, and the Government determined to
bring it to a speedy settlement. We see from the
following letters how great was the pressure of Sir
Richard Bethell's official duties at this period :—

Hackwood, Jan. 27 [1861].

'Dear Lord Palmerston—I have had the honour of receiving
your Lordship's letter on the subject of my Bankruptcy Bill.

'I did not know that any section of the Cabinet had been
appointed to consider it. If I had, I should have been glad to
have discussed with them two or three subjects. It will not be
possible to send them a complete copy of the Bill until Monday,
the 3d February, as it will not be completely printed before that
time ; but that is immaterial, as although the Bill is entirely recast
and rearranged, its principal features remain the same as last year.

'I shall be happy to see any members of the Cabinet either
on Wednesday or Saturday, but as there are many books and
papers which it may be necessary to refer to, I hope they will do
me the favour to come to Lincoln's Inn at any hour convenient
to themselves. Your Lordship is pleased to add that the Cabinet
desire me to give notice of the Bill on the first day of the session,
and to bring in the Bill a few days afterwards. It was my intention so to do. But it would have been more acceptable to me
if this intimation from the Cabinet had been less mandatory in
its form of expression. The laborious duty I have undertaken
of bringing in measures of legal reform is a self-imposed voluntary
obligation, discharged at great personal sacrifices, and must not
be the subject of peremptory communications.

'In the hope that I may receive some satisfactory assurance
from your Lordship on this subject, I will remind you that there
is another measure hardly less important than the bankruptcy
reform, which has engaged much of my time, and in which I am
most anxious to have a meeting with your Lordship and the Chief
Commissioner of Works—I mean the Law Courts Concentration
Bill.

'I had hoped that this and the Bankruptcy Bill might have been brought in during the first week or ten days of the session.

'The Artistic Copyright Bill is another measure which has also engaged much of my attention, and I shall be glad of an opportunity of explaining it to you.—Believe me, yours faithfully,

RICHARD BETHELL.'

Lord Palmerston's reply has not been preserved, but it was of a nature to appease the Attorney-General's discontent, for two days later he wrote again :—

'*Lincoln's Inn, Jan.* 29, 1861.

'My dear Lord—Many thanks for your kind conciliatory letter. I have been unwell lately, and feel much the weight of the load on my shoulders, and I suppose that I had become more than usually irritable.

'Remember I have no one to help me, even by the application of a finger, for all these matters are out of the line of thought of the Solicitor-General,[1] and the Chancellor does nothing but tease me with constant exhortations to have *all* the Bills ready by the commencement of the session.[2]

'I am obliged too, personally, to do all the Government business that requires anything more than common attention. Forgive me, therefore, if I have been peevish. Remember I have been described by Gladstone as "a hewer of wood and drawer of water to the Cabinet" (*servus servorum*, "a servant of servants shall he

---

[1] Sir William Atherton, who had succeeded Sir Henry Keating on the appointment of the latter as Justice of the Common Pleas in December 1859, was of the common law bar.

[2] In Lord Campbell's diary, under the date December 23, 1860, is the entry :—' Mr. Attorney and I have hitherto gone on very amicably ; but, in spite of his magniloquent professions about the law reforms he is to bring forward next session, I have not yet been able to get from him a draft of any of his Bills, and I am afraid that when Parliament meets we may fall into disrepute and may be driven to disparage each other.'—*Life of Lord Campbell*, vol. ii. p. 387.

be "), and every paltry Chamber of Commerce in the country thinks itself at liberty to abuse me in the newspapers if I do not accord to its members the palm of absolute wisdom.

' *Satis superque de hoc.* I will come down to the Cabinet and bring the Bankruptcy Bill with me on Saturday, and will wait until you are at leisure to call me in. I will write to William Cowper and beg him to give me a meeting then, whilst the Cabinet is engaged on the Law Courts Bill.

' I have begged the Lord Chancellor to take on his shoulders the Land Transfer Bill, and introduce it in the Lords (which ought to be the course), and I have offered to explain it all to him, but " Jock is too canny," and so I must do it myself. As soon as the other Bills are well forward, I will bring it in.

' Of course it will be a great pleasure to me to dine with you on Monday.—Yours sincerely,   RICHARD BETHELL.'

The Bankruptcy Bill was very well received both by the legal and mercantile communities, and the Attorney-General, unassisted, took it through Committee at an almost unprecedented pace, his conciliatory tone and clear explanations doing much to recommend it to both sides of the House. In the Lords more difficulty was encountered. Lords Brougham, Cranworth, and Chelmsford were notoriously hostile to the measure as it stood, and Lord Campbell, single-handed, was no match for his opponents. It seemed only too likely that the Bill would again have to be abandoned. Sir Richard Bethell wrote to Lord Palmerston :—

' I have made such representation to the other side as to the determined course we would adopt if the Tory Lords attempted to do any material damage to the Bankruptcy Bill in their House, or to refer it to a Select Committee (that they may mutilate it without public responsibility), that I think you will find Lord Derby will not make any attempt of the kind. At least I was so assured on Friday by a leading member of their party.'

But the representation was ineffectual. The Bill was referred to a Select Committee, when official assignees were substituted for the creditors' assignees, and the provisions relating to the Chief Judge, which were the most valuable part of it, were struck out. The Bill came back sadly mutilated, much to the disgust of its projector, who made no concealment of his opinion that, in its altered shape, it was absolutely useless. Before, however, the Lords' amendments came to be considered in the House of Commons, the sudden death of Lord Campbell removed Sir Richard Bethell to the Upper House.

No one now questioned his right to receive the reward to which his distinguished public services and unrivalled position at the Equity bar plainly entitled him. On the 27th of June 1861 he received the Great Seal, and was raised to the peerage by the title of Baron Westbury, of Westbury, in the county of Wilts. He took his designation from the town nearest to Bradford, as he was precluded from assuming that of his native place. There was some fitness in connecting the name of Westbury with a legal peerage, for another distinguished lawyer, Sir William Blackstone, had been associated with the borough as its representative in Parliament a hundred years before.

Much curiosity was expressed as to the way in

which the eminent advocate would acquit himself in the exalted station of 'prime man of the State.' Uniting the highest qualifications of lawyer and jurist with the advantages of a considerable political experience, Lord Westbury had an excellent opportunity of associating his name with those great reforms of the law which he had already inaugurated, and the completion of which he considered essential to the establishment of a simple, uniform, and comprehensive system of jurisprudence. With respect to the discharge of his political duties as President of the House of Lords no very confident expectations were expressed. The permanent majority by which the Government were opposed in the Upper House made the position of the Chancellor one which demanded peculiar tact, good temper, and firmness.[1]

[1] The following formed the Cabinet on Lord Westbury's appointment :—

First Lord of the Treasury .	Viscount Palmerston.
Lord Chancellor . . .	Lord Westbury.
Lord President of the Council .	Earl Granville.
Lord Privy Seal . . .	Duke of Argyll.
Home Secretary . . .	Sir George Grey.
War Secretary	Sir George Cornewall Lewis.
Foreign Secretary . . .	Lord John Russell.
Indian Secretary . . .	Sir Charles Wood.
Chancellor of the Exchequer .	Mr. Gladstone.
First Lord of the Admiralty .	Duke of Somerset.
President of the Board of Trade .	Mr. Milner Gibson.
Postmaster-General . . .	Lord Stanley of Alderley.
Chief Commissioner of the } Poor Law Board } .	Mr. Villiers.
Chancellor of the Duchy of } Lancaster } .	Mr. Cardwell.

The predominant feeling of the Chancery bar was undoubtedly one of relief at the removal of the great leader. He had been in the full swing of practice for nearly forty years—such a practice as for duration and success, taken together, was unexampled. For almost twenty years he had enjoyed unquestionable supremacy, and at the time of his elevation to the woolsack his professional income very nearly approached £30,000 a year.

His own feelings on his appointment found some expression in a letter to a lady who was his oldest friend :—

'I well knew the pleasure that you would feel on hearing of my elevation to the dignity of Lord Chancellor of Great Britain. You remember my dear father's prophecies and the confidence with which he used to announce that his words would be fulfilled. You, my dear friend, were my earliest playmate, and will recollect the struggles and anxieties of early years. I shall be sure therefore that your good wishes will accompany me in my elevated position. It is indeed a place of great anxiety and responsibility,—to me especially, because much is expected of me. God grant me grace and strength to be useful in my generation.

'No doubt it is a noble thing to live in a country where industry and moderate ability can accomplish so much, and that without sacrificing one iota of manly independence. For from my youth up I have truckled to no man, sought no man's favour, but both at the Bar and in politics have been independent even to a fault.'

To another friend he wrote : 'The duties of my office are very onerous and extensive, and I regret to say that all useful measures now encounter so much factious and bigoted opposition, that I very

much doubt being able to be of much public
utility.'

Strange to say, even at the very time of
attaining this proud elevation, Lord Westbury's
mind turned to anticipations of rest and freedom
when he should have retired from public life.
'Everything,' he wrote to one of his sons-in-law,
'has been most gratifying to me since my accession
to office. The heap of congratulations and eulogies
is more than I ever supposed I should live to receive.' He added, 'I have taken a fancy to a house
in Hayling Island—Lennox Lodge. It is to be had
very cheaply, and as soon as I am out of office it
would suit me for yachting excellently well. . . . You
know I hate a crowd and a multitude of people,
and deserted Hayling seems to be the only place
to ensure retirement.'

Sir William Atherton succeeded to the post of
Attorney-General, and Sir Roundell Palmer became
Solicitor-General. There was some idea of promoting Palmer to the higher office, and leaving Atherton, whose powers were of a more superficial kind,
in his former place. It was said that some one re-
monstrated with the Lord Chancellor on this subject: 'Surely, you are not going to put Palmer over
Atherton's head;' a remark which drew from Lord
Westbury the characteristic rejoinder: 'Certainly
not; I never attempt impossibilities. I did not
know that Atherton had a head.' For Sir Roundell
Palmer's ability as an advocate Lord Westbury

entertained the greatest admiration : he observed
on one occasion : ' If Palmer could get rid of the
habit of pursuing a fine train of reasoning on a
matter collateral to the main route of his argument,
he would be perfect.'

The Chancellor's first speech from the woolsack
was delivered in circumstances of some perplexity.
The House of Commons had disagreed to the serious
alterations made by the Lords in the Bankruptcy
Bill, and when their amendments came on for consideration at the end of July, Lord Westbury was in
this dilemma : either he must place himself in antagonism to the majority of the peers, or surrender
what in the other House he had declared to be some
of the most valuable provisions of his own Bill.
With his usual self-confidence he chose the former
alternative, but the tone of his address was ill
designed to induce the peers to abandon their
position. After drawing a sarcastic contrast between
the proceedings of the two Houses with regard to
the measure, he insinuated that the alterations which
had been made in it were due to party motives rather
than regard for the administration of justice. This
line of observation was interrupted by cries of
dissent, and elicited from Lord Chelmsford a warm
disclaimer on behalf of the Opposition. In his reply
the Chancellor, fairly roused, displayed more temper
than discretion. He lectured Lord Cranworth on
his want of apprehension, and ironically expressed
satisfaction at making the discovery how the Select

Committee had arrived at their conclusions : ' If they had no further information before them as to the contents of the Bill than the knowledge of the subject, and of the subject of bankruptcy generally, which has been exhibited by my two noble and learned friends, I have no right to be at all surprised at that conclusion ; and when I consider the irresistible effect of the witticisms with which their lucubrations ended, I may assume that in the Committee *solvuntur tabulæ risu,* and so the Chief Judge was dismissed.'

The peers were unused to this kind of language, though probably, if Lord Westbury had been more conciliatory, the result might have been the same. They adhered to their amendment relating to the Chief Judge, but waived the others.   Mutilated as it was, the Bill seemed too valuable to be lost.   At that late period of the Session it was useless to prolong the struggle; accordingly the Lords' amendment was accepted by the Government and the Bill passed.   Lord Cranworth's dogged opposition to the reform on which the Chancellor was intent had been the chief source of his irritation.[1]

Lord Westbury always objected to the Act

---

[1] ' We happen to know from the lips of the late Lord Westbury that, in his opinion, Lord Cranworth had the unhappy knack of making such proposals for their amendment as would entirely defeat some of Lord Westbury's most masterly measures.   He particularly expressed to the writer this opinion with reference to the plans for reforming the Court of Bankruptcy and for effecting a digest of the law.'—*Law Magazine,* 1873, vol. ii. p. 724.

. being called by his name, and compared it to a
watch from which the mainspring had been taken.
A few months later he declared that for every hydra
head of abuse which he hoped to have destroyed,
seven new ones had arisen, and that he despaired of
seeing the bankruptcy business properly conducted
until there was an efficient official superintendence.[1]
The alterations which had been introduced during
its discussion made the provisions of the Act inconsistent and unworkable.

As soon as Parliament was prorogued the Chancellor turned his attention to the question of his
Church patronage, and wrote to explain to Dr.
Jeune the scheme which he had formed for its
improvement :—

'Weymouth, Aug. 19, 1861.

'My dear Vice-Chancellor—I enclose you a letter just received. I wish I had more Christian charity. Being abused I
think hardens the heart.

'I am devising a great scheme, so at least I think it. No
doubt it will be attributed to the worst motives. You know, as
Chancellor, I am patron of about 150 livings, each under £150
per annum. My great desire is to augment them. Very many
wealthy persons in the country would, I am assured, be glad to
buy them on the following terms :—I propose to get an Act of
Parliament enabling me to transfer the advowson of any living
not exceeding £150 per annum to any person gratuitously on his
engaging at once to augment the income by one-third, and on the
church becoming vacant, to add as augmentation another third,
in each case a proper investment being made. Thus if the
living of A is worth £100 per annum, and is held by Parson B,

---

[1] This superintendence has been provided by Mr. Chamber
lain's Act of 1883.

aged fifty, I transfer the advowson out and out to Squire C,
who at once increases the £100 by £33 per annum, and on the
death of Parson B makes the living worth £166 per annum,
the advowson being Squire C's property.

'I put the terms low, as I think, to secure purchasers. Do
you think it will succeed? If it does, I shall have done more for
the Church in one year than certain Commissioners have done in
twenty. Give me your opinion, but you must not mention it, as
the Queen's consent must be obtained.—Yours sincerely,

WESTBURY.'

In reply, Dr. Jeune made the following observations :—

'Now as to your great plan, great like all your plans. You
will be met with the objection that the only means of keeping up
the influence of Government, and so of public or lay opinion on
the Church of England, and of preserving it from the hierarchical
spirit, which in this country would be fatal to it, is to keep patronage in the hands of the Crown ; that the higher patronage is not
sufficient for this, and the patronage of benefices is too scanty
already ; that if you diminish it you will have again the deplorable
spectacle of the last century when the bishops thought one way
and the clergy another ; the result being that episcopal power,
which is really one of opinion and paternal influence, wholly died
away, and the result was a dead Church. You will be told too
that the Ecclesiastical Commissioners will in due time augment
all the small livings in Crown patronage.

'These arguments do not prevail with me. I think that one
of the securities of the Church is the vast amount of individual
and lay interest connected with it, and that your proposed extension of private patronage would, take it for all in all, be bene-
ficial. But I would not *fix a price* for the benefices—or, at least,
only a *minimum ;* I would give away the advowson (*even during
a vacancy*) to *the best bidders.* Some livings there are greatly
coveted for their position or their power; some for the consequence
which the patronage would confer on a neighbouring country
gentleman. Some would be contended for, though of little value,

in towns between rival schools. Some might be endowed highly
in order to keep in a favourite curate as incumbent. . . .

'Bad motives will doubtless be attributed to you, if ingenuity
can devise them; but I do not see how your scheme can appear
otherwise than as a large and generous one.

'But, my dear Lord Chancellor, you must pay the penalties
of greatness. *Macte virtute istâ.* Do not become weary of man's
ingratitude. You remember the fine lines of Horace—

> '" Invidiam placare paras, virtute relictâ ?
>   Contemnere miser."

'Your conscience, your thoughts of posterity, your very success
must support you.

'Yet lying and misrepresentation are hard to bear. . . .'

In the autumn of this year the new library of
the Middle Temple, of which Mr. Abraham, Lord
Westbury's brother-in-law, was the architect, was
opened by the Prince of Wales, who was then called
to the bar and made a bencher of the Society. Lord
Westbury hoped that the honour of knighthood
might be conferred on the treasurer in connection
with this ceremony, and wrote to Lord Palmerston
to make the suggestion :—

'Being myself a member of the Middle Temple, I am not fit
to judge whether any such request should be made to the Sovereign. Honours were conferred by Queen Elizabeth when she was
entertained in the Hall of the Middle Temple. There is therefore, as lawyers say, an abundance of authority to warrant the
hope that a similar course will be adopted on the present
occasion.

'I have been for some time constantly occupied by the
numerous arrangements necessary for the proper working of the
new jurisdiction in bankruptcy, but I am anxious to see you on
two important subjects : one is the building of the new Law

Courts, which I beg of you to take into your own hand, or to give it into mine; without some such control nothing will be done. The other subject is the recent decision of the American Courts condemning British subjects for breach of blockade, which requires immediate attention.'

In reply Lord Palmerston informed the Chancellor that 'honours are not conferred when the Sovereign is not present, and not always when the Sovereign is present.'

Lord Westbury's attachment to his own Inn received a pleasing tribute in the request of the benchers that he would sit for his portrait, to be added to the possessions of the Society. 'I speak with great truth,' he wrote to the treasurer,[1] 'when I tell you that I never felt so proud of being Lord Chancellor before. There is no distinction, no mark of honour, I could receive that would give me more sincere pleasure than this compliment which I have received at your hands.'

The year 1861 closed amid profound gloom. The untimely death of the Prince Consort cast a deep shadow over the land, and the apprehensions caused by the Civil War in America were greatly increased by the affair of the Trent, which threatened a rupture with the Federal Government. On the 15th of December Lord Westbury wrote: 'How sad a thing is the death of the poor Prince Consort! He died last night at ten minutes before eleven. The Queen is, or rather was before the event, more collected than could have been supposed, but I dread

[1] The late Mr. James Anderson, Q.C.

the consequences. It is a most inauspicious event, and at a most unfortunate time. A bad and gloomy year is before us. God send light to break through the darkness. My visit to Windsor now will be a very different one from what I expected.'

His personal knowledge of the Prince Consort gave him a true appreciation of the irreparable loss which the country had sustained. The system of educational training adopted for the children of the Royal family received his hearty approval, and he had the highest opinion of their intellectual powers, particularly in the case of the late Princess Alice. On his visits to Windsor or Osborne he conversed with the Princess several times on classical subjects, and used afterwards to speak of her character and abilities with enthusiastic admiration, and declare that she could have taken any university degree with a little study.

During this season of mourning and anxiety Lord Palmerston was confined to his house with a violent attack of gout, and in the excited state of the public mind a rumour that his illness had proved fatal readily obtained credit. Lord Westbury wrote to him :—

'*Belgrave Square, Dec.* 19 [1861].

'My dear Lord—There used to be a game at cards when I was a boy at which the cry was "Pam's alive," and I am thankful to find that we can cry that cry and win at that game. I wish I could have the perpetrators of the abominable falsehood of yesterday publicly whipped. The report reached my Court and so alarmed me that I hastened up to Cambridge House, though I did not think it right to disturb you. Poor Lady Westbury

nearly fainted in a shop where she heard the report. . . .—Ever
yours sincerely,   WESTBURY.'

The Chancellor was now preparing himself for
the vigorous prosecution of the most difficult of his
projected law reforms.   On the 10th of January he
writes to one of his daughters :—

'My anxiety and sense of responsibility are certainly greater
in my present office than when Attorney-General, and I cannot
say the labour is much less.   This morning I lit my fire before
the clock struck five.   I wish you could induce M—— to get up
and read in the morning very early; reading by candle-light in
the morning is much less trying and injurious to the eyes than
at night.   The organ is stronger after the night's rest, and three
hours in the morning are equal to five at night.   No man has
injured his health by getting up early, but many by sitting up
late at night.'

As soon as Parliament met, he presented a
measure for facilitating the proof of title and the
transfer of land.   Almost every occupant of the
woolsack during the previous thirty years had
undertaken to cheapen and simplify transfer and
give greater security of title by a system of registration ; and the undertaking had baffled them all, as it
has hitherto baffled their successors.   It might have
been supposed that a subject hedged round with the
difficulties arising from the intricate system of tenures
which has grown up in this country would have
belonged exclusively to real property lawyers ; but,
strange to say, the Chancellors promoted from the
common law bar have displayed an equal readiness
to take it in hand.   Lord Campbell in 1851 intro-

duced a Registration Bill which, he declared, with a
happy innocence, ' is likely to pass, and ought to
immortalise me.'[1]   It was well for Lord Campbell
that his hope of immortality rested on a surer basis.
His Bill, which was for the registration of deeds,
not of title, did little more than extend the objectionable system of the Middlesex Registry to the
whole country.   The opposition of the profession
was so strong that the Bill, after passing through
the House of Lords, was dropped in the Commons.
Lord Campbell told the peers, in his chagrin, that
'there was an estate in the realm more powerful
than either their lordships or the other House of
Parliament, and that was the country solicitors ; and
it behoved their lordships to beware of it.'

Animated with the same prospect of fame,
Lord St. Leonards, Lord Cranworth, and Lord
Chelmsford now presented measures of their own
with similar objects.   No less than six Landed
Estates Bills lay on the table of the House at the
same time.   *Sic itur ad astra !*

For the existing system of conveyancing Lord
Westbury had always expressed the heartiest contempt and dislike.   He was reported, with some
show of probability, to have said that when he came
to deal with the question of the transfer of real property, he would make the position of a conveyancer
such that he should not be able to earn his salt.
He was too fond of a short cut through everything,

[1] *Life of Lord Campbell*, vol. ii. p. 292.

and, it must be added, too confident in his own more
excellent way of doing things, to look with any
veneration on a system which rested on mouldy
precedents, and found exposition in obscure forms
and endless tautology.   His own conveyancing was
generally done on a sheet of notepaper ; settlements,
wills, and agreements were alike concisely framed
in clear, untechnical language ; the appointment of
executors he held to be a useless testamentary
provision, and an attestation clause wholly superfluous.

He always advocated the registration of estates
and titles, not of deeds.   The objects which he
proposed to accomplish by the Act of 1862 were,
first, to ascertain whether there was a good title ;
then to place the estate by precise description on
the register, and separately record the existing
position of the 'title ; next, to preserve by entry in
the register evidence of the subsequent dealings
with the property ; and finally, to provide a simple
means of transfer.   The register was to consist of
two parts—one a register of estates with indefeasible
titles, guaranteed to be valid and marketable, the
other of titles not so guaranteed, but registered by
owners proving undisturbed possession for a period
of ten years, with the view to such possessory titles
ripening into an indefeasible ownership by a further
period of possession.   There were also to be a
record of title and a separate register of incum-
brances.   The record was to give a *précis* of the

estates, powers, and interests in the land, so that the register might be, to adopt his own expression, ' a perfect mirror of the existing ownership.'

' I want,' he said, ' to construct a legal instrument that shall not only enable a man to obtain a statutory title at the present time, but which shall enable him to give from time to time entries of the results of all future dealings and transactions with the land ; so that the owner of the estate may at any time send to the registry, and if he wanted to sell might obtain a special certificate of title. He can then go into the market with that certificate, and a purchaser may safely deal with the estate, the simple certificate obviating the necessity for the difficult and cumbrous and expensive investigations that are now required.'

A minor provision, to which Lord Westbury attached much importance, was that all future deeds should be printed, to get rid of what he designated 'the tyranny of parchment.' The Bill differed materially from Sir Hugh Cairns's measure of 1858, which had proposed to create a new Court, and to put upon the record a nominal possessor with a system of caveats to provide for the real ownership. It was intended to make registration compulsory.

The several competing Bills were sent to a Select Committee, and the Chancellor's Bill, slightly amended, was accepted by the House and read a third time almost without opposition. Lord St. Leonards alone expressed his disapproval of it. The objections he took were that the Bill was in disguise a Bill for the registration of assurances, that it would wantonly expose private affairs, and lead to much litigation, trouble, and expense, without corresponding advantage. As for preserving the chain of title on the register, the necessary entries, he said, would be so incessant, and the consequences of neglecting them so fatal, that, instead of the land-owner receiving the visits of his medical man every morning to feel his pulse, and ask him two or three questions, he would stand much more in need of a daily visit from his attorney, to see if anything had happened on the previous day that ought to be put upon the register. In the House of Commons Sir Roundell Palmer took charge of the Bill, and after some slight objection from the legal members of the Opposition, who naturally expressed a preference for Sir Hugh Cairns's measure, it became law. Lord Westbury's opinion of its value is shown by his letter to the Prime Minister :—

'*Hackwood, Oct.* 9, 1862.

'My dear Lord—I have the pleasure of sending you a copy of the orders I have made under Registration of Title Act. The system comes into full operation on the 15th October inst.

'On my first introduction into Parliament in 1851, I stated at the hustings that I hoped to make land and freehold estates as easily transferable as consols. This was laughed at as a fond conceit. But I am happy to say it *has been* effected. You will see by the orders and scale of fees that as soon as any land has been put upon the registry, it may (with the exception of the stamp duty payable to Government) be transferred on sale, mort-gage, or settlement, as quickly and cheaply as an amount of stock of equal value.

'And the rules I have made, with the assistance given to proprietors by the office, will render it more easy and economical for a landowner to prove his title and put it on the registry, than it would be for him if he has contracted to sell a farm or estate to make out his title to the satisfaction of the purchaser according to the present state of the law and practice.

'No landowner will in future (if he is rightly advised) bring any estate for sale into the market until he has first put his title on the registry.

'When registered, his estate will be worth much more in the market, and he can name an early day for completion of the purchase, secure that his receipt of the purchase-money cannot be delayed by any requisition of title or difficulty in settling a conveyance.

'The purchaser too will have no anxiety, he will be under no necessity of employing any attorney or incurring any expenditure beyond his purchase-money and the small charge of transfer (not exceeding what he would pay to a broker on an investment of the same sum in consols), and he will know with certainty the day on which he can take possession with perfect security.

'It is quite true, therefore, that the occupation of the attorney will be in great measure gone. Hence "the wailing and gnashing of teeth" which you have heard, and the unmeasured abuse of your Lord Chancellor.

'There will be great opposition to the system and an attempt to obscure it by a cloud of falsehoods and misrepresentations, but it will notwithstanding win its way.

'In fact it will appear hereafter to be so plain and obvious a thing that people will hardly believe there would be any difficulty in the introduction of it.'

In reply Lord Palmerston wrote, 'It must be a source of great satisfaction to you that your name will be connected with all the important law reforms and improvements which have rendered the last few years so remarkable an era in legal arrangements.'

Lord Westbury undoubtedly attached more value to the Registration Act than to all the other legal reforms in which he was interested, and was convinced of its perfect success. Never were

sanguine predictions more completely falsified by
the result. The attempt to change the existing
practice of transfer proved almost entirely abortive,
and conveyancers, like other men threatened by
legislation, have survived the author of the Act
which was to decree their extinction. This failure
was due partly to a radical defect in the scheme
itself, and partly to the over-elaborated machinery
constructed to work it. The scheme attempted
too much in combining a register with a record
of title. The very simplicity and certainty which
are the first essentials of registration were lost in
the endeavour to add an analysis of the title, however doubtful or obscure it might be.

Another cause of its non-success was the hostility
or apathy with which the profession regarded it. Acting on legal advice, the landowners showed a reluctance to avail themselves of the Act, which from the
first deprived it of much of its utility. It was soon
discovered that the trouble and cost of registration
were in most cases greater than the advantages
derived from it. If the title was free from suspicion, there was little use in putting it on the register ;
if open to doubt or objection, the effect of the application might be to stir dormant claims and expose
flaws which, on a transfer of the property, could
have been covered by special stipulation. Moreover, the necessity of determining the identity of
the property, which is the *crux* of many a title,
brought prospects of litigation with neighbouring

owners over boundaries, as no provision was made
for a general map, the cost of which was variously
estimated at one or two millions sterling. Lord St.
Leonards declared that the remedy which the Act
provided reminded him of the Italian epitaph :
' I was well, wished to be better, took physic,
and died.'

It is probable that the measure might have succeeded better if, as Lord Westbury desired, it had
been accompanied by a change in the mode of
solicitors' remuneration, and provision had been
made for a system of mutual insurance. Whatever
the cause, some five hundred titles only were registered during the first five years, and subsequently
the number greatly decreased, so that the Act had
become almost a dead letter when it was superseded
by Lord Cairns's Act of 1875, which in its turn met
with an even smaller measure of success.

Lord Westbury was slow to recognise the failure
of the scheme upon which he had expended so much
thought and labour. Writing to Lord Palmerston
nearly three years later, he says :—

' I really think (thanks in very great measure to Delane [1]) that
my Land Registry Act will soon be very generally adopted. The
benefit to every landowner (taking them on an average) will be
at least double their income tax, so that when they come again
for a reduction of the malt tax Gladstone will have nothing to do
but send them to my Land Registry, if they want relief from their
burthens.'

---

[1] The *Times*, of which Mr. Delane was then editor, constantly
expressed approval of the Act.

At a subsequent date, when taunted by Lord Chelmsford in the House of Lords with the comparative failure of the Act, Lord Westbury himself referred it partly to the refusal by Parliament to make registration compulsory, as he had wished, and partly to the system of remuneration under which solicitors, instead of receiving an *ad valorem* payment, regulated by the amount of the purchase-money, were rewarded for prolixity and fined for brevity, so that it was opposed to their interest to support the new system of conveyance.[1] The result had been that all sorts of legal hobgoblins had been conjured up to deter the lawyer-ridden landowner from putting his title upon the register. The success of the measure would, he admitted, be gradual, but its failure was impossible. ' I have had the good fortune,' he said, ' to assist in the passing of some measures of reform, and of originating others ; but if there is one measure on which I could put my finger with the hope of being hereafter remembered, it will undoubtedly be this Act, when its utility and the relief which it is calculated to give to the owners of landed property shall have been fully developed.'[2]

[1] This obstacle to registration has been removed by the Orders and Rules under the Solicitors' Remuneration Act, 1881.

[2] The Commission appointed in 1868 to inquire into the operation of the Act reported that the causes of its failure, in addition to the delay, trouble, and expense of registering, were the fear of litigation during the process, and the sense that a registration of all interests would neither protect owners nor facilitate transfers, but prove a hindrance and burden. Of this

Dis aliter visum. That land transfer by means
of registration is feasible is however shown by the
success of the system which has been established
in Prussia for upwards of fifteen years, to say nothing of that introduced by Sir Robert Torrens into
the Australian colonies, and based on the principle
of the registration of British shipping. The failure
of the Acts of 1862 and 1875 has, by calling attention to the exigencies of the law of real property,
afforded a strong argument in favour of simplifying
titles before compelling registration.

Any very elaborate observations on the judicial
capacity of Lord Westbury would possess little
interest for the general reader, and for members of
the profession they are hardly necessary. It may
suffice to say that his decisions reflected the peculiar
vigour of his mind, and were marked by a complete
individuality. His profound experience of the doctrines and practice of the Courts of Equity made
him independent of the assistance of the Lords
Justices, which some of his immediate predecessors
had found indispensable. On the first day of his
taking his seat on the bench, an application was
made to set down an appeal before the full Court.
'The case,' said Lord Westbury, 'will be put into
the Lord Chancellor's list. The Court *is* full.'

Impatient of the authority of cases, he preferred,
like Lord Hardwicke, to ground his decisions on

Commission Lord Westbury was a member, but he took no part
in its proceedings, and did not sign the Report.

elementary principles, and perhaps took rather too
arbitrary a view, when we consider how much
attention must be paid by the legal adviser to
the unwritten legislation of judges. 'Notwithstanding the elaborate and ingenious arguments,'
he would say, 'this case is clearly governed by
rules which have been very long established ;' or,
'this appeal certainly does not stand upon any other
ground than one of purely technical reasoning, and
has no merit in point of justice or in point of
equity.' Thus in the leading case of *Holroyd* v.
Marshall,[1] which determined the effect in equity of
a mere contract as amounting to an alienation of
property, he brushed aside the decision of Lord
Campbell with the observation, 'The question may
be easily decided by the application of a few elementary principles long settled in Courts of Equity.'
The case had been twice argued, through a difference
of opinion among the law lords, but Lord Westbury's
masterly judgment changed the opinion which Lord
Wensleydale had formed on the previous hearing,
and secured unanimity of decision. Several similar
instances of the independence of his judicial character
might be cited.

The case of *Gann* v. *Free Fishers of Whitstable*[2]
affords a striking illustration of his disregard of

---

[1] 10 House of Lords Cases, 191. If judgment had been
given after the first argument in Lord Campbell's lifetime, the
appeal would have failed instead of succeeding.

[2] 11 House of Lords Cases, 192.

precedents to which he was not absolutely bound to
defer.   On all such occasions 'his own opinion was
his law.'   The action was brought to try the right
claimed by the Company of Free Fishers to levy a
toll of one shilling for every vessel casting anchor
within the limits of their oyster beds.   The payment
had been made from time immemorial in respect of
the land covered by the sea, which the Company
were entitled to under a grant from the Crown.
The Court of Common Pleas and the Exchequer
Chamber, comprising in all eight or nine judges,
held unanimously that the plaintiffs were entitled to
the payment, but, on appeal to the House of Lords,
the Lord Chancellor, and Lords Wensleydale and
Chelmsford reversed the decision.   In moving the
judgment of the House Lord Westbury said :—

'The case appears to me to depend on principles which
have long been settled.   The bed of all navigable rivers where
the tide flows and reflows, and of all estuaries and arms of the
sea, is by law vested in the Crown.   But this ownership of the
Crown is for the benefit of the subject, and cannot be used in
any manner so as to derogate from or interfere with the right of
navigation, which belongs by law to the subjects of the realm.
The right to anchor is a necessary part of the right of navigation,
because it is essential to the full enjoyment of that right.   If the
Crown, therefore, grants part of the bed or soil of an estuary or
navigable river, the grantee takes subject to the public right, and
he cannot, in respect of his ownership of the soil, make any
claim or demand, even if it be expressly granted to him, which
in any way interferes with the enjoyment of the public right. . . .
Anterior to Magna Charta, by which such grants were prohibited, a several fishery, in an arm of the sea or navigable river,
might have been granted by the Crown to a subject.   The

present fishery of the respondents must be taken to have been so granted. And the grant might include a portion of the soil for the purpose of the fishery. But this, like every other grant, whenever made, must have been subject to the public right of navigation ; and I cannot suppose that the establishment of oyster beds for the private emolument of the proprietors could be regarded by the law as an equivalent to the public for the imposition of this tax (at its commencement not inconsiderable) on the right of navigation.'

In another case in the House of Lords[1] Lord Westbury, in dissenting from the judgment of his two colleagues, drew attention very forcibly to one of the anomalies of our judicial institutions. The Court of Queen's Bench, consisting of four judges, unanimously gave judgment in favour of the plaintiff. The case was taken on error to the Exchequer Chamber, where four of the judges were for reversing, and two for affirming the judgment below, the majority overruling by their decision two similar cases previously decided, so that in effect the opinions of six judges prevailed over the opinions of ten or twelve. 'It is a striking example,' said Lord Westbury, 'of the uncertainty of the law which rests on judicial decisions.'

The case was a simple one. The plaintiff was the occupier of a public-house situate in a thoroughfare. In the course of making their railway the Company obstructed the access to his premises, whereby he sustained temporary damages to his

[1] *Ricket* v. *Metropolitan Railway Company*, 2 English and Irish Appeals, 175.

business. Lords Chelmsford and Cranworth held that the plaintiff was not entitled under the Lands Clauses and Railway Clauses Acts to recover compensation for this injury. Lord Westbury, on the other hand, expressed an emphatic opinion that, though the plaintiff might not have had a right of action at common law, there was no warrant for the position that he should have no compensation for an injury occasioned by the act of a company done in exercise of statutory powers. Loss of custom was damage to the business premises, which were, therefore, 'injuriously affected' within the Acts. His views on the question were perhaps more approved at the time than those of the other judges.

In cases of ancient lights and other prescriptive easements Lord Westbury delivered some masterly judgments. And he was entitled to the credit of removing the last of the anomalous restrictions which limited the right of a married woman to dispose of every species of her equitable separate estate. He was at his best when the case fell outside the ambit of well-settled authority, to which indeed he was not always, as we have seen, very deferential.

His contempt for Lord Campbell's equity decisions once placed him in a somewhat ridiculous position. During the argument of an appeal,[1]

---

[1] *Ex parte Potter*, 3 De Gex, Jones and Smith's Reports, 240.

which raised the question whether an unstamped
deed of assignment for the benefit of creditors was
admissible evidence of an act of bankruptcy, a case
was inadvertently cited as a decision by Lord
Campbell.   Lord Westbury in delivering judgment
said that he was not satisfied as to the correctness
of the opinion which had been cited, and he should
require considerable argument before he should be
prepared to support it.   When it afterwards turned
out that the decision, thus impugned, was one of his
own, there was a hearty laugh at his expense.[1]
The earlier decision was afterwards held to be the
better law.

On the whole, it may be said that Lord Westbury's vigorous grasp of facts, and the readiness
with which he tore the heart out of a case, stripped
it of its technicalities and irrelevancies, and brought
it to the test of scientific principle, made him a very
strong judge.   Broom's *Treatise on Legal Maxims*
is a storehouse of clear and concise definitions by
Lord Westbury of such principles.   He regarded
law rather as an elevated science than an ingenious
collection of a mass of enactments and cases.   His
ambition was to build up a great philosophical structure, resting on the foundations of principles derived
from the civil law, and from which all excrescences
of superfluous precedent would be discarded.   Com-

---

[1] 'Lord Westbury,' said *Punch*, 'is always understood to
consider one person at least as infallible.   If that infallibility is
divided against itself, what *are* the Courts of Equity to believe in?'

paratively few of his decisions have been disturbed
or questioned.

During the four years of his Chancellorship a
difference of opinion among the law lords was of
rare occurrence. The resolute logic of his reasoning,
the force and felicity of his illustrations, and what
Mr. Frederic Harrison has well called his 'genius for
clear-cut phrases,' made his judgments models of the
judicial style. Critically examined as expositions of
the law, they may, perhaps, be regarded as occasionally erring on the side of overmuch ingenuity. When
right, Lord Westbury was splendidly right; but he
was rather apt to be led away by some brilliant
fancy.

Though he held it to be the duty of a judge, as
trustee of the time of the public, to prevent counsel
from talking nonsense, his patience and courtesy
were generally acknowledged by those who appeared
before him. No one would acknowledge with more
genial grace than he that the argument of counsel
had had some effect in forming his opinion. Occasionally the tedious irrelevance of an address provoked a flash of satire, as when at the conclusion
of a long argument he said : ' There are only two
objections to the elaborate argument of the learned
counsel. It supports a principle of equity that has
never been disputed and is indisputable ; and it is
utterly irrelevant to the application he has made.'
He liked to tell the story of a learned lord who was
in the habit of sitting in the evening in the Court of

Chancery, and now and then nodded. Somebody asked, ' How came you to do so ? '—' Why,' he said, ' it mattered not ; for when I awoke I always found the counsel at the same point where I left him when I went to sleep.'

This story recalls another, which may be given here, though it belongs to an earlier period, when Lord Westbury was at the bar.   He was engaged in an ecclesiastical appeal which had lasted several days.   The   case   involved   some   very   abstruse technical questions, with which the spiritual lords who were members of the Judicial Committee were obviously unfamiliar.   Coming into the robing-room at the conclusion of his argument, the Attorney-General said to his junior : ' Did you observe the dear Bishop ?   On the former argument he slept only on one side ; but this time he slept quite impartially.'

CHAPTER II

1862–1863

Amendment of Lunacy Law—Lord Westbury provokes opposition in
the House of Lords—Collisions with Lord Chelmsford and Bishop
Wilberforce—Game Laws—Official relations—Church patronage
—Revision of the Statute law—Lord Westbury's speech—His
plan for digest of case law—Authorised law reports.

IN the early part of 1862, the Windham case drew
public attention very forcibly to the defective condition
of the law of lunacy. An inquiry into Mr. Windham's capacity to manage his affairs extended
over more than thirty days, in the course of which
one hundred and fifty witnesses were examined, and
it resulted in the subject of the inquiry vindicating
his right to be considered sane at a cost of upwards
of £30,000.[1] The case was an exceptional instance
of combined eccentricity and profligacy, but it proved
the necessity for some revision of an anomalous
and expensive procedure, and Lord Westbury took
advantage of the feeling it aroused to propose a

---

[1] The finding of the majority of the jury was, that Mr.
Windham was capable of managing himself and his affairs. He
afterwards squandered a large fortune and became hopelessly
insolvent.

general revision of the law by a Bill which he introduced.

It had been the absurd practice to defer the
examination of the alleged lunatic till all the other
evidence had been taken, and to carry back the
inquiry through the whole of his past life.   This
encouraged much speculative flight in the medical
evidence — a species of scientific testimony which
Lord Westbury held ought only to be received, as
in other inquiries, when the subject is removed from
the ordinary sphere and knowledge of men.

'The introduction of medical opinions and medical theories
into this subject,' he said, 'has proceeded upon the vicious
principle of considering insanity as a disease; whereas the law
regards it as a fact which can be ascertained by the evidence in
like manner as any other fact.   The conclusion should be a
judicial one, not a conclusion of natural science; but to derive
it from the opinions of medical professors is to base it upon mere
matter of speculation, instead of upon matter of moral certainty.'

He had a particular objection to the use of the
expression, disease of the mind.   In arguing the
Duchess of Manchester's case before Vice-Chancellor
Page Wood in 1854 he said : ' Men talk of disease
of the mind, but *we* know that the mind, which is
divinæ particula auræ, is never diseased ; it is the
organisation of the mind.'[1]   Nor did he attach much

[1] Bishop Wilberforce's Diary gives a story which illustrates
this view of the subject.   The Bishop introduced a Bill into the
House of Lords for enabling clergymen to resign their livings
when incapacitated by age or infirmity from performing their
duties, and sent a draft to Lord Westbury, asking him to
revise and support it.   'This drew forth a very characteristic reply.

value to the scientific disquisitions of ' mad-doctors.'
In one of his speeches on the Lunacy Bill he ridiculed with amusing effect a list of the characteristics laid down by one of the most eminent of these
authorities as *indicia* of chronic mania, and from
which the writer drew the conclusion that the effect
of all forms of insanity was to stamp upon the patient
a remarkable degree of ugliness. ' That,' said the
Chancellor, ' is a very dreadful announcement for
plain men ; but let not the ugly man hope to escape
the conclusion by clothing his face with a smile of
good - nature, because ' — quoting again from the
medical authority—' nothing is a surer proof of
insanity than a pleasing smile always present.'

The Bill proposed to limit the inquiry to the
previous two years, and gave the Lord Chancellor
power to order the issue whether the alleged lunatic
was incapable of managing himself and his affairs to
be tried before one of the Common Law Judges. It
reduced the number of the jury, which had been
any number between twelve and twenty-three, and
provided for the examination of the person whose
sanity was in question both at the commencement
and the close of the proceedings. Provision was

Lord Westbury said he would cordially support the Bill, but
added, that he perceived the Bishop referred to "diseases of the
mind." This, he said, was a difficulty, because, in the first place,
there could be no such thing as disease of the mind ; and,
secondly, if there were, he had never yet met a clergyman, "with
the exception of your lordship, who had a mind."'—*Life of Bishop
Wilberforce*, vol. iii. p. 340.

also made for the regular visitation of lunatics, and reports of their condition. The Bill passed with little amendment, though not without a smart passage of arms between the Lord Chancellor on the one side, and Lord Derby and Lord Chelmsford on the other, which drew from Lord Westbury the complaint that though continual appeals were made to his duty to expound the law, he found a constant disposition on the part of those who were desirous of obtaining his expositions to question their accuracy. On a similar occasion he observed that he was there to explain the law, but not to instruct amateur lawyers.

From the first his peculiar propensities of speech provoked some antagonism among the peers. The solemn artificial atmosphere of the Upper House seemed to oppress his energetic temperament and induce acrimony. His manner, probably without intention on his part, gave the impression of one who, having no excessive veneration for the order to which he now belonged, felt it to be his duty to enliven the prevailing dulness of his surroundings by the occasional display of a rather caustic wit. In this he succeeded only too well, but being apparently heedless whether his tongue offended or not, he could scarcely escape censure. It has been said with much truth that, strong and keen as a man's wit may be, it is not so strong as the memory of fools, nor so keen as their resentment: one who has not strength of mind to forgive, is by no means so

weak as to forget; and it is much easier to do a
cruel thing than to say a severe one.   Lord Westbury, unfortunately for himself, had not the happy
art, which has been justly ascribed to one of his
colleagues, still living, of keeping even his opponents in good temper.   He certainly would have
done well to lay to heart Lord Derby's warning
that if he desired not to excite animosity in the
House, he must forbear the use of language which
appeared to intimate his belief that he was infinitely
superior to all those he was addressing.

Lord Chelmsford added personal hostility to
party opposition in a degree which made collision between the two rivals from time to time inevitable.   It was a case of natural antipathy,
or at least of imperfect sympathy; each had the
unlucky faculty of rousing what has been happily
termed the travelling acids in the system of the
other.   Early in the Session of 1862 Lord Chelmsford made a very deliberate and violent attack on
the Chancellor.   Relieved of its personalities, the
matter was simple enough.   Under the new Bankruptcy Act, the officers of the late Insolvent Court
had been transferred to the Bankruptcy Court without due provision being made for continuing the full
payment of their remuneration, which was previously
met partly by salary and partly by fees.   Some one
had blundered, and the unfortunate officials were left,
it appeared, without proper compensation.   They
applied to the Lord Chancellor, who naturally re-

ferred them to the House of Commons for relief, and so the matter stood.

In calling the attention of the House of Lords to the subject, Lord Chelmsford exhibited a surprising amount of acrimony, considering the nature of the subject, and even imputed to the Chancellor, as the person responsible for the Bankruptcy Act, grave neglect of duty.   He could not believe, he said, that, as far as the majority of the members of the Government were concerned, this wrong had been done knowingly—thus fixing on Lord Westbury by implication a deliberate intention to ignore the just claims of public servants. The whole of a long speech was marked by a sneering tone which made it peculiarly offensive, and roused Lord Westbury's deep indignation.   With the most deliberate coolness he proceeded to administer a well-deserved castigation to his assailant.

'It is evident,' he said, 'that if Lord Chelmsford pities the clerks much, he hates the Lord Chancellor more.   The noble and learned lord in bringing forward his attack has not shrunk from charging the Lord Chancellor even with falsehood, and yet he has actually been during several weeks, and even during the present week, in daily and confidential intercourse with me ; yet not one word, not one intimation of an attack of this malignant description have I received from him, not even to the extent of enabling me, by inquiry, to ascertain the facts of the case, that I might come prepared even with an explanation of them.'

His speech on this occasion was described as the outpouring upon Lord Chelmsford's head of a pellucid, calm-flowing stream of vitriol which lasted for about an hour. The Opposition benches were crowded with Lord Chelmsford's friends, who had assembled in anticipation of a scene. 'If I had known,' Lord Westbury said afterwards, 'that he was going to bring his ladies with him, his discomfiture should have been still more complete.' Viewed as a party manœuvre, the attack could not be considered effective.

A little later the Chancellor came for the first time in collision with Bishop Wilberforce, and, it must be admitted, found his match. The Bishop brought in a Bill for the purpose of constituting bishoprics in heathen countries without the necessity of procuring the license of the Crown. To this Lord Westbury offered an earnest opposition, alleging that the measure was quite unnecessary and sought to alter the relations between Church and State. The grave authority with which the perils of such legislation were foreshadowed was altogether too much for the Bishop's equanimity. It was hard to have to withdraw a Bill to which much attention had been given ; to be accused of endangering the supremacy of the Crown over the Church was intolerable. The Chancellor's provoking calmness betrayed the Bishop into expressions which appeared, by mere force of the contrast, the more violent, and which, with less excuse, he afterwards summarised in his diary. *Tantæne animis cælestibus iræ ?*

Subsequent encounters with Bishop Wilberforce

led people to suppose that Lord Westbury had an
imperfect appreciation of the Bench of Bishops as a
constituent part of the Upper House.   One of the
bon mots attributed to him was represented as made
at their expense.   On his elevation to the woolsack,
some one remarked that after the heated atmosphere
of the House of Commons, he must fancy himself in
Paradise when presiding over the peers.   ' I might
indeed do so,' the Chancellor was said to have
replied, ' but for the predominant and excessive display of lawn-sleeves, which at once dispels the pleasing illusion.'   On a later occasion he is reported to
have objected to a Bishops' Resignation Bill as
unnecessary, giving as his reason : ' The law in its
infinite wisdom has already provided for the not im-
probable event of the imbecility of a bishop.'

One of the most marked features of his political
life was a conscientious, and as it seemed, overstrained
dislike and fear of any concessions made to the
Roman Catholic Church in England.   An illustration of this is afforded by the objection he made on
constitutional grounds to Lord Palmerston's proposal
to confer the Order of the Thistle on Lord Lovat,
a Roman Catholic.   A difficulty having arisen from
the form of the oath of the Order, Lord Westbury
wrote :—

' The Order of the Thistle is of very remote antiquity, and there
are several mythical traditions with respect to its origin.   Its
ancient constitution, statutes and oath (if it had any) do not appear
to be known.   But it is clear that it had fallen into desuetude

long before the Reformation, at which time there was not (I believe)
any knight of the Order. The Order was revived and re-established
in Protestant times. The constitution of the existing Order was
settled at the time of this renewal or refoundation. The form
of the present oath was then (in the reign of Queen Anne)
devised.

' Now it is true, that to the Sovereign, as the fountain and head
of the Order, is reserved the power of making new statutes or regu-
lations for the government of the Order. But this power must
have some reasonable limit. It cannot be taken as extending to
the right of entirely altering the constitutional basis, the corner-
stone of the foundation of the Order. Such, at least, will be the
argument of those who will question the validity and propriety of
what your Lordship proposes to do. They will say that all these
Orders of knighthood partake of · a religious or ecclesiastical
character, such as were the Templars and the Knights of St. John.
Taking the language of the oath, it will be said that the Order
was to be a bulwark and defence (" fortify and defend ") of the true
Protestant reformed religion. This, it will be contended, is its
constitutional basis, and that it is *ultra vires* of the Sovereign,
under the power of making new statutes for better government
of the Order, to alter this basis. It will be urged that the
Sovereign can no more alter the Order from Protestant to Catholic,
than she could change it from Christian to Mahommedan.

' Such and many other more vicious attacks will be made on the
act proposed by your Lordship, and, without saying positively that
the objections are well founded in law, I am certainly of opinion
that they are plausible enough to render it, in my judgment, very
unsafe and inexpedient to advise any such alteration in the
statutes of the Order. As the oath stands, no honest Roman
Catholic can take it. Not to require the oath of Lord Lovat, or
to give him a special dispensation, would be to make a *privilegium*
in favour of a Roman Catholic, a thing more objectionable than
an attempt by a new statute to alter the nature of the oath.
Looking at the sensitive and irritable character of the Scotch on
all things relating to their religion, and their bigoted and unreasonable temper on such subjects, I would advise your Lordship not to persevere in your intention.'

The condition of the game laws was the only topic which gave rise to any considerable parliamentary struggle in 1862.   An alarming prevalence of night poaching by armed gangs, resulting not unfrequently in murderous affrays, gave rise to the impression that a more stringent law was needed for the prevention and punishment of such depredations.[1]   There was a difficulty in apprehending the marauders unless they were seized *in flagrante delicto*, which their superior force usually rendered impracticable.   Many people thought it desirable, therefore, to give the police power to stop and search persons suspected of being in the unlawful possession of game, and to summon the offenders.   The Home Secretary, Sir George Grey, on behalf of the Government, strenuously opposed the proposed enactment,

---

[1] The earlier law was by no means deficient in severity.   By a statute of Edward I., 'To the intent that trespassers in forests . . . may more warily fear hereafter to enter and trespass in the same,' it was made lawful to kill trespassers who would not yield themselves to the foresters, 'after hue and cry made to stand unto the peace,' but fled or defended themselves with force and arms.   An Act passed just two centuries later (1494) shows that poaching was still a common offence, for it recites that 'divers persons, having little substance to live upon, use many times as well by nets, snares, or other engines, to take and destroy pheasants and partridges,' by which the owners of lands 'leese not only their pleasure and disport,' but also 'the profit and avail that by that occasion should grow to their houshold, to the great hurt of all lords and gentlemen, and others, having any great livelihood within this realm.'   It is evident that poaching is not, as is often represented, the outcome of the over-preservation of later days.

on the ground that it would turn the county police into gamekeepers. Eventually, after a great deal of controversy, in which every device was exhausted in attempts to defeat the Bill, it became law through the persistent support of the county members.

Lord Westbury disapproved of the distinction which the law draws between game and other kinds of private property, and, as appears from the following letter to Lord Palmerston, would have made game the subject of larceny, treating the poacher as a common thief rather than an irregular sportsman :—

> ' 1 *Upper Hyde Park Gardens,*
> ' *Dec.* 26, 1862.

' Grey (*more Greyorum*) raises all sorts of difficulty, which, however, on being examined resolve themselves into this kind of reasoning : you cannot give to game all the incidents of property, and therefore you must not give it any, even though those rights, which may be imparted to it, are sufficient for the purpose you have in view.

' Sir George says, What do you mean by calling game property ? Is a man to follow and reclaim his pheasants and hares as he may his ducks and turkeys ? The answer is, No such thing ; live game shall by enactment be declared to be the lawful property of the owner of the soil (including in the term "owner" tenant by agreement to have the game) whilst it is on his land ; when it quits the land of A and is found on the land of B, it is in like manner the property of B. By the law of England game is classed as things *feræ naturæ* in which there can be no property. It is only necessary by statute to remove the legal affix and to define the extent to which the rights of property shall attach. Live game, if taken on and removed from my soil by the hand of man, may be followed and reclaimed where it can be identified. Dead game, if capable of identification, may always be followed.

' For the purposes of identification, the Bill must lay down certain rules of presumption which will be laws of evidence in proceedings under the Act. Thus I propose to enact, that if persons are seen trespassing on my land, and being followed, are found to have game in their possession, they shall be presumed to have possessed themselves of such game on my land—that is, stolen my property, until the contrary be shown. So, if persons are found on my land in pursuit of game between sunset and sunrise, a constable may enter the houses of such persons to search for game, and if game be found there, it shall be presumed in like manner to have been stolen. Observe how such a provision would destroy poaching, for the poacher would know that a single keeper would be able to follow, and with the aid of the first policeman repossess himself of the game, and convict the whole of a gang. There may be a more stringent enactment as to persons found trespassing with the evident intent of killing—that is, stealing game.

'The great benefit of the law would be the change it would effect on the minds and feelings of the lower classes. At present they see no immorality in poaching; but when it becomes theft, and the law, with a just scale of punishment, is administered firmly and consistently, the present feeling would wholly disappear. This is, of course, a very imperfect statement of the subject.'

He goes on to refer to the standing grievance which the heads of the other great departments of the State have against the Treasury :—

'If the Cabinet agreed to the introduction of such a measure, I would gladly charge myself with it; but for that which renders my position irksome, namely, the necessity of resorting to the Chancellor of the Exchequer. The parsimony of former times has stripped the high office of Lord Chancellor of all that was requisite to enable the Lord Chancellor to act in a suitable manner as head of the law. Thus I have not a person in my service, nor the means of employing a person, to whom I could commit the preparation of such a Bill and the duty of making such researches as are necessary before preparing it. If any amendment of the law seems to me desirable, I must beg for the approval

of the Home Secretary, and, through him, the sanction of the
Chancellor of the Exchequer. My secretary writes to Sir George
Grey requesting him to move the Chancellor of the Exchequer
to consent that the Lord Chancellor may have a small sum of
money to pay the gentlemen he may employ to effect the necessary reform. After weeks of delay, an official letter comes from
Mr. Peel or some subordinate, doling out some niggardly sum,
as if it were a favour, and often with the most absurd stipula-
tions.

'Such is the *circuitus officialis* for which Dickens has substituted felicitously "circumlocution." I am waiting now for the
time when the Chancellor of the Exchequer will be pleased to
tell me whether he will consent to my request, that the barristers
engaged in the great work of the expurgation of the Statute-Book
may have slightly increased emoluments to enable them to devote
to the work a much longer period of their time. I must appeal
to you to emancipate the Lord Chancellor from a necessity so
humiliating, and to establish a rule that, when the Cabinet has
agreed to a measure of improvement of the law and committed
it to the Lord Chancellor, that great officer shall have credit given
to him, that he will not waste the public money, and will not
incur any greater expenditure than is fit and necessary for the
desired end. As an illustration of this, let me remind you of
our position as to the New Law Courts. This the greatest improvement, whether regarded in a legal, moral, sanitary, or archi-
tectural point of view, has been utterly defeated, and, as I have
been compelled to give it up for the reason above given, now lies
utterly derelict. In lieu of it, I suppose Mr. Gladstone proposes
to expend £700,000 in a building for the surplus rubbish of the
British Museum. I do hope, my dear Lord, that these things
may not be.

'I enclose you the Dedication to yourself in 1803 of Gavizzotti's
Grammar. My copy is very old and torn, or I would have sent
you the book. The language pleased me much, and it may
remind you of early days. Pray give it to Lady Palmerston with
my kind remembrances, for she will justly value this early tribute
to you.—Yours sincerely,   WESTBURY.'

No Lord Chancellor ever worked more un-
selfishly or untiringly than Lord Westbury in the
public service. Almost the only relaxation he
allowed himself was some occasional shooting in the
Hackwood coverts, or a day's trout or grayling fishing with Lord Palmerston at Broadlands. Fishing
of the less ambitious kind he delighted in, and he
loved to explain to his grandchildren the niceties of
catching roach or perch in the Thames, or 'tickling'
trout in the stream at Old Basing. He was very
fond of rook and rabbit shooting, and did not despise
a day's ferreting with the boys in the Christmas
holidays. In the mysteries of this latter art he may
be said to have been a past-master. Despite the
hardest frost, or the bitterest wind, he would
patiently stand by the hour over a well-populated
burrow, seldom missing a shot. Though generally
slow in firing when 'walking up' game, he was an
extraordinarily quick shot at rabbits crossing a ride.
At one time he kept a small pack of beagles, which
he was very fond of following on his speedy Arab
cob, 'Pearl.' The numerous hares in the neighbourhood of Hackwood afforded excellent opportunities
for this kind of pursuit, which was sometimes varied
by running a 'drag' round the park. Coursing also
gave him great pleasure, and he was generally first
up at the kill.

He was very scrupulous about having a precise
line kept by the beaters in shooting, and in working
a field for partridges liked to give the signal to

wheel from his place in the centre. He was often much put out when a day's sport turned out badly, and woe betided the unlucky keeper who failed to show the expected amount of game in his coverts. But though strict in his requirements, and of a hot temper, he was kind to subordinates, and they were much attached to him. He was fond of walking round with the gun, attended by a single keeper, to whom he would impart a variety of curious information on subjects of natural history.

A Greek nobleman, Count M——, an old friend of his, used to shoot sometimes at Hackwood. The Count, besides being a very bad shot, was wont to fire in a wild and dangerous manner, and Lord Westbury delighted in 'wiping his eye.' One day the Count, after missing every shot he had, severely peppered one of the dogs, and then twice claimed for himself birds which had dropped to his host's gun. He capped this performance a few minutes later by nearly bagging the whole line of shooters, keepers, and beaters in a turnip-field—his previous misdeeds, and the wiggings he got for them, having made him completely lose his head. This was too much for Lord Westbury, who at once ordered a keeper to take from the excited and protesting Count his gun and cartridges, and sent the offending sportsman home to the ladies, to the great amusement and relief of the rest of the party.

The following letters addressed to Mr., afterwards Sir Robert, Phillimore on his appointment as

Queen's Advocate, may be given as specimens of the geniality of Lord Westbury's official relations with his colleagues :—

'*Sept.* 22 [1862].

'My dear Queen's Advocate—I hope you are by this time perfectly at home in your new office. Do not be too anxious or too zealous at first. Talleyrand's *point de zèle* is a most useful maxim. Eschew long opinions and much reasoned opinions—the authorities in office desire little beyond a clear definite rule of action ; the opinion is not to convince ; it is to guide, conduct, and relieve from responsibility. I doubt much whether the Q. A. ought or ought not to be in Parliament ; but on the whole, remembering that he is a permanent officer, and ought to be the disinterested impartial adviser of all administrations, I think he ought not. What is your opinion ?

'I have applied to the Treasurer of our Inn to allow me to have my levee on the first day of next term in the Middle Temple Hall. You know I receive on that day not only the profession, but the Lord Mayors (both the setting and the rising suns) and Aldermen. I find Belgrave Square so relaxing that I have been compelled to remove to the other side of Hyde Park, but I can find no house large enough now vacant, save one in Upper Hyde Park Gardens, which will not be complete for me by the first day of Term, and in November it might be too far, though in the finer weather of Easter Term it might be accessible enough.

'It is a great shame that the Lord Chancellor has no official residence. It detracts much from the dignity, and much more from the emolument of the office. Lord Eldon slighted our Society and its noble hall and held his levees in Lincoln's Inn, which was glad to welcome him, as it seemed to give them a pre-eminence. But I desire to adhere to my Inn, and to bring the profession there to do it homage. I hope you and the other benchers will agree that it is a legitimate use of the hall ; and as it will place your brother-bencher, the Lord Chancellor, in a right position, I trust it will not be displeasing for any. If you think there should be a parliament, pray write to the Treasurer and kindly ascertain for me the feelings of those benchers you can see or communicate with.

'I need hardly say the Society is not to incur one farthing expense. I hope you have had a pleasant vacation.'

'My dear *Sir Robert*—As I have just had the honour of affixing the Great Seal to the patent conferring upon you the most ancient and the greatest distinction of knighthood, I desire to be the first to offer to yourself and Lady Phillimore my sincere congratulations. I think the Queen should have given me authority to dub you personally, to give you the accolade, and admonish you to be faithful, true, and valiant. In one sense I rejoice to be able to say—

> ' "'Twas my blade
> That knighthood on thy shoulder laid."

Whence comes that quotation, most doughty knight? Remember, this is only the first step on the ladder of dignity. Excelsior be the cry, and let the name of Robert Phillimore be added to the Peers of England. Adieu, "sweet knight."—With my kind regards, yours sincerely,   WESTBURY.'

Another letter, addressed to the Lord Advocate, Mr. (now Lord) Moncreiff, with respect to magisterial appointments and Scottish appeals, is a pleasant example of the same style :—

'. . . I think it right to consult you, first, as to the necessity of new appointments ; secondly, as to the manner of the appointment, if necessary ; thirdly, as to the persons proposed.

'In England I judge, first (in cities and boroughs), of the sufficiency of the existing number ; secondly, in cities, I submit the proposed names to the Town Council ; thirdly, I endeavour to keep an even hand between Conservatives and Liberals, giving *a little* preponderance to the latter.

'But I never appoint attorneys, clergymen (if others can be found), vintners, brewers, owners of public-houses ; for the latter three have a direct interest in the decisions of the magistrates.

'Will you kindly give me your opinion on the several subjects to which I have adverted, and your judgment as to the men proposed?

'I hope the Court of Session is in great force, and that it receives the decisions of *Dom. Proc.* as dutiful children do paternal admonitions and corrections. So shall its days be long in the land. When Brougham, Lyndhurst, and St. Leonards are gathered to their fathers, if we are still on the face of the earth, I think we must reconsider the question of the appointment of a Scotch Peer for the House of Lords and Privy Council.

'The lieges talk of injustice to Scotland in the diminished length of the Unicorn's tail; but I am more true to her interests, and point to the injustice done to her Bar, and to the anomaly of her being driven to seek justice wholly at the hands of foreign jurists.

'When this act of justice is done, will you at some future day please to remember and record that it was I who first insisted on it in 1847 (on the restoration of the Liberal Government, when the proposal was quashed through ——'s opposition), and that I have never ceased to advocate it as a thing due to the great learning, talent, and position of the Scottish Bar, and as a measure eminently conducive to the judicial interests of the empire?'

The appearance of grave dignity and lofty bearing of Lord Westbury found fitting exhibition on high state occasions. In the splendid ceremony of the Prince of Wales's marriage the Lord Chancellor, described by an eye-witness as 'a perfect pageant in himself,' bore his official part, though his own home was at this period of national rejoicing overshadowed by the approach of a great sorrow, marking the contrast which is never absent from human affairs. Lady Westbury, who had been for upwards of twenty years in failing health,

died on the 17th of March 1863, loved and mourned
by all who had experienced her gentleness, simplicity,
and tender solicitude for others. A most devoted
wife and mother—admirable indeed in every relation
of life—her memory lived in the hearts of her many
friends as that of a true and perfect woman.

The late Edward Lear, well known as the gifted
landscape painter, and still better as author of
the delightful *Books of Nonsense*—the E. L., whose
travels in Greece were the subject of one of Lord
Tennyson's minor poems—was very intimate with
Lord Westbury and his family. On the death of
Lady Westbury he wrote to one of her daughters :—
'To me your mother had always been a most kind
and unchanged friend. No difference of worldly
position had the least power of altering her uniform
and unaffected friendliness to those she cared for ;
therefore I must always love the memories of the
many years in which I have known her. Truly, she
was one who is missed rather more than less, as one
finds that constant quiet sympathy is not only one
of the most lovable of qualities, but one of the very
rarest.'

The scheme which Lord Westbury had devised
for increasing the value of the Church patronage
vested in the Lord Chancellor, and by this means
converting very small livings into a source of strength
to the Church, took shape in the Augmentation of
Benefices Bill, which he himself presented early in

the Session of 1863. Of the 720 small livings in the
Chancellor's gift he selected upwards of 300 of the
worst endowed, and proposed to take power to sell
them and apply the purchase-money in the augmentation of those livings or of other livings small in
value.

Successive holders of the Great Seal had found
much embarrassment in dealing with this part of
their patronage. The livings were so small that
it was difficult to find a proper incumbent willing to
take one, and the church and parish suffered from
the absence of any resident proprietor interested in
the living. Moved by these considerations, Lord
Westbury desired that these livings, instead of
being held in the barren hand of the Lord Chancellor,
should be sold and transferred to landed proprietors
who would be likely to take an interest in them,
while the value of the livings would by the sale itself
be increased by one-half, or in some cases, two-
thirds of their former value. He writes to the Rev.
Charles, afterwards Canon, Kingsley :—

‘Of course the whole value of the plan consists in the purchase-money being returned to the purchaser in the augmented
value of the living. My tables are wholly of my own devising, as
the Bill is, every word of it, my own composition. I tried various
actuaries, but found them inconsistent with each other to an
absurd degree, and incapable even of estimating anything out of
the ordinary routine.’

After explaining that his tables were framed on
the principle of always giving a purchaser a clear
income of 10 or 11 per cent for his purchase-money,

so that after deducting from the income 4 per cent
on the purchase-money, as the proper return on
money permanently invested, 6 or 7 per cent remained as the remuneration of personal labour and
duty, he continues :—

'Many persons are willing to embark money in trade, and
work at it if they can make 12 per cent. But in buying a
living it must be remembered that you obtain for a young man
a profession, the social status of a gentleman, and a sphere
for useful exertion, possibly distinction. I certainly should
recommend every father who has a son destined for the Church
to buy one of my livings. All this proceeds on mere worldly
principles, wholly independent of higher and nobler feelings.
I am dilating on the merits in the language of the votaries
of Mammon. But I trust that many will take advantage of
this opportunity thus afforded of benefiting the Church with
more exalted feelings. I neither desire nor expect to be long in
my office, but if this first attempt works well, I shall certainly
carry it much further. It would surprise you if I could tell you
how much opposition and prejudice I had to surmount even to
get this reduced measure sanctioned.'

The measure received the unanimous approval
of the bishops and clergy, who hailed it as a most
valuable piece of ecclesiastical legislation. Lord
Shaftesbury wrote :—

'I have read through your Bill with satisfaction and gratitude.
It will, be assured, be joyfully received by the clergy. Dr. Sin-
clair, the Archdeacon of Middlesex, right-hand man to the late
Bishop of London, has written to me in delight, and saying that
"he had given testimony to some purpose before the Bishop of
Exeter's Committee, but that he had not hoped that he should
live to see so generous a Lord Chancellor."

'I have seen Lord Palmerston this morning. He highly
approves the measure, and he will tell you so.'

The only objections raised to the Bill went to
its principle.   It was said that it was an extension
of the system of trafficking in livings, and that patronage in the nature of a public trust ought not to
be delegated.   Dr. Jeune, referring to the amendment of the Bill by a Select Committee, wrote :—

'It has been altered, as I think and probably as you think,
for the worse.   But your sacrifice of so much more patronage
will give you a present and future reputation in the Church.
Two centuries hence shall you loom largest as a law reformer
or a friend to the Church?   I think the latter.   It will be a
peculiar glory.

'The following extract from a letter written to me by our new
Dean of Gloucester will show how the clergy are looking up
to you :—

' " May I whisper that Bristol is in a sad state of dissatisfaction ?
They would depose Ellicot in a moment if only they could elect
a bishop of their own.   It would be a most popular act to dissever
it from Gloucester.   Ellicot will consent, could you persuade the
Lord Chancellor to carry through the Bill.   Funds are ready.   If
at the same time Cornwall could be parted from Devon, the satisfaction to the Church would be immense.   Time should not be lost."

'The thing has been often mooted, and probably Lord P——
has made up his mind.   Nor can I tell whether more bishops are
needed.   But sure I am that Dean Law is right as to the pleasure
which the matter would give to Bristol and the clergy generally,
and think that it would be well if you, or a ministry in which you
are, should prepare a measure which will eventually be carried.

'Do you know the following lines from Mandeville's *Fable of
the Bees*, A.D. 1714 ?—

' " The lawyers of whose arts the basis
Was raising feuds and splitting cases,
Opposed all registers, that cheats
Might make more work with kept estates,
As wer't unlawful that one's own
Without a lawsuit should be known." '

The Bill quickly received the assent of the Peers, and in the House of Commons Lord Palmerston himself, at Lord Westbury's special request, moved the second reading with a strong recommendation of its provisions, and a very complimentary reference to its projector. An attempt was made in Committee to prohibit the sale of the next presentations, but it failed, and the Bill passed. 'The effect of the Bill is this,' wrote Lord Westbury to Lord Palmerston, 'that if all the livings made saleable are sold on the most reasonable terms, there will be a fund for the augmentation of poor livings amounting to £800,000. It is therefore a gift by the Crown of that sum for the benefit of the Church.'

The success of the Act surpassed the Chancellor's most sanguine expectations. Such excellent prices were obtained for the livings sold, that it may be regretted that the operation of the statute has not been further extended.

The following letter from Dr. Tait, then Bishop of London, shows how the more moderate section of the clergy at that time looked to the Chancellor for ecclesiastical reforms :—

'*Sept.* 23, 1863.

'My dear Lord—In your letter of the 5th you alluded to ecclesiastical legislation for next session. I am distinctly of opinion that it is discreditable both to Church and State to leave certain matters which require settling in their present unsatisfactory condition.

'1. Clergy discipline. If the opposition and divergence of opinion on the subject of the Court of Final Appeal makes it very difficult to have a thoroughly satisfactory measure of reform carried, at all events let the procedure of the Ecclesiastical Courts be reformed.   This, with a satisfactory settlement of the question connected with registries and fees, would do much, even if a more complete reform were delayed.

'2. As to dilapidations, I earnestly trust that your Lordship will take the matter in hand.

'It has been discussed *ad nauseam ;* the innumerable Bills proposed and the Report of the Select Committee of the Lords have left very little more to say—we need action.

'3. It will be a great blessing to have the Church Building Acts not only arranged, but greatly simplified.   I hope the new legislation will go the length of cutting out all that is at present useless, and giving some new facilities in directions not hitherto much encouraged, *e.g.* as to building and endowing Chapels of Ease.

'4. Why in the world are the sensible majority to allow two foolish minorities to prevent a settlement of the Church Rate question?   There never was a time when all moderate men of all parties were so well disposed to a compromise—why in the world is such an opportunity to be lost because Mr. D'Israeli has thought it would suit his purpose to make a stalking-horse of Archdeacon Hale, and, aided by Archdeacon Denison, joins with the extreme Dissenters in declaring that there shall be no compromise?   If we cannot have the guidance of Government in all these matters, let us at least have their help and support to the efforts made by private members.

'But, after all, what do Governments exist for except to steer us safely through difficult straits?

'Your Lordship has carried one very useful ecclesiastical reform this session.   Let us have some more next.—Believe me to be yours very truly,   A. C. LONDON.'

The only other important reform in which Lord Westbury took a leading part this year was effected by an Act for the further revision of the Statute-book by the removal of obsolete or unnecessary statutes.   His celebrated speech in introducing the

Bill must be considered his most successful parliamentary effort. Taking advantage of the occasion to advocate a complete revision of the whole law—written and unwritten—he devoted a great part of his speech to an elaborate exposure of the evils of the existing system under which, it has been well said, the only thing certain about the law is its uncertainty. He disclaimed at the outset the idea that the subject belonged to lawyers exclusively. 'A great philosopher, who was also a great lawyer, has said, "*Juris consulti tanquam e vinculis sermocinantur*"—lawyers, when speaking of legislation, discourse in chains and shackles; and what are they? They are the professional prejudices, the narrow horizon within which their views are bounded, and their blunted sensibility to evils with which they have been long familiar.'

In clear and simple language he explained the distinction between the written or statute law and the unwritten or common law created by the decisions of judges, who thereby became not only legislators, but the worst of legislators—legislators *ex post facto*. He proceeded to trace the history of the growth of this system, which Sir William Blackstone had unsparingly condemned. The reports of these decisions were in early times compiled under the direct superintendence of the judges themselves, and great care was taken in sifting and ascertaining the proper grounds of decision. But though this was an approach to certainty in the law, it led to the practice of appealing to former decisions for the determination of similar cases, and thus originated what Lord Westbury termed ' that distinctive peculiarity of the English mind—a love of precedent, of appealing to the authority of past examples rather than of indulging in abstract reasoning.'

He pointed out that as reports multiplied and the personal superintendence of the judges was withdrawn, there was no security for revising or digesting the reports, and inconvenience arose, which led to Bacon's celebrated proposal to amend the laws. Through the singular *inertia* that characterises our Legislature, nothing had been done to give effect to so excellent a proposal. The 50 or 60 volumes of reports which existed at the beginning of the seventeenth century had grown to 1100 or 1200 volumes. ' Nay, more,' said Lord Westbury, ' at this time there are at least 40 or 50 distinct sets of reports pouring their streams into the immense reservoir of law, and creating what can hardly be described, but may be denominated a great chaos of judicial legislation.' Lord Coke had said that our bookcases are the best proofs of what the law is, and it was the rule that precedents must be followed, unless plainly founded on erroneous principles. Each succeeding judge has it in his power to determine what is absurd, what is unjust, what is the measure of erroneous principle.

' Nor is this,' the Chancellor continued, ' the only evil inherent in the present system, for there is another necessarily

inherent also, and it is this—in the language of Lord Bacon—
that the unlearned age governs the more learned, because you
take your rule as it is laid down in an early and undeveloped stage
of society, and you are compelled to abide by that rule, if, for
instance, it has regulated the disposition of property, until the
Legislature intervenes to rescue the law from the necessity of following that which is often unreasonable and absurd.   But the
contradiction and anomaly do not end there, as I will render
plain to your Lordships by citing one or two instances of the
manner in which decided cases are occasionally dealt with by
courts of justice.   We have all heard the vulgar phrase, " the
glorious uncertainty of the law."   It is the common opprobrium
of our system, which has passed into a proverb, and the saying has
taken its rise in the fact that no man can tell with certainty whether
a particular case which he finds recorded, and which is supposed
to govern the particular case in which he is interested, will or
will not be followed by the judges.'

After citing several striking examples of this uncertainty, he passed on to a further peculiarity in
the law of England :—

' By a legal fiction,' said Lord Westbury, ' it is supposed that
the law contains within itself the materials for the decision of
every case, however novel its circumstances ; and, accordingly,
when the judges have a new case before them, they do not
profess to arrive at the law by reasoning, by theory, or by
philosophical inquiry, but they profess to discover it by searching
among the records of former decisions for cases which are supposed to be analogous to the case before them ; and they derive
from those analogies the rule which they desire for the determination of the particular case.'

A judicial opinion, he declared, is also a judicial
enactment.   It decides a particular case, and it sets
a precedent for all future cases.   Therefore the
judges become legislators—legislators *ex arbitrio ;*

and with such a vast mass of material from which to select, what an impossibility for any one to ascertain beforehand the nature of the law that will be enacted! ' There is a flow of the tide one way, to be succeeded by a revulsion another way, and the refluent wave, consequent upon the alteration of the judicial decision, in its turn brings ruin to many who have trusted to the former exposition of the law. That is an example of the evil consequences of men being left without rudder, without light, without compass or chart, in traversing the immense sea of judicial precedent, whenever a new combination of circumstances arises.'

The Chancellor also took the opportunity which the subject offered to dilate in language of much force and cogency on the evils and inconveniences of the existing system of unofficial law-reporting, and the necessity of obtaining some guarantee that the judicial decisions of the Superior Courts, which were part of the law of the land, were accurately recorded. Then turning from the common law to the statute law, he pointed to the remarkable similarity of their condition. The statutes were printed chronologically, without the least regard to arrangement. Amid the great variety of matter, enactments on the same subject were scattered over an immense extent of ground. He continued :—

' Unfortunately our legislation has been always extemporary. We wait till a grievance is intolerable, and then we apply ourselves to a remedy which does not go beyond the grievance. Our legis-

lation has always been on the spur of the moment ; nay, more, it
unfortunately happens that the manner in which the legislation is
conducted contributes more than anything else to the evils that
lie so palpably on the surface of the Statute-book. . . . When
you address yourself to a new statute, after having considered the
general principle of the proposed measure, the Bill is subjected
to the process of Committee, and then it constantly happens that
things are grafted upon a statute under misconception, at
variance altogether from the original conception of the framer.
Your new Acts are patches on old garments. You provide for the
emergency, but you pay not the least regard to the question
whether the piece you put into the old garment suits it or not.
Such being the mode of your legislation, it would be utterly impossible that your Statute-book should be other than it is,—a mass
of enactments which are in a great degree discordant and irrecon-
cilable.'

Lord Westbury proceeded with admirable boldness to sketch the outlines of a scheme of revision
of the case law, which might, he thought, lead to a
digest of the whole law—statutory as well as judicial.
He proposed to revise all the reports ; to weed them
of contradictory decisions, and where there were
doubtful cases to decide on those which ought to
remain. So, too, with the Statute-book : he proposed
to get rid of enactments which were no longer in
force, to classify the remainder under proper heads,
bringing dispersed statutes together, and eliminating
jarring and discordant provisions, so as to obtain an
accurate and methodical analysis, from which, with
the addition of the revised reports, a digest of the
whole law might be framed.

While he did not disguise his opinion that the
law ought ultimately to be reduced to a code, the

Chancellor confessed that so long as the absurd
division between the province of common law and
the province of equity existed, and due precision of
language, a complete and settled legal vocabulary,
and accuracy in legislative construction and composition were wanting, the law of England was
not fit for that process. The revision might, in
his opinion, be properly entrusted to a Department
of Justice.

This speech was highly praised by Lord
Brougham, and the Bill was taken very much on
trust in both Houses, upon the recommendation of
Lord Westbury and Sir Roundell Palmer, as a
useful extension of the Revision Act of 1861. No
labour had been spared to make the reform as
extensive and accurate as possible. It is worth
mentioning that the Act of Richard II., imposing
a penalty 'for telling slanderous lyes of the great
men of the realm,' was carefully excluded from
the schedule comprising the repealed statutes.
The penalty was imprisonment till the offender
brought into Court the author of the tale, but the
punishment of the author when captured was left to
the imagination. This admirable Act was, strangely
enough, repealed by the Statute Laws Revision Act
of 1887—at a time when it seemed most needed.

Lord Westbury more fully explained his plan of
revision in the following letter to his eldest son :—

' I shall organise a body of *rédacteurs*, of whom six will be
working, paid barristers, chiefly young men of proved ability, who

will work under the superintendence of myself, the Attorney and Solicitor-General, Queen's Advocate, Vice-Chancellor Wood, and, I think, Mr. Justice Willes. Each of the six expurgators will have a particular portion of the reports assigned to him and his superintendent, and it will be their duty to eliminate every case that does not enter into, or illustrate, or show the application of some portion of living law. With respect to the cases that are allowed to remain, great liberty may be taken in reducing useless arguments or omitting points no longer necessary or useful. What remains after this pruning will be arranged under heads according to the most perfect analysis that can be framed, and thus there will be formed a complete digest of the cases which embody, or illustrate and teach the application of the existing law. Every doubt and question that may arise in this process will be carefully noted, reserved, and discussed before the six superintendents. In matters of great importance, I propose to have the nature of the question, the discussion, and decision of the superintendents made public (by the aid of some periodical), as was done in the discussions on framing the Code Napoleon, so that the opinion of the profession may be obtained. When the digest is complete, then (subject to the difficulty I am about to mention) I would have it published by the authority of Government with money obtained from a vote of the House of Commons. Looking to the sale it would command, a small sum (say £10,000) would be sufficient. I do not propose any enactment to annul or prohibit the citation of the rejected cases. That must be effected by the Judges of the different Courts. But any case not found in the digest would hardly be ventured on. (The difficulty I alluded to is the possibility of objection by the owners of existing copyright in modern reports, but the objection might not hold, any more than it did when the "Leading Cases" were published.)'

He thought that in little more than three years the entire digest of the case law, under the same titles as he proposed to arrange the statute law, might be completed.

'The digests of the statute law and case law are not regarded by me as final works; they are materials only, to serve for the formation of a Code.

'Such is an imperfect sketch of one part of my design. You will see how easily this might have been accomplished, if the plan I submitted (when Attorney-General) to the Government for the formation of a Department of Justice had been carried into effect. A staff of practised, well-trained, legal artisans would have been formed, by which the expurgation and revision of the statutes and reports would have been steadily and uninterruptedly pursued, with all the advantages resulting from a system of co-operation and constantly improving experience.'

Lord Westbury's speech gave a valuable impetus to the movement which was then gathering force for the publication of a system of authorised reports. There was a difference of opinion among members of the Bar on the question whether the work ought to be undertaken by the State or by the profession? Soon after the delivery of the speech, a deputation waited on the Lord Chancellor to request him to obtain the assistance of the Government in establishing official reports. He, however, expressed his preference for a system of voluntary enterprise under judicial sanction. He reminded the deputation of the fable of the waggoner appealing to Jupiter for aid to get his waggon out of the ruts, and added that reporting was the privilege of the Bar, and the Bar must devise whatever remedy was required. He subsequently suggested to the Committee formed to carry out the Bar scheme, that a reporting Council should be appointed, and a guarantee fund opened.

This advice was adopted, and the publication of the present authorised law reports soon after commenced.[1]

[1] *Vide The History and Origin of the Law Reports*, by Mr. W. T. S. Daniel, Q.C., pp. 26, 137. Mr. Daniel's book gives an interesting account of the many difficulties which beset the matter, and of the steps taken to overcome them.

CHAPTER III

1863-1864

Appellate jurisdiction in ecclesiastical matters—Judicial appointments —Difficulties of patronage — Lord Westbury's kindness in its bestowal—*Essays and Reviews*—Proceedings against Dr. Williams and Mr. Wilson—Judgment of Privy Council—Synodical condemnation — Debate thereon in the House of Lords — Encounter between Lord Westbury and Bishop Wilberforce—Greek Professorship Bill.

SINCE the decision in the *Gorham Case* in 1850 the constitution of the Court of Final Appeal in ecclesiastical matters had become unacceptable to the Anglican party. An agitation now arose, in which the Bishop of Oxford took a leading part, for removing the spiritual lords from the Judicial Committee of the Privy Council.[1] It was proposed that the Court should be constituted exclusively of lay judges, so that its decisions might have no appearance of ecclesiastical sanction. Issues of fact would be tried by the Courts, and matters of doctrine might be referred to the authorities of the Church.

[1] The two Archbishops and the Bishop of London, as Privy Councillors, were members of the Judicial Committee for hearing Ecclesiastical Appeals.

As will be gathered from the subjoined letter, Lord Westbury was opposed to any such change.[1]

'*June* 27, 1863.

'My dear Lord Chancellor—I am greatly obliged by your kindness about the first presentation to Hornton, though *that* was not my object; but that I think there are more opportunities of *nursing* a bishop's living into something than one in the patronage of so inaccessible a height as the Great Seal, I should have been sure that you would not surrender any patronage. But as this is really new patronage, and delivery of your existing patronage from an impediment, I thought you might feel at liberty to suffer it to be created as a *nullius filius*.

'The latter part of your letter fills me with dismay. I should quite have expected that having to preside at that most anomalous Court would convince one of so clear an intuition and so masterly an intellect that it was an intolerable mixture of iron and clay (I do not distribute the predicates). But you will pardon me if I maintain that all I have asked in altering the Court is the creating no *imperium in imperio*, but is simply necessary to give entire efficiency to the working of the purely legal Court. I propose not that the ecclesiastics should be asked how the Court is to decide, but that, whenever a question of the divine law is involved in the decision, ecclesiastics should be asked what is the doctrine of the Church of England on that question. The fact of this answer would satisfy the Church that *doctrine* remained intact under the legal decision, *e.g.* in the Gorham case the lawyers would still, it may be, have decided that Mr. Gorham's book did not so categorically contradict the formularies and articles as to subject him to deprivation. But with this would have gone out the ecclesiastic answer that the Church of England taught that every rightly baptized infant was regenerate, and this would have saved us from the great schism under which we have ever since languished.

'But my dismay is for the present. If, constituted as it now

---

[1] The latter part of this letter is printed in the *Life of Bishop Wilberforce*, vol. iii. p. 109.

is, with its mischievous semblance of being "a Court Christian," the Committee or Council advise Her Majesty to revoke the sentence of the Court below, then *actum est de Ecclesiâ Anglicanâ.*

'I admit all the folly and self-contradiction and ignorant annoyance of Dr. Lushington's judgment, and yet I maintain that, whilst casting out the plainest grounds of condemnation, and retaining and straining the weakest, yet that enough remains to condemn both of these misty men on the simplest legal grounds to the common sentence of mistiness—that these in their period of suspension must wait till the sun shines on them before they publicly teach.[1]   And I am sadly convinced that if this be not done it will not be that the reasonable liberty of thought for which I am deeply solicitous, and for which you plead, will be preserved to the Church of England, but that, on the one hand, her faithful members will receive a blow which will send a multitude more to Rome, and, on the other side, that her own belief will be most deeply endangered.

'May God avert such a blow from us.—I am, my dear Lord Chancellor, most truly yours,   S. Oxon.'

It was not likely that Lord Westbury would approve of a scheme which, professing to distinguish between the doctrine and the law of the Church, would either have reduced the Judicial Committee to the position of a common jury or have created a dual jurisdiction, exercisable by ecclesiastical referees on the one hand and lay judges on the other, whose decisions on matters of orthodoxy it might be impossible to reconcile.

In the summer of 1863 the judicial bench sustained a heavy loss in the death of Sir Cresswell

---

[1] The 'misty men' referred to were Dr. Williams and Mr. Wilson, who had been condemned by the Dean of Arches for heretical doctrines in *Essays and Reviews, vide* p. 74 *post.*

Cresswell, and on Lord Westbury's recommendation Baron Wilde, now Lord Penzance, was appointed Judge of the Probate and Divorce Court in his place. It was intended that the Attorney-General, Atherton, should succeed Baron Wilde in the Exchequer; but Atherton refused the appointment, and some difficulty arose through the rival claims to promotion of several of the other lawyers who supported the Government. Lord Westbury, in a letter to Lord Palmerston, discusses their several qualifications, and continues :—

'I propose, therefore, either to take a very learned and distinguished man, who in point of learning is superior to both, but has never been in Parliament, and so far as I know has no politics at all — Mr. Lush, Q.C., or the present Recorder of London, Mr. Russell Gurney.

'Gurney has been out of practice in the Civil Courts, and is inferior to Lush as a lawyer, but on the other hand is an experienced and able criminal judge. The appointment of Lush would be solely on the ground of professional merits. . . .

'I wish the appointments of the puisne judges to be made exclusively on legal merits, as this principle affords the greatest inducement to exertion at the bar.'

While the mattter was in suspense the health of the Attorney-General utterly broke down, and he was compelled to retire. Lord Westbury thereupon appointed Mr. Pigott, and subsequently Mr. Lush, to the vacant judgeships. It may be safely asserted that no more admirable appointment than that of Mr. Justice (afterwards Lord Justice) Lush was ever made to the judicial bench.

For Lord Westbury may also be claimed the honour of appointing the late Mr. Justice Shee, the

first Roman Catholic Judge in England since the
Emancipation Act. The appointment was very
pleasing to the profession, though scruples on the
part of some politicians who considered that it
would damage the Government by offending Protestant feeling in the constituencies had first to be
overcome. Following the excellent principle he had
laid down for himself, he subsequently appointed to
the Common Pleas bench a political opponent, Sir
Montague Smith, late a paid member of the Judicial
Committee of the Privy Council, simply on the
ground of his pre-eminent qualifications for judicial
rank.

The disposal of his patronage gave Lord Westbury much difficulty and anxiety, and in this respect
the Church patronage was the worst of all. Great
pressure was continually put upon him by persons
whose high position ought to have preserved them
from such use of their influence.

The claims preferred by the candidates themselves were occasionally of a ludicrous nature. One
clergyman wrote to ask for a vacant living. He
frankly acknowledged that he had no right to expect
any patronage from the Chancellor; still he might
just mention that some years before he had lodged
in the same crescent at Littlehampton, and often
saw Mr. Bethell, surrounded by his young family, on
the green in front of the house. Another application was tragically ridiculous. A lady wrote on
paper with the deepest mourning border. Her

husband had lately died, she said, and his death lay at the Lord Chancellor's door. A living in Wiltshire had become vacant, and the deceased applied for it. So certain was he of success that he took a long journey to view the parish, put up at the village inn, lay in damp sheets, and died from a cold in consequence. His widow was nearly destitute, and as the Lord Chancellor was clearly, though not wilfully, the cause of so untimely a death, he would surely, she supposed, make some provision for her.

In view of the calumnies which were afterwards heaped upon Lord Westbury in connection with the Chancellor's patronage, an extract from a letter written by Mr. John Stuart (son of the late Vice-Chancellor), his private secretary, may be given :—

'He was indeed a generous, tender-hearted man. During the time I had the honour and pleasure of acting as his secretary, I always found him most anxious to assist the poor and friendless.

'Frequently, when handing me a large bundle of letters, he would say, "There is a letter this morning from a very poor man. Stuart, you must write a very kind letter to him." I never knew him direct his great power against any but the proud and overbearing. One morning Lord Westbury said to me, "Stuart, here is a letter from the Bishop of ——, recommending a clergyman for one of my livings. Stuart, if that clergyman is as good a man as the Bishop says he is, he should have been presented to one of the Bishop's livings long ago." A Lord-Lieutenant of one of the western counties wrote a rude letter declining to place in the Commission of the Peace a gentleman recommended by the Lord Chancellor. When the Lord Chancellor read the letter he said in his calm, slow tone: "This Lord-Lieutenant takes a peculiar view of his duty. I must reduce him to his proper dimensions."

'The best of the patronage at his disposal was admirably bestowed. The accusations made by the worst part of the news-paper press were utterly false. When Lord Westbury resigned, Mr. Christie, the eminent conveyancer, said to me that he did not believe that any Lord Chancellor had retired from office having done so little for members of his own family. I know that that remark was true.'

The late Earl of Shaftesbury, writing to the Hon. Mrs. T. E. Abraham after Lord Westbury's death, bore similar testimony. He said :—

' . . . Along with the rest of the world I was a great admirer of his intellectual power, and specially in legal state-ments and debate ; and although he frequently indulged in pleasantries, both in public and in private, he always seemed to me more under the irresistible influence of great natural wit than of any disposition to irritate or give pain.

'I ventured at different times to advance opinions on certain things that I thought might be beneficially done. I was struck by the attention he paid to my suggestions, and the desire he evidently had to hear and to say all that could be heard and said upon it.

'I must give you an instance of his anxiety to forego the exercise of preferments (which he might have claimed for his friends), with a view to the public weal. I presumed, as having been many years connected with lunacy, to remark that the Chancellor ought to have his own medical inspector for Chancery patients exclusively devoted to that duty. He agreed to it, and brought in a Bill accordingly. The Bill having been passed, he desired me to make the nominations, as one who had more experience than himself on the subject. These were places with salaries of £1500 each.'

Another letter shows very pleasantly that Lord Westbury was not unmindful of the friends of his early days. The delicacy with which the offer was made is particularly noticeable :—

' My dear "Joe Griffiths "—You are apt to suppose that I have forgotten you and the time when we read the Hellenics together in the garrets at Wadham. That is not so, as this note will prove to you.

'This morning brought me news of a small living, Norton Bavant, being vacant. It is near Warminster, where you were born and bred, and *therefore*, though a very small living—not exceeding clear £200 per annum,—I thought it might be accept- able to you, and if it is worth your attention I will present you to it.

'If it be too small, you must wait till I have some better opportunity of serving you, and take my present letter as a proof of my recollection of former times. Pray send me an immediate answer, and believe me yours very sincerely,   WESTBURY.'

Mr. Griffiths, an ex-fellow of Wadham, being at the time without preferment, accepted the living. 'My object,' wrote the Chancellor in a subsequent letter, 'is to give you a quiet and comfortable haven for life.'

Lord Westbury's correspondence gives frequent proof of how gracefully he could do a kind action. But like the rest of the world he found that grati- tude too often meant little more than a lively expectation of future favours. Few were contented. His experience was similar to that of the French king who complained that whenever he bestowed a piece of patronage, he made a hundred persons dis- satisfied and one ungrateful.

The publication of the *Essays and Reviews* in 1860 had excited a warm controversy between the principal parties of the Church, and eventually led to proceedings being instituted under the Church Dis-

cipline Act against two of the writers, Dr. Rowland
Williams and Mr. Wilson, on charges of heresy.
Both were charged with denying the plenary
inspiration of the Holy Scriptures.   Dr. Williams
was also charged with maintaining that justification
by faith meant only 'peace of mind, or sense of
Divine approval which comes of trust in a righteous
God, rather than a fiction of merit by transfer;'[1] and it
was alleged against Mr. Wilson that he had denied the
doctrine of everlasting life or death.   The Dean of
Arches, Dr. Lushington, found these charges proved,
and condemned each of the accused to one year's
suspension.   From this sentence both appealed to
the Judicial Committee of the Privy Council.

The judgment in the *Gorham Case* in 1850 laid
down the principle that in such proceedings the
Court had no jurisdiction to determine matters of
faith or doctrine on which the Church had prescribed
no definite rule of opinion.   It had only to ascertain
the true construction of the Articles and formularies,
with reference to the charges preferred, according to
the legal rules for the interpretation of written documents.   The proceedings against Dr. Williams and
Mr. Wilson were an attempt by the High Church
party to obtain the condemnation of unorthodox
views as inconsistent with the written law of the
Church.

---

[1] In the argument at the bar Dr. Williams explained that he
used the word 'fiction,' not in the sense of 'feigning,' but as a
phantasy or idea in the mind of an individual.

The appeals were heard together, both defendants appearing in person, and in February 1864
Lord Westbury delivered the written judgment
of the majority[1] of the Committee, reversing the
decision of the Court below on all points.[2]　The judgment was prefaced by a distinct avowal that the tribunal had no power to pronounce any opinion on the
character, effect, or tendency of the *Essays and Reviews*.
'If, therefore, the book, or these two essays, or either
of them as a whole, be of a mischievous and baneful
tendency, as weakening the foundation of Christian
belief, and likely to cause many to offend, they will
retain that character, and be liable to that condemnation, notwithstanding this our judgment.'

Stress was next laid on the fact that the proceedings were of a criminal nature, which required that the
accusation should be stated with precision and dis-
tinctness, and made it competent to the accused to
explain from other portions of his work the meaning
of the passages challenged.　With respect to the legal
tests of doctrine by which the soundness or the un-
soundness of the passages must be tried, the Court
adopted the rule laid down by the *Gorham Case*,
the Lord Chancellor observing :—

'It is obvious that there may be matters of doctrine on which
the Church has not given any definite rule or standard of faith or
opinion ; there may be matters of religious belief on which the
requisition of the Church may be less than Scripture may seem to

---

[1] The Lord Chancellor, the Bishop of London, Lord Cranworth, Lord Chelmsford, and Lord Kingsdown.

[2] 3 New Reports, 494.

warrant; there may be very many matters of religious speculation
and inquiry on which the Church may have refrained from forming
any opinion at all. On matters on which the Church has
prescribed no rule, there is so far freedom of opinion that they
may be discussed without penal consequences.

'Nor in a proceeding like the present are we at liberty to
ascribe to the Church any rule or teaching which we do not find
expressly and distinctly stated, or which is not plainly involved in
or to be collected from that which is written. . . . That only is
matter of accusation which is advisedly taught and maintained by
a clergyman in opposition to the doctrine of the Church.'

Passing on to consider the specific charges, the
Committee, on a careful examination of the passages,
strictly construed and taken with their context,
held that they did not contravene the teaching of
the Church. The charge of denying the inspiration
of the Scriptures involved the inquiry whether the
Church has affirmed that every part of every book
of the Bible was written under the inspiration of the
Holy Spirit. The judgment disposed of this question by showing that the framers of the Articles, in
their caution, had not used the word 'inspiration,'
as applied to the Scriptures ; there was therefore no
warrant for ascribing to them 'conclusions expressed
in new forms of words involving minute and subtle
matters of controversy.'

With respect to the charge against Mr. Wilson
of denying the eternity of reward or punishment, the
Court held that the mere expression of the hope that
the perverted may ultimately be restored did not
warrant the accusation. This part of the judgment
was expressed with great caution.

'We are not required, or at liberty, to express any opinion upon the mysterious question of the eternity of final punishment, further than to say that we do not find in the formularies to which this Article refers any such distinct declaration of our Church upon the subject, as to require us to condemn as penal the expression of hope by a clergyman that even the ultimate pardon of the wicked who are condemned in the day of judgment may be consistent with the will of Almighty God.

'In the first place, we find nothing in the passages extracted which, in any respect, questions or denies that at the end of the world there will be a judgment of God, awarding to those men whom He shall approve everlasting life or eternal happiness; but, with respect to a judgment of eternal misery, a hope is encouraged by Mr. Wilson that this may not be the purpose of God. . . .'

The Archbishops did not concur in those parts of the judgment which related to the charges of denying the inspiration of the Scriptures. Referring to the diversity of opinion among the Episcopal dignitaries, Lord Cranworth wrote to Lord Westbury :—

'I hope the differences among lawyers on legal points will cease to be a subject of merriment when among the three highest theological authorities, one thinks the judgment below right on both points as to both defendants,[1] another thinks it wrong on both points as to both defendants, and the third thinks it as to each defendant wrong on one point and right on the other.'

The judgment raised a storm of indignant protest from the Anglican party. Notwithstanding the care which had been taken to make the dose less unpalatable to clerical lips, the law lords were assailed with furious abuse. Lord Westbury in

[1] The Bishop of Oxford was probably the authority thus referred to.

particular was singled out for attack, as if, because he delivered the judgment, he alone was responsible for it.[1]

The extreme bitterness of Church politics has seldom been more plainly or painfully evinced. It was natural that those who thought strongly on these burning questions and were actively engaged in the contest should express themselves with vigour. Several lately-published biographies set forth utterances of leaders of the High Church party at that period, with respect both to the judgment and the tribunal responsible for it, which would, however, be ludicrous in the intensity of the rage and hatred they convey had they proceeded from men less entitled to veneration. Even the Missionary Bishop

---

[1] The judgment gave rise, among more serious literary efforts, to the following suggested epitaph, which has been sometimes attributed to the late Sir Philip Rose :—

RICHARD BARON WESTBURY,
Lord High Chancellor of England.
He was an eminent Christian,
An energetic and merciful Statesman,
And a still more eminent and merciful Judge.
During his three years' tenure of office
He abolished the ancient method of conveying land,
The time-honoured institution of the Insolvents' Court,
And
The Eternity of Punishment.
Towards the close of his earthly career,
In the Judicial Committee of the Privy Council,
He dismissed Hell with costs,
And took away from orthodox members of the
Church of England
Their last hope of everlasting damnation.

of Melanesia (Bishop Patteson), in whose character
humility and charity were pre-eminent, reflecting, it
would seem, the opinions of Bishop Selwyn, though
taking, as he said, 'a calmer view of what is agitat-
ing the Church at home,' assumed a deliberate intent
on Lord Westbury's part to offend by 'gratuitous
extra-judicial remarks.'

As for Bishop Gray of Capetown, his views found
the most violent expression.   Referring to what he
elsewhere termed 'this awful and profane judgment,'
he declared that if the Church did not denounce it
she would cease to witness for Christ.   'She must
destroy that masterpiece of Satan for the overthrow
of the faith, the Judicial Committee of the Privy
Council as her court of final appeal, or it will destroy
her;' and again: 'I believe that if the Privy
Council can throw the Church, it will. . . . In that
body all the enmity of the world against the Church
of Christ is gathered up and embodied.'[1]   Among
such words as these we find no trace of that charity
which has been declared the perfection of all virtues
and the greatest ornament of religion.

Those who were able to view the subject with
minds free from the warp of an *odium theologicum*
found in the judgment a recognition of the right to
liberty of thought and opinion on matters of religious
speculation, and considered that it would tend, as
undoubtedly it has tended, to enlarge the compre-
hensiveness of the Church.

[1] *Life of Bishop Gray*, vol. ii. pp. 113, 137, 158.

Foiled in this attempt to subject individual
writers of the *Essays and Reviews* to legal penalties for their alleged violation of ecclesiastical law,
the Anglican party, relying on the strong influence
in Convocation of Bishop Wilberforce, proposed the
formal condemnation of the whole book as heretical
by means of a judgment of the Synod. Such a
course had only once been adopted during the past
three centuries, and it was opposed by the Bishops of
London and Lincoln on the ground of its inexpedi-
ency. But the Bishop of Oxford and his friends
triumphed, and the condemnation was pronounced.

Thereupon Lord Houghton in the House of
Lords asked a series of questions as to the powers
of Convocation to pass a synodical judgment on
books, and as to the immunity of its members from
legal proceedings consequent thereon. The subject, he said, involved a practical grievance and an
immediate danger, and his concern in it was for the
freedom of opinion and the liberties of literature. He
enlarged upon the injustice of condemning *in toto* a
work containing several essays in some of which no
one had ever pretended to find anything objectionable. Those who pronounced the censure meant
that it should punish, and by punishing injure, and
he deprecated the unfairness in the case of such men
as Dr. Temple and Professor Jowett of a sentence
pronounced by a body which possessed none of the
attributes of a court of justice. It was an attempt
to limit freedom of expression and thought in this

country. He concluded by saying : ' If Convocation persists in proceeding in this path, I fear the
result will be a reversion to the constitutional form
which has been adopted before to check its eccen-
tricities ; whereas if they will employ argument to
meet argument, knowledge to meet knowledge, and
intellect to meet intellect, they will do all which will
be best for their Church and their country.' The
Lord Chancellor in reply said :—

'There are three modes of dealing with Convocation since it
has been permitted, which I deeply regret, to come into action
again and transact business. The first is, while they are harm-
lessly busy, to take no notice of their proceedings ; the second is,
when they seem likely to get into mischief, to prorogue them
and put a stop to their proceedings ; the third, when they have
done something clearly beyond their powers, is to bring them to
the bar of justice for punishment.'

After referring to the laws passed to secure the
royal supremacy, under which the Crown is the
fountain of all jurisdiction, spiritual and temporal,
and particularly to the Act of 25 Henry VIII. c. 19,
which prohibited Convocation from pronouncing any
sentence without the consent of the Sovereign under
the penalties of a *præmunire*, he proceeded :—

'I am afraid my noble friend has not considered what the
pains and penalties of a *præmunire* are, or his gentle heart would
have melted at the prospect. The most rev. primate and the
bishops would have to appear at this bar, not in the solemn state
in which we see them here, but as penitents in sackcloth and
ashes. And what would be the sentence? I observe that
the most rev. primate gave two votes—his original vote and a
casting vote. I will take the measure of his sentence from the

sentence passed by a bishop on one of these authors—a year's
deprivation of his benefice.   For two years, therefore, the most
rev. primate might be condemned to have all the revenues of his
high position sequestrated.   I have not ventured—I say it seriously—I have not ventured to present this question to Her
Majesty's Government ; for, my lords, only imagine what a temptation it would be for my right hon. friend the Chancellor of the
Exchequer to spread his net and in one haul take in £30,000
from the highest dignitary, not to speak of the *oi polloi*—the
bishops, deacons, archdeacons, canons, vicars—all included in
one common crime, all subject to one common penalty.   I cannot
contemplate that possibility, and therefore your lordships will not
be surprised to hear that I have refrained from approaching the
subject—that I have shrunk altogether from taking the first step
of asking counsel of the law officers of the Crown in the matter.
Had I taken that step, I have no doubt I should have been
advised that if there was a synodical judgment it would be a
violation of the law ; I should then have been placed in the disagreeable position of having to advise a prosecution ; and, entertaining as I do a sincere affection for the Episcopal bench, and
a sincere personal regard and affection for many members of the
Episcopate, I am happy to find myself relieved from such great
difficulty and embarrassment.'

Lord Westbury went on to ridicule the judgment in the following terms :—

'I am happy to tell your lordships that what is called a
synodical judgment is a well-lubricated set of words—a sentence
so oily and saponaceous that no one can grasp it.   Like an eel,
it slips through your fingers. . . . Convocation could not have
been more successful if they had synodically sat down to produce a sentence of no meaning, than they were when in their
labour they produced this *ridiculus mus*.   As a judgment this
sentence has no meaning whatever—this judgment is no judgment at all.'

Therefore, as no one was injured by 'this oily
form of words,' in view of the impotency of the thing,

the Government, he said, intended to take no action in the matter. The intention of the Legislature declared by the statutes was to marshal ecclesiastical jurisdiction for trying ecclesiastical offences in this order—first, the diocesan ; then the Archbishop in Court of Appeal ; and lastly, the Crown, as the supreme head and final administrator. By interposing Convocation they interposed an anomalous body exercising jurisdiction uncontrolled by any court of appeal and not amenable to the Crown. After pointing out that a bishop by declining to institute the author of any of the essays might involve himself in the serious consequences of a *duplex querela*, he concluded by saying :—

'Those who do not concur in these proceedings may probably think that, by protesting against such a course, they may save themselves from consequences ; but, if they will take my recommendation, whenever there is any attempt to carry Convocation beyond its proper limits, their best security after protesting will be to gather up their garments and flee, and, remembering the pillar of salt, not to cast a look behind. I am happy to say that in all these proceedings there is more smoke than fire, though they do not, probably, proceed from a spirit that is equally harmless.'

The transparently personal nature of this attack drew the Bishop of Oxford into a reply more remarkable for invective than argument. The Chancellor's speech had been listened to with an amused surprise, if not enjoyment, by many of their Lordships ; the Bishop's was received with repeated cheers from the Opposition benches. He said :—

'I have good ground to complain of the tone of the noble
and learned lord on the woolsack. If a man has no respect for
himself, he ought, at all events, to respect the tribunal before
which he speaks; and when the highest representative of the
law of England in your lordship's House upon a matter involving
the liberties of the subject and the religion of the realm, and all
those high truths concerning which this discussion is, can think
it fitting to descend to a ribaldry in which he knows that he can
safely indulge, because those to whom he addresses it will have
too much respect for their character to answer him in like sort,
—I say that this House has ground to complain of having its
high character unnecessarily injured in the sight of the people of
this land by one occupying so high a position within it.'

The Bishop proceeded to argue that the very
fact that Convocation sat under the Queen's Writ
negatived the presumption of any claim to a jurisdiction independent of the Crown.   He continued :—

'I know enough of this House, and of the people of England, to know that it is not by trying, in words which shall blister
those upon whom they fall, to produce a momentary pain on
those who cannot properly reply to them, that great questions
will be solved; but that it is by dealing with them with calmness, with abstinence from the imputation of motives, and, above
all, with the most scrupulous regard to stating upon every point
that which shall prevent any man in this House being led to a
conclusion other than that which the facts warrant.'

He justified the action of Convocation as necessary for the maintenance of truth upon the following
ground :—

'We had to deal with this question : Shall the Church of
England see these false doctrines stated by those who hold her
ministry; and shall we, her highest ministers, having under our
Queen the opportunity of, for the ministry of that Church, dis-
avowing these errors—shall we timorously hold our tongues,

because if we speak we may be subject to ribald reproach? or shall we, in the name of the Church of England, clear that ministry from being supposed to be at liberty to declare one thing as the condition of taking it, and then to speak another as the habit of its exercise? It was not, my lords, to put down opinion; it was to prevent men breaking their solemn obligations that this step was taken.'

In defence of the course taken in condemning the book instead of individual writers, he maintained that as long as each author allowed his name to appear in the company of others whose essays were at variance with the religion of the country, he rendered himself morally responsible for the contents of the whole book, though he had the opportunity of disclaimer or explanation as edition after edition was published. In conclusion he said he was satisfied that the best way to avoid the recurrence of such a state of things was to allow the Church in her authorised manner to pronounce for her followers that she disclaims for her living ministry erroneous teaching.

In a few words of reply the Lord Chancellor complained, with some bitterness, of the construction put upon parts of his statement, and of the excited manner and license of language which had characterised the Bishop's speech. With regard to the charge of having misrepresented a passage in the Act, which the Bishop had attempted to fasten upon him, he simply observed, 'My apology for him, I think, must be that he himself does not quite understand it.'

This much-to-be-regretted incident was at the time viewed in greatly differing lights by the rival partisans in the bitter feuds then growing up within the Church. The truth was, that there was little love lost between the two high dignitaries.[1] The same high spirit and combativeness which had led Lord Westbury to single out Mr. Gladstone in the House of Commons as a foeman worthy of his steel now brought him into conflict with Bishop Wilberforce, and when it came to personal invective there was little to choose between the two combatants.[2]

Still it must be conceded that the Bishop had good reason for complaint. Admitting that it was desirable to discountenance the claim of Convocation to a novel jurisdiction, and to point out their mistake in attempting to limit freedom of thought and expression; admitting also that the Chancellor was justified in refusing to take steps which might lead to his being coerced by the force of public opinion

[1] Mr. W. P. Frith, R.A., in his lately-published *Autobiography and Reminiscences*, tells an amusing story of an incident which occurred when he was engaged upon his picture of the Marriage of the Prince of Wales, painted by command of the Queen : ' When the Lord Chancellor sat for me, his eye caught the form of the Bishop of Oxford, and he said : "Ah! I should have thought it impossible to produce a tolerably agreeable face and yet preserve any resemblance to the Bishop of Oxford." And when the Bishop saw my portrait of Westbury, he said : "Like him? Yes; but not wicked enough." '—Vol. i. p. 43.

[2] In describing the encounter, *Punch* observed that although the celestial mind was above personalities, ' in the interest of the Church and truth and humility, the Bishop did blaze out with uncommon fury.'

into hostile proceedings, and that therefore it was
his object to treat the matter lightly, and convey,
under cover of good-natured badinage, advice which
might prevent the recurrence of the mistake, yet
the tone of his observations cannot be excused. Personalities so plainly levelled at the acknowledged
leader of a powerful and ambitious section of the
Church, added to expressions which evinced some
contempt for the whole bench of bishops, gave just
offence to many who disapproved of the proceedings
of Convocation, while some of Lord Westbury's
friends who heard the speech felt that he had been
fatally misled by his dangerous gift of satire. The
debate interrupted for a time the friendly relations
which had previously existed between the Chancellor
and the Bishop. After an interval Lord Westbury
showed his regret for what had passed by expressing a desire for a reconciliation, and the quarrel was
made up.[1]

The bitter feeling aroused by the Chancellor's
attack on Convocation had an unfavourable influence on the chance of passing the measure referred
to in the following letter :—

> '1 *Upper Hyde Park Gardens, W.*
> '*March* 12 [1864].
>
> 'My dear Gladstone—I did not forget my promise to you

---

[1] 'Lord Westbury forced a reconciliation upon me, sending
Lord St. Germains to ask me to speak to him on the woolsack ;
and then asking me "to take once more his hand," and hoping
" I had enjoyed my vacation and shot many pheasants." '—*Life
of Bishop Wilberforce*, vol. iii. p. 143.

about examining the subject of the Suffragan Bishops. I have done so, and am now (as becomes a judge, who never ought to be ashamed of modifying his former opinions, whenever he thinks they have been extreme) prepared to discuss the subject *æquiore animo.*

' Suppose we ask the Cabinet to refer it to you, me, Sir George Grey and Cardwell, to report what is best to be done ?

' I want to bring in a Bill to endow the Greek Professorship of Oxford with one of my canonries, enacting that to the first canonry in the gift of the Lord Chancellor which shall become vacant, the Regius Professor of Greek in the University of Oxford shall be appointed, and thenceforth from time to time the professor for the time being, provided he be a clergyman in full orders, shall succeed to and enjoy such canonry.

' In the present instance it would be an act of great justice, and for the future a very appropriate provision.

' I do not want you openly to support this proposal, but I am confident nothing could be more acceptable to right-minded men, and zealots would not be angry at the thought that an heretical Lord Chancellor is stripped, even though it be for an heretical professor.—Yours sincerely,   WESTBURY.'

The Greek chair was the only one of the five Regius Professorships at Oxford which had no other endowment than its original stipend of £40 a year. To the Regius Professorship of Greek at Cambridge a canonry was annexed, and Lord Westbury desired to provide the chair at Oxford with a similar endowment. The proposal excited much opposition. It was represented that it would practically exclude laymen from the Professorship, though they might be as eminent for scholarship as Professors Porson and Conington. Lord Westbury met this objection by declaring that if a layman were appointed for his peculiar eminence, the Uni-

versity might reasonably be expected to make the
necessary provision for him.   In his view the
University received certain pecuniary exemptions
on the understanding that it would make proper
provision for its professors.   His observations on
this point gave some offence to the University, and
Lord Derby, as its Chancellor, brought the matter
before the House, and obtained from Lord Westbury
a disavowal of any imputation of breach of faith.

After considerable debate the Bill was thrown
out.   The Bishops opposed it on the ground that
it was the duty of the University to provide the
requisite endowment, and that it was unfair to withdraw a valuable piece of Church preferment from
the rewards of purely clerical service.   But a great
part of the opposition was unquestionably due to
the dislike felt for what were supposed to be the
views of Professor Jowett, the occupant of the
chair.   One eminent Church dignitary went so far
as to declare that to refuse the endowment was the
best way to counteract the mischief of the decision
of the Privy Council with regard to the *Essays and
Reviews*.

Two other reforms, attempted by the Lord
Chancellor in this session, also failed.   One was a
Bill for extending the jurisdiction of County Courts
and reducing the period for the recovery of simple
contract debts, to which reference will be made in
the next chapter.   The other was a measure repeal-
ing the existing Church Discipline Act, and intro-

ducing a very simple, short, and inexpensive mode
of procedure, both with respect to charges of
immorality and matters of doctrine and discipline.
In trials of the latter character the Bishops were to
be entitled to the assistance of the advice of the
law officers; and unless the Court decided to the
contrary, their costs were to come out of the funds
of the Ecclesiastical Commissioners. The Cabinet
were not much inclined to meddle with the subject,
and although the Chancellor had drawn the Bill with
his own hand, it was thought that as there was no
pressing public call for any measure of the kind, it
was better not to introduce it. 'To tell the truth,'
wrote Lord Westbury, 'I think some of my friends
were afraid of leaving it in my hands.'

Some ground for this apprehension may, no
doubt, have existed in the attitude of the High
Church party towards the Chancellor. But apart
from personal considerations, the question of enforcing Church discipline has long been one of extreme
difficulty. The partial attempt to settle it made by
the Public Worship Regulation Act of 1874 resulted
in one of the greatest legislative blunders of modern
times. Even the problem of how to deal with
'criminous clerks' in a speedy and effectual manner
has for half a century defied solution.

CHAPTER IV

1865

THE opening of the session of 1865 gave promise of a golden opportunity for further amendment of the law by a reforming Lord Chancellor. Party spirit was in a state of comparative tranquillity, and no burning question threatened to obstruct domestic legislation. Lord Westbury's ambition to utilise the final session of the expiring Parliament in the completion of the legal reforms he had already suggested seemed likely to be realised. Little could he have supposed that the most stirring event of that session would be the debate on motions of censure on himself. Early in January he wrote to Lord Palmerston :—

'I am anxious to send you a statement of the different legal measures which I am desirous of submitting to Parliament during the ensuing session, and which, if you approve, can be stated to the Cabinet at our next meeting.

'They are almost all of them measures of great importance, and which will lead to much improvement in the administration of justice.'

The following list of measures, with the Lord Chancellor's observations on them, accompanied the letter :—

' 1. A Bill to complete the expurgation of the Statute-Book, being the final conclusion of the work on which the Lord Chancellor has been engaged during the last five years, and by which the statutes of the realm, now extending over forty-six large quarto volumes, will be reduced to one-fourth of that bulk.

' This will be followed by a proposal to appoint a Commission for making a complete digest of the whole body of English law, the nature of which the Lord Chancellor has already stated to the Cabinet.

' 2. Bills for the concentration of all the Courts of Justice on one site, with their attendant offices, and the appropriation to this purpose of certain large funds in the Court of Chancery.

' These Bills *are prepared* and will be immediately brought in by the Attorney-General and Mr. Cowper ; they must begin in the Commons.

' 3. Bill for the reform of the law relating to patents and the better administration of justice in actions and suits respecting patents.

' This Bill is provided mainly on the recent Report of the Royal Commission, but with some alterations.   The Lord Chancellor wishes to have a Committee of the Cabinet, consisting of Earl Granville, Sir George Grey, and Milner Gibson, to consult with him on the details of this measure.

' *Note.*—These three measures may be mentioned in the Queen's Speech.

' 4. A Bill for investing the County Courts with equitable jurisdiction in causes below a certain amount, and also for reducing the period of time allowed by the present statutes of

limitation for the recovery of simple contract debts (six years)
to three years.

'This is the Lord Chancellor's Bill of last session, but in a
reduced and amended form.

' 5. A Bill to alter the law relating to attorneys and their clients
with respect to costs.

'This is a most important measure.   It must be well considered, because it is the first measure of the Lord Chancellor
which has the hearty assent of the great body of solicitors ; that
the interest of solicitors should also be the interest of the public
is hard to believe, but the Lord Chancellor thinks that this
measure will be found to be an exception to the general rule.

' It will certainly place the profession of the attorney on higher
ground, and tend to introduce better and more equitable rules for
their remuneration.[1]

' 6. Two smaller Bills for the removal of some anomalies and
defects in the law, and the administration of justice, which will
tend to remove some of the causes of litigation.

'Among the details, which are purely technical, will be a
measure for carrying out the agreement made with the Belgian
Ambassador, that where land or any interest in land in the
United Kingdom comes to an alien, it shall not be forfeited to the
Crown, but shall be sold and the proceeds paid to the alien.'

In reply Lord Palmerston said :—

' I have sent in circulation your list of proposed measures, the
whole of which with the exception of the last seem very good.
But why are we to alter our laws about landed property to please
and oblige Van de Weyer ? why is a foreign minister to have our
standing law changed for his private convenience ?   If he wants
some change to suit his own peculiar case, let him apply for a

---

[1] The Bill empowered solicitors to make bargains with their
clients as to remuneration, and to take security for their costs.
It also enabled a solicitor trustee to charge his costs to the trust,
and gave any person power to appoint the Court of Chancery his
trustee for the administration of his personal estate.   It was
referred to a Select Committee and afterwards withdrawn.

private Bill, just as the King of Prussia did about the Prussian Embassy House on Carlton Terrace.

'I am all against letting foreigners be landowners in England, and as to the case of a landed estate being left by will to a foreigner, such a case must be rare indeed, and may be dealt with on its own merits when it happens. The bequeather could easily do himself that which you propose to do by law—that is to say, he might by his will devise the estate to be sold and the proceeds to be paid to the favoured foreigner, so that your Bill would be not only objectionable but unnecessary.'

Upon this question, which had been much pressed by the Belgian Minister, Lord Westbury held more liberal views than the Prime Minister, who declared that the alleged inconvenience felt by British subjects in Belgium, upon which the demand for an alteration in the law was based, was a mere pretence.   Lord Palmerston put the matter thus :—

'The greater part of British subjects who go to Belgium are people who go thither to live cheap, and whose means are devoted to buy bread, and are not available for buying land. There are a few manufacturing establishments set up in Belgium by British subjects, but the only complaints I have ever heard about them have arisen from the jealousy of their fellow-countrymen engaged in similar industry at home.   Van de Weyer has a house near Windsor and has been buying land around it, or rather Bates has been buying it for him ; and Van de Weyer would like to be able to hold this property in his own name, especially in the event of Bates's death ; but I do not think that we ought to alter the long-established law of our land to suit the private purposes of a foreigner, however respectable or entitled to consideration, and the more especially if the law proposed to be repealed is one for which there are good reasons.

'Now according to our social habits and political organisation the possession of land in this country is directly or indirectly the source of political influence and power, and that influence and power ought to be exercised exclusively by British subjects, and not to pass in any degree into the hands of foreigners. It may be said that the possession of landed property by a few foreigners would produce no sensible effect on the working of our constitution ; but this is a question of principle and not of degree, and you might on the same ground propose a law to allow foreigners to vote at elections, as well as to allow them to purchase the means of swaying the votes of other persons at elections. You could not repeal the present law in favour of Belgium without doing so for every other country, and you may depend upon it you would find a greater number of alien squatters come and settle here than might by some be anticipated.'

In deference to these views Lord Westbury dropped the proposed Bill. ' I should have been very glad,' he wrote in reply, ' to have altered the law, because I regard it as a relic of feudal barbarism which nearly every other country has repudiated ; but your Lordship has such an instinctive perception of what would suit the public mind, that I could not venture to press my opinion for a moment in opposition to your judgment.' The disabilities of aliens with respect to the acquisition of land have since been removed by the Naturalisation Act of 1870, without giving rise to any of the evils which Lord Palmerston apprehended.

In the previous year the Chancellor had laid before the House a measure to confer a limited jurisdiction in equity on the County Courts. He explained that the existing systems confined their functions to the authority exercised by the Courts of Common Law, and thus in a great number of matters in which the poorer classes were interested justice could only be obtained by resort to the more expensive process of the Court of Chancery. Lord Westbury considered that this often amounted to a practical denial of justice to persons in humble circumstances, and he wished to give the inferior tribunals power to deal with such matters, subject to certain limitations as to the value of the property and other matters.

The Bill of 1864 embodied a still more ambitious scheme. By the Bankruptcy Act of 1861 the Lord Chancellor had done something to mitigate the severity of the law with respect to imprisonment for debt. He declared he would give no countenance to the principle of treating every debtor as a criminal. The state of the law as then administered in County Courts in the case of small debtors differed from that which existed with regard to other classes of the community. There was one law for the rich, and another for the poor. No bankrupt could be kept in prison, except for fraud, for more than fourteen days; but a poor man, against whom a judgment had been obtained in the County Court, might be imprisoned fifty times over for the same debt. The creditor was always on the watch to find where he was employed, in order to pounce down upon him and send him to prison, in the hope of wringing from him some further payment. 'The result is,' said Lord Westbury, 'that the law has mortgaged the labour and earnings of the poor to their creditors for an indefinite time, mercilessly and without possibility or hope of relief.'

Imprisonment for small debts was, in his opinion, as disastrous to society as to the debtors. The artisan or labourer had no resources except his ability to labour. By shutting him up in prison he was deprived of the power of exercising his skill or strength, condemned to enforced idleness, and degraded by contaminating influences; while the country sustained a loss of a part of its wealth-productive labour. Lord Westbury had therefore proposed to abrogate the law which gave the judge power of imprisonment if satisfied of the debtor's ability to pay, and to confine the power to cases where the debt was contracted by false pretences or without reasonable expectation of ability to pay it. He considered that the system of extended credit which had grown up under the County Court Acts was a serious evil to be checked. It led poor men into habits of improvidence, and placed them too much at the mercy of retail dealers.

'For my own part,' he said, 'I confess that I do not think a man, if he chooses to give credit, is entitled, morally or upon grounds of good policy, to anything more than an equitable distribution of all the means in the possession of his debtor at the time when he gives him credit. It is not, it seems to me, a just or a politic course so to legislate as to induce a creditor to speculate on the future profits of the person whom he trusts.'

He therefore proposed that the period within which debts under £20 were recoverable should be reduced from six years to one year. The opposition to this last proposal as totally destructive of credit, and therefore injurious to small traders and their cus-

tomers alike, was so strong that the Chancellor agreed
to an amendment making the period of limitation
three years. But even this concession proved insufficient, and the Bill was withdrawn.

The provisions as to debtor and creditor were
omitted from the measure again brought forward by
the Chancellor in 1865 to extend the jurisdiction of
the County Courts. Notwithstanding the adverse
criticism of Lord St. Leonards, it was accepted by
the Lords. In the Lower House it received the
cordial approval of Sir Fitzroy Kelly, and became
law. It may perhaps be said that none of the
reforms with which Lord Westbury's name is connected has proved of greater value. The Act
popularised the equity system by bringing it home
to every man's door, and entitled its author to the
gratitude of the community.

At a later date he evidently favours a still
further extension of local jurisdiction. Writing to
his youngest son, who was acting as marshal to one
of the Judges on Circuit, he says :—

'The great tendency of modern opinion appears to be that
the Circuits are a very inconvenient mode of administering justice
in civil causes; that great delay and expense arise from the
necessity of compelling suitors to resort to the assize with much
uncertainty when their causes will be heard, or whether they will
be remanets, or whether, if called on, time will allow of their
being satisfactorily heard, or whether the counsel and the judge
will not, in truth, drive many parties to a reference who desired to
have their causes heard and decided in open court ? It is not
impossible that we may ultimately come to local courts of the
première instance as in France, in fact, enlarging the county courts

into general courts of civil causes without limitation as to amount. I wish you very much to form an opinion on this subject. Of course it would very much augment the number of local barristers. The Courts at Westminster Hall would then become Courts of Appeal. Pray attend Court constantly, that you may become thoroughly imbued with the practice and conduct of causes.'

One of the newspapers, referring to the Lord Chancellor's measures and the opposition to them, humorously complained that he was taking away the breath of the ancient law reformers :—

'He has skipped along at such a pace that all his competitors are tailing off in the rear. He has reached such high acclivities that his friends are beginning to draw up and pant. Lord St. Leonards, who received such an excellent character from Lord Brougham as a law reformer a few days since, has given up, and has seized his too active leader by the coat-tails, trying with all his might to draw him back. Lord Cranworth has lost his first wind, and now declares that he is half for going up and half for standing still. Even Lord Brougham complained the other day of the pace, and seems now inclined, like an elderly gentleman half-way up the Righi, to turn round frequently and admire the prospect below. As to Lords Chelmsford and Wensleydale, and such like Law Lords, of course they do but abide in the valley below and shout out warnings and prophecies. The active Chancellor, however, steps deftly over boulders, scorns the zigzag, climbs the steep alone, and waves his pocket-handkerchief at the top of his alpenstock, inviting all to follow him who will. The fact is that the nation has in Lord Westbury, for the first time, a law reformer who is terribly in earnest.'

The concentration of the Law Courts on their present site—'the umbilicus of the legal locality,' as he called it—gave Lord Westbury an opportunity, which he turned to admirable account, of explaining a valuable reform which he had long urged. The change involved a comprehensive financial scheme which demanded careful advocacy. 'Law and Finance,' wrote Mr. Gladstone, 'are two beautiful damsels. How charming to see them hand in hand!' The chief source of the money required to be expended was afforded by the Chancery Suitors' Fund—representing the accumulations of dividends resulting from the investment by the Court of cash belonging to suitors. The Chancellor held that the profits of an investment made at the risk of the State were public money; and his argument on this point convinced many who had previously opposed this part of the scheme as inequitable. To meet this sentimental objection, he had proposed, as an alternative mode of obtaining the money required, that the site should be bought by the Court of Chancery, and let with the buildings to be erected upon it to the Government at a rent which would be capitalised, the cost of site and buildings being raised by debenture bonds.

'No sensible person,' he wrote, 'would think of resorting to this latter plan. But there are certain morbidly sensitive and non-apprehensive people who start at the notion of the Government plundering (as they call it) the Court of Chancery; and some of these persons imagine that there may be found persons, but whom they know not, that may by some possibility, but what they cannot describe, have a claim to this £800,000; and it is possible that their timid, but ignorant, consciences might be better

satisfied with a scheme that seems to retain and hold
the £800,000—treating it as invested only, and not
parted with.'

About two-thirds of the million and a half
appropriated to the work was eventually taken from
the so-called Suitors' Fund, or, to speak more
correctly, the accumulated banking profits of the
Court of Chancery. A vast deal of cold water was
thrown on the scheme, and the measures which embodied it ran the gauntlet of many perils, especially
in the House of Lords. But they became law, and
under them our Palace of Justice was erected. To
Lord Westbury and Sir Roundell Palmer was due
the credit of finally removing the greatest obstacle
of modern times to the proper administration of
justice.

Lord Westbury expressed his sanguine belief
that the concentration of the Courts was a long step
in the direction of the fusion of law and equity,
which he had steadily advocated since his entrance
into Parliament. Upon this anomaly he was never
weary of descanting. 'It is a lamentable thing,' he
said in one of his judgments, 'to observe how much
of the litigation in this country, and how much of
the difficulty in the administration of justice, is due
to the fact that the jurisdiction is divided between
different Courts and conducted upon different principles. The justice of a court of law is one thing,
the justice of a court of equity is another, the justice
of the court of bankruptcy is a third ; and it is from

that confusion that this very simple case has become complicated.'

On another occasion he declared 'it was unreasonable that one court should be bound to commit injustice, and that another court should be instituted, the functions of which should be to watch the proceedings of the first court, to run after it and stop it in its course.'

Lord Westbury's career furnishes abundant proof of Balthazar's assertion that

> ' Slander lives upon succession,
> For ever housed, when once it gets possession.'

He had already given deadly offence to a strong party of Churchmen, and the Colenso case once more exposed him to the bitter hatred of dogmatical theologians, whose exclusive pretensions were declared to be inconsistent with the law of the realm. The case, which had long been the subject of discussion, was finally disposed of by the judgment of the Privy Council in the spring of 1865.   Dr. Gray, the Bishop of Cape Town, claiming to exercise jurisdiction as Metropolitan of the Colony, had sentenced Dr. Colenso to be deposed from his office of Bishop of Natal upon charges of heresy and false doctrine. Dr. Colenso refused to recognise the validity of the proceedings, and presented a petition to Her Majesty in Council, which was specially referred to the Judicial Committee.

The question of the jurisdiction of the Metropolitan mainly depended upon the power of the

Crown to create a Metropolitan See, or confer
coercive jurisdiction over a suffragan bishop. By
the unanimous judgment of the Committee[1] it was
held that the sentence pronounced by the Bishop of
Cape Town was null and void. The status of Colonial
Bishops was defined with a precision which swept away
for ever the pretensions on which the inhibition of Dr.
Colenso was founded. Even the Bishop of Oxford
declared: 'I think that Westbury's judgment on
Colenso, bristling with Erastian insults to the Church
as it purposely is, is yet the charter of the freedom of
the Colonial Church, so is the modern Ahithophel
overruled.'[2] Surely 'the modern Ahithophel' was a
singularly inappropriate designation for Lord Westbury, for his ecclesiastical judgments were most
strongly denounced by many at that period on the
particular ground that it was *not* 'as if a man had
enquired at the oracle of God.'[3] Nor to the un-
prejudiced lay reader of the judgment are the 'insults'
apparent ; but whatever its language, the Bishop and
those who acted with him might have remembered,
in common fairness, that the judgment was the
deliberate expression of the opinion of men so widely
differing as Lords Cranworth and Kingsdown, Sir
John Romilly and Dr. Lushington. With the subsequent excommunication of Dr. Colenso by the Bishop

[1] The Lord Chancellor, Lord Cranworth, Lord Kingsdown, the Master of the Rolls (Sir John Romilly), and Dr.
Lushington.

[2] *Life of Bishop Wilberforce,* vol. iii. p. 126.

[3] 2 Sam. xvi. 23.

of Cape Town, and other proceedings arising out of the case, we need not here concern ourselves.

The voluntary confession in the Road Murder case gave rise to much discussion as to the right of a clergyman to withhold evidence of facts which had been disclosed to him 'under seal of confession.' This privilege had been claimed by Mr. Wagner during the proceedings before the magistrates, and some doubt was expressed as to whether the witness could be compelled to answer the questions put to him. Lord Westbury, in replying to an inquiry on this point, declared very plainly that no such privilege was conferred by the law of England. This led to an interesting correspondence between the Lord Chancellor and the Bishop of Exeter, then in his eighty-eighth year. Dr. Phillpotts wrote :—

'I need not assure your Lordship that it is with great diffidence I presume to intimate any doubt of the entire accuracy of a statement of your Lordship with respect to a point of law; but as that point is specially connected with the Church and the duty of its ministers, I shall be forgiven if I thus venture to intrude upon your Lordship.

'That I have the highest confidence generally in any such statement, even when extra-judicially made, as it was on Friday last in the House of Lords by your Lordship, I need not say; but as a Bishop of the Church of England, and in discharge of the last duty to it I am likely ever to be called upon to discharge, I must not forbear to hazard the appearance of presumption. Your Lordship is reported to have said, "That there can be no doubt that in a suit or criminal proceeding a clergyman of the Church of England is not privileged to decline to answer a question which is put to him for the purposes of justice, on the ground that his answer would reveal something that he has known in

confession ;" in other words, that nothing which has passed between a clergyman and his penitent in confession can be regarded
as a privileged communication. This is contrary to a canon of
the Church of England—the 113th canon of 1603, entitled
"Ministers may present," which concludes with the following
words : "Provided always that if any man confess his secret and
hidden sins to the minister for the unburdening of his conscience,
or to receive spiritual consolation and ease of mind from him,
we do not any way bind the said minister by this our constitution,
but do straitly charge and admonish him that he do not at any
time reveal and make known to any person whatsoever any crime
or offence so committed to his trust and secrecy (except they be
such crimes as by the laws of this realm his own life may be
called into question for concealing the same) under pain of irregu-
larity "—one of the gravest canonical offences.

'This canon is, I trust, a sufficient excuse for a bishop to take
the step which I am now presuming to take. I am far from
suggesting that any canon made by Convocation, even though it
have received the sanction of the Crown under the Great Seal (as
those of 1603), could be deemed valid against any pre-existing
law of the State, or against any Act of Parliament passed subsequently to the making of such canon ; but I am not aware that
any Act of Parliament, before or since the making of that canon,
is at all at variance with its provisions.

'But this is not all. The proviso in the 113th canon is the
more entitled to observance as being in accordance with the old
Canon Law of the Church, which was accepted in this country
without gainsaying or opposition from any temporal Court in the
land. But this canon is not the only nor the highest authority
for the principle which I maintain. It seems to me to be con-
firmed irresistibly by the Book of Common Prayer, carrying with
it all the weight of an Act of Parliament—the Act of Uniformity,
which is specially declared in the Articles of Union with Scotland
as a fundamental part of the Union.

'In the office of the "Visitation of the Sick," which existed in •
almost the same terms in the Book of Common Prayer at the
time when this canon was made, we find the following rubric :
"Here shall the sick person be moved to make a special con-

fession of his sins, if he feel his conscience troubled with any weighty matter.   After which confession the priest shall absolve him (if he humbly and heartily desire it) after this sort." Such was and is the law both of Church and State in respect to the duty, as regards confession, both of the clergy and the penitent. Can it then be urged that the law which enjoins confession does yet require the minister to whom confession is made to disclose such confession, even though a canon of his Church absolutely forbids it?   Would such a condition of law be tolerated in any country where justice and reason are more than empty words?'

The tenour of Lord Westbury's reply may be gathered from the Bishop's rejoinder to it :—

'I most sincerely thank your Lordship for your letter of the 16th inst. with which you have honoured me.   If I make one or two remarks on it, your Lordship will, I am sure, think them not wholly unnecessary.

'First, you, my Lord, with the candour which characterises you, say that the 113th canon of 1603 appears to you to be "that the clergyman must not *mero motu* and voluntarily, and without legal obligation, reveal what is communicated to him in confession."

'To me it seems that this construction of the canon is not warranted by its words.   That canon, instead of admitting *any* legal obligation, excludes all, even *legal* obligation, "except they be such crimes as by the laws of this realm his own life may be called into question for concealing the same."   All minor legal obligation is manifestly excluded.

'Secondly, I should say that the rule of evidence, which is contrary to this canon, not only ought not to *have been* established, but cannot be said really *to be* established.   Such a *rule* of evidence is contrary to the *law* of evidence.   Nothing short of an Act of Parliament, I submit, can make such a law.   Immemorial usage cannot be claimed for such a rule; for before the Reformation it is notorious that the law was contrary to it, and even in very modern days the rule has not been acknowleged by great legal authorities.   In the case *Du Barre* v. *Lisette* (Peake's *Cases of*

Nisi Prius, p. 78) it will be found that a case on the Northern
Circuit, which had been then lately determined, viz. *King* v.
Sparkes, in which a confession to a clergyman was permitted to
be given in evidence, Lord Kenyon says : " It is sufficient for me,
sitting here, to say, that this case materially differs from that
cited ; but *I should have paused before I admitted the evidence there
admitted.*" This shows that Lord Kenyon did not recognise
as binding the rule cited by your Lordship. He adds, " The
Popish religion is unknown to the law of this country." This
further shows that Lord Kenyon implies that the law of the
Church of England (being known to the law of England)
ought to regulate the proceeding of a Court in making rules of
evidence.

'With regard to your Lordship's observation that the public
is not at present in a temper to bear any alteration of the rule, I
trust to your forgiveness if I say that you are the last man from
whom I should have expected such a reason for reticence. It
must be apparent to every one that your Lordship's statement in
the House of Lords on Friday last has done more than has ever
been done in a Court of Justice to fix the authority of the supposed rule. To leave the matter as it stands would be, in fact,
to give the very highest sanction to the mischievous delusion of
the public, and which, because mischievous, ought to be without
delay removed.

' Forgive anything that may seem presumptuous in this letter,
and believe me, with high respect for you, on whom I look as
the soundest and ablest living expositor of our law, your much
obliged and most faithful servant,   H. EXETER.'

Several of Lord Westbury's letters at this time
have reference to international matters, particularly
the attitude of the Government on the Sleswig-
Holstein question. He heartily approved of the
course taken by Lord Palmerston with respect to
the threatened entry of the Austrian fleet into the
Baltic, and had for some time advocated a more

decided line of foreign policy. He wrote to the
Prime Minister :—

'*May* 3, 1864.

'My dear Lord—I thank you most sincerely for your great
kindness in sending me a copy of your letter to Earl Russell,[1]
which I return, and am rejoiced to find that it is to go to the
Queen.

'I admire with all my heart the manly, straightforward, and
honest course of sincerity and plainness which you have adopted,
and which I am confident is the most likely mode of producing
good results. The result we must of course leave to Providence,
but it is exactly what our honour and the interests of humanity
required.—Ever yours sincerely,   WESTBURY.'

Some mention should here be made of the unsatisfactory working of the Bankruptcy Act of 1861,
as it had an important bearing on the events related
in the next chapter, which ultimately led to Lord
Westbury's resignation. From the returns presented to Parliament it appeared that the sums
squandered in realising bankrupt estates were in-
credibly large. During 1864 the whole of the
property collected was less than £700,000, and upwards of £140,000 was expended in dividing little
more than half a million. The official assignees
had in 1862 returned only £1,390, in respect of the
fees which they ought to have paid into the Court
of Bankruptcy ; in 1863, in consequence of inquiries
which the Lord Chancellor instituted, the sum
increased to £13,620 ; but in 1864, after he had
directed a more searching investigation, the amount
paid in was £45,158. In calling the attention of

---

[1] Printed in the *Life of Lord Palmerston*, vol. ii. p. 432.

the House of Lords to the subject, Lord Westbury
cited as an example of the grave irregularities which
had come under his notice the case of a defaulting
assignee, whose accounts had been audited for years
by the usher of the Court, under the direction of the
Commissioner, whose duty it was to check them.
This, he said, was a very hopeless picture of the
state of the Bankruptcy Court, and he trusted that he
should be able to provide some remedy for such a
monstrous state of things.

At a later date he denounced, in his usual incisive
style, the system of official extravagance which had
become inseparable from the bankruptcy process,
and forcibly invited public attention to 'the swarm
of auctioneers, accountants, messengers, and other
creatures who now feed and crawl upon the body of
the bankrupt estates.'

CHAPTER V

Causes of Lord Westbury's unpopularity—Edmunds case—Outcry
raised against the Chancellor—Select Committee of Investigation
appointed on his own motion—Attitude of Opposition Peers—His
wish to resign—Lord Palmerston refuses to entertain it—Lord
Westbury's explanation—Report of Committee—Censure of the
Chancellor for errors in judgment.

'CENSURE,' said Dean Swift, 'is the tax a man
payeth to the public for being eminent.' A Lord
Chancellor's career is watched with jealous scrutiny
by a host of men anxious to magnify his failings
and misrepresent his actions.

> ' " He who ascends to mountain tops shall find
>   The loftiest peaks most wrapped in clouds and snow ;
> He who surpasses or subdues mankind
>   Must look down on the hate of those below.
> Though high above the sun of glory glow,
>   And far beneath the earth and ocean spread,
> Round him are icy rocks, and loudly blow
>   Contending tempests on his naked head,
>   And thus reward the toils which to those summits led." ' [1]

The liability to hostile criticism which is inseparable from a high position was increased in Lord

---

[1] *Childe Harold,* canto iii. stanza 45.

Westbury's case by his thoughtless indifference to public opinion. The lectures which had been received with an amused complacency in the House of Commons were less tolerable when coming from the newly-ennobled lawyer. A peer who asked a question as to the effect of the decision in the Colenso case received the reply, that it would require more time than the Chancellor could spend, and perhaps greater effort than he could employ, to render the judgment of the Privy Council intelligible to his interrogator's mind. The most thick-skinned felt that they did well to be angry under such treatment, and attempted reprisals.

The attacks which began to be unsparingly levelled at Lord Westbury in the public prints were not altogether without the effect they were intended to produce. Though he professed utter indifference to criticism on his public actions, he was in reality of a sensitive nature, and some of the 'slings and arrows' found their mark and struck home. He had made many enemies, who showed an evident desire to find something censurable in his public conduct. ' He that hath a satirical vein, as he maketh others afraid of his wit, so he had need be afraid of others' memory.' But apart from his peculiarities of speech and manner, Lord Westbury's marked defiance of conventionalities at this time naturally exposed him to obloquy. It is necessary to premise thus much in order to fully understand the public events which must now be related.

In the spring of 1865 the Edmunds case began
to attract considerable attention.   The material facts
showing Lord Westbury's connection with the matter
were shortly as follows :—

For many years Mr. Leonard Edmunds had
held the office of Reading Clerk and Clerk of the
Committees in the House of Lords, in addition to
the offices of Clerk of the Patents and Clerk to
the Commissioners of Patents.   As Clerk of the
Patents it was his duty to pay the fees he received
into the Exchequer, but there was no statutory provision for the audit of his accounts.   The superintendence of the Office of Patents was entrusted to
Commissioners, including the Lord Chancellor, the
Master of the Rolls, and other legal dignitaries.

In 1864 various complaints were made to the
Lord Chancellor of the conduct of Edmunds in the
Patent Office, and after consultation with the other
Commissioners he directed an inquiry, and appointed
two Queen's Counsel, one of them being the Solicitor
to the Treasury, to conduct it.   It is but fair to add
that Edmunds himself courted the fullest investigation.   The investigators made a preliminary report,
from which it appeared that Edmunds, as Clerk of the
Patents, had misapplied public monies to the amount
of £2681, and that there were various other grounds
of claim against him.   The report stated that the
facts seemed to justify, if not to require, the immediate removal of Edmunds from his offices with
respect to patents.

Upon the receipt of this report Lord Westbury and the other Commissioners deemed it their duty to summon Edmunds before the Lord Chancellor and two Chancery Judges, to answer the charge of misapplication of the public monies. By the Chancellor's direction charges were framed by the Attorney-General accusing Edmunds of applying to his own use discounts upon stamps purchased for the Patent Office, improperly retaining large sums for fees on patents which ought to have been paid into the Exchequer, and transferring to the credit of his private banking account divers other sums of public money. Before, however, these charges came on for hearing, Edmunds, acting under the advice of his own solicitor, applied to be permitted to resign his offices in connection with patents.

The Lord Chancellor consulted the Master of the Rolls, and they agreed in thinking that it would not be an improper thing in the circumstances to permit the resignation. Upon this the Chancellor directed his secretary to inform Edmunds that if he thought proper to surrender his offices with regard to patents, and would undertake to account for all sums due to the Treasury, the proceedings contemplated would not be taken. Lord Westbury added that he should take the opinion of Lord Cranworth and Lord Kingsdown as to the course which it would be his duty to adopt with reference to the office held by Edmunds in the House of Lords. He made this statement under the impression that the power of removing

Edmunds from this office rested with the Chancellor,
and not, as the fact was, with the House. The
undertaking was accordingly given, and the offices
with respect to patents surrendered. At the same
time Edmunds expressed the hope that the Lord
Chancellor would not take the opinion of the Law
Lords as to the office of Reading Clerk until he had
considered his (Edmunds's) answer to the statements
made against him. To this reasonable request Lord
Westbury assented ; Edmunds put in the answer,
and afterwards, to the surprise of every one, voluntarily paid into the Treasury the sum of £7872,
which he represented to be the entire amount of his
indebtedness, though a further report, subsequently
made, found that he still owed the sum of
£9100.

Meanwhile some of Edmunds's friends persuaded
him that he had better resign his other office of
Clerk to the House in the hope of getting a pension.
In reply to that suggestion the Lord Chancellor wrote
declining to offer any opinion on the case. 'All I
can say is, that if he thinks proper to resign, I will
do all I can with propriety to obtain for him a pension ;' and he added that he could with truth certify
that Edmunds had properly discharged the duties of
that office.

In these circumstances the Lord Chancellor took
the opinion of the Government whether it was incumbent upon him to communicate to the House of Lords
what had taken place. The Government being of

opinion that it was, he gave Edmunds notice of his
intention to lay the papers upon the table of the
House, and to move for a Committee to inquire into
the subject. Edmunds asked for a short delay,
which was granted. On the very day on which
Lord Westbury was to bring the matter before the
House, a petition from Edmunds, asking leave to
resign the office of Reading Clerk, was brought down
to the House, and put into the Lord Chancellor's
hands immediately before the House sat. The
petition not only prayed for leave to resign ; it stated
that Edmunds had been for eighteen years a servant
of the House, and that his conduct in that capacity
had never been questioned, and it prayed the usual
reference to the Parliament Office Committee in
order that a pension might be granted in accordance
with custom. This petition Lord Westbury himself
presented, and an order was made in conformity
with its prayer. From his point of view he could
not refuse to present the petition ; still the information which, but for the resignation of Edmunds, he
would have laid before the House, might have been
communicated to the Committee to whom the question
of the pension was referred. This, he said, he could
not bring his mind to do, because Edmunds's defal-
cations were, in the opinion of the Law Officers, a
matter of civil liability. If it turned out that Edmunds had paid the full amount due from him, it
would have been wrong to deprive him of his
pension ; but if he was still indebted, the pension

would be taken in satisfaction of the debt. At any
rate the Chancellor volunteered no information, and
the Committee did not ask for any. The irregularities in the Patent Office were a matter of
notoriety, but the Committee probably thought that
Edmunds's delinquencies in another office ought not
to debar him from receiving the usual acknow-
ledgment of his services in the House of Lords.
Without further inquiry they granted him a retiring
pension of £800 a year.

As soon as the circumstances of Edmunds's
retirement transpired, the matter became the subject
of much comment in the public prints. It was said
that if Edmunds was innocent of the charges against
him, he should not have been forced to resign ;
but if his conduct made him unfit to hold his office in
the House of Lords, a pension, the reward of faithful
service, ought not to have been granted. It was also
insinuated that Lord Westbury had in some way or
other prevailed on Edmunds to resign, in order that
two offices might be vacant to which he might appoint connections of his own. It was true that the
office of Reading Clerk had been filled up by the
appointment of one of his family, but the insinuation
that Edmunds's resignation had been brought about
in order to create a vacancy was certainly not borne
out by the facts. Referring to this, Lord Palmerston
wrote to the Chancellor :—

'The only matter in doubt was whether Edmunds should be
dismissed and prosecuted, or should be allowed to resign. The

Master of the Rolls and your colleagues in the Cabinet were of opinion that, as the matter stood, Edmunds should be allowed to resign. But his resignation or his dismissal, one or other of which had become inevitable by reason of his own conduct, would equally make vacant the patent offices which he held, and those offices did not become more vacant nor more at your disposal in consequence of his resignation than they would have been if he had been dismissed. The insinuation therefore to which I allude has not the shadow of a ground on which to rest, and the decision taken as to allowing Edmunds to resign had no bearing whatever upon your power to appoint successors to his offices in the Patent Department.

'As to his pension, that was given to him, not for the patent offices with regard to which he was a defaulter, but with reference to his House of Lords office, in which there was no charge that he had misconducted himself, and that pension might, I presume, be made to cease if it should be found that he is still a debtor to the Crown.'

The Treasury authorities were throughout the proceedings thoroughly alarmed by the prospect of the loss of the monies belonging to the Consolidated Fund and alleged to have been misappropriated by Edmunds. For this loss they might probably be called to account in the House of Commons, and, with more policy than generosity, they now manifested a strong desire to throw the main responsibility on the Lord Chancellor, though all the time they had expected him to act as their legal adviser. Lord Westbury at once expressed his desire to give the fullest public explanation, while some of his colleagues thought it better that he should wait for any attack that might be made in Parliament. He wrote to Lord Palmerston on the 7th March :—

'Do you not think that it is my duty to the Government and to myself to make a statement, particularly after the language of the papers this morning?   Granville refers me to your Lordship, and begs me to be guided by your opinion.   I will not have the slightest imputation rest on your Lordship or the Government in consequence of anything that I have done or omitted to do.   I entreat and implore you with that frankness and sincerity which characterise you to tell me at once if there be anything open to the least reproach, for if there be, I shall beg you the next moment to accept my resignation.   I am quite sincere in this, and shall certainly not shrink from what I have written.'

On the same day he made a full personal statement in the House of Lords, and obtained the appointment of a Select Committee to inquire into all the circumstances connected with Edmunds's resignation and the grant of the pension.   Though Lord Derby commended this as 'a straightforward and manly course,' it was evident from his speech and the speeches of other peers on this occasion that the Opposition recognised their opportunity of making party capital out of the incident, by attacking the Government through the Lord Chancellor. The tone of their observations was so hostile to Lord Westbury personally, that he at once requested the Cabinet to accept his resignation.   Lord Palmerston refused the request in the following letter :—

'My dear Lord Westbury—Granville has just been with me and has read to me your letter to him expressing your wish to resign your office of Chancellor.   I can quite understand that a person of keen and sensitive feelings like yourself should be sharply stung by the personal attacks which have been aimed at you ; but you should bear in mind that the higher the position which a man holds the greater is the temptation to his opponents

to assail him, and when facts are wanting invention is summoned
to their aid.

' As to your resigning, I must be allowed to say that it is out
of the question—we cannot spare you.   Your loss would be a
source of weakness to the Government, and though the labours
which press upon you are no doubt severe, you ought to reflect
that they have been productive of much good to the public service,
and you ought to persevere with your wonted energy in the career
which you have so successfully pursued.'

The Select Committee proceeded to examine
witnesses, and amongst them the Lord Chancellor.
He explained that after the tender of Edmunds's
resignation, he resolved not to lay the papers relating to the charges on the table of the House,
and they would not have been brought before the
House if public attention had not been drawn to the
subject out of doors.   He said he had acted throughout upon this principle—that he would do nothing
against Edmunds but what public duty required.
He had asked Lord Cranworth and Lord Kingsdown whether it was his duty to discharge Edmunds
from the patent offices if the alleged facts were true ;
when they said it was, he directed the inquiry to
proceed.   When he found that the House of Lords
was the tribunal to judge their officer, the Reading
Clerk, he had asked the Cabinet whether it was his
bounden duty to bring the matter before the House.
They said it was, but that, in his view, was only in
order that the House might no longer have that
officer.   When Edmunds retired, he (the Chancellor)
determined for himself (and he took all the responsi-

bility of it) that he would not interfere actively to prevent his having a pension.

It may be added, though the fact was not in evidence, that one of Lord Westbury's reasons for this leniency was that Edmunds had to support two sisters who were in circumstances of distress. He was anxious not to press too hardly upon a ruined man after fulfilling his duty by relieving the public service of an unsatisfactory officer.

Pending the inquiry, the Chancellor wrote to his two youngest children, who were travelling in Italy :—

'I am delighted to find that you still continue to enjoy your tour, and I am most thankful that you are away from all the trouble with which I am surrounded. I did not suppose that I could have so many enemies as this event has revealed; but all persons appear to be delighted to join in the howl against me. It has so thoroughly disgusted me, that although it is not at all probable that the report of the Committee will be at all unfavourable, yet I am determined to take advantage of it and to resign my office, which I have long wished to do, as you know, but which has now become so hateful to me that I could not bear to continue in the possession of it. You see the world is determined, and perhaps very justly, to denounce and condemn nepotism in public men. Unfortunately I have been induced to appoint a number of connections and relatives to small offices. The value is little compared with the value of two or three gifts made by Lord Eldon, Lord Ellenborough, and others, for their own sons and relatives; but the number seems large, and there is a long parade of the numerous names and offices in all the newspapers.

'I hope you will not be vexed, therefore, if I lay down an office which, whilst I keep it, will constantly expose me to all these attacks. . . . To me it is a matter of perfect indifference, because if it had not happened, I should certainly

never have taken office again, if I had remained till the
resignation of the Ministry, which cannot be far off. It would
shock you if I were to tell you the scandalous and wicked stories
that are circulated about me. All this distresses me, because I
think it will distress and vex you and W——   Otherwise I
should really attach very little importance to it. But you will be
mortified and annoyed. Perhaps it is better that I should leave
office now, for I find its duties and the kind of life it renders
necessary are beginning to have a very injurious effect upon my
health ; and I trust, and believe it likely, that my life will be
longer than it would be if I remained another year in office.
You must, my darling children, be very philosophical about the
matter, and whilst we regret what has passed, we must endeavour
to convert it into good. Do not hurry home. If I resign I
shall endeavour to meet you and go to the Italian lakes.'

In view of the virulence and pertinacity with
which the charge of nepotism was made, it should
be mentioned that Lord Westbury, out of a patronage larger than that possessed by any single individual, had given at the most six or seven appointments, chiefly of small value, to his own relations
and connections, and in this respect his record
would probably compare not unfavourably with that
of the majority of his predecessors, if not of his
successors in office.

On the 4th of May 1865 the Committee presented
their report. They expressed their regret that Edmunds was allowed to resign, and thereby withdraw
himself from the impending inquiry before the Lord
Chancellor and Vice-Chancellors. They were of
opinion that the inquiry ought to have proceeded ;
and if the charges which Edmunds had been formally
called upon to answer had been proved, as in the

judgment of the Committee the principal part of them must have been, he should at once have been dismissed, leaving it open to future consideration whether ulterior proceedings ought to be taken against him.

With respect to the pension, the Committee said that they could not coincide with the Lord Chancellor in the view taken by him of his public duty. In their opinion 'it was incumbent on him who presented the petition of Mr. Edmunds to the House of Lords in some manner to have apprised the Parliament Office Committee of the circumstances under which the resignation of the clerkship had taken place, and with which the Lord Chancellor was officially acquainted, and not to have left them to decide the question of a pension with no clearer light than could be derived from vague and uncertain rumours.' They added: 'The Committee have, however, no reason to believe that the Lord Chancellor was influenced by any unworthy or unbecoming motive in thus abstaining from giving any information to the Committee.' In conclusion, they expressed their regret that the Parliament Office Committee did not consider it their duty to act upon their general knowledge or impression so far as to interpose some delay before the question was finally settled in favour of a pension, which, had the circumstances been fully known to them, would probably not have been recommended.

The report thus acquitted Lord Westbury of

improper motives, but attributed to him an error in
judgment and a wrong view of his duty. It was
anticipated that he would address the House in
deprecation of this censure, but he made no observation upon it. The resolution by which the pension
was granted was afterwards rescinded, and the matter
for the time dropped.

CHAPTER VI

1865

IT happened, unfortunately for Lord Westbury, that another case for inquiry with respect to the resignation of a public official and the grant of a pension arose almost immediately after the report of the Committee in the Edmunds case was made known. The prejudice which he had sustained in popular opinion by the censure passed by that Committee gave an impetus to the attack, while it placed him at some disadvantage in the subsequent proceedings. *Non licet in bello bis peccare.*

On the 15th of May 1865 Mr. Bousfield Ferrand, one of the members for Devonport, Lord Westbury's opponent when he first contested Aylesbury, put a series of questions to the Attorney-General with reference to the registrarship of the Leeds Bankruptcy

Court, and he subsequently gave notice of a motion
for a Select Committee to inquire into the matter.
It being the wish of the Lord Chancellor that a
searching inquiry should take place, the motion was
not opposed by the Government, and a Committee
was nominated. The facts of the case were extremely
complicated, and all that is proposed here is to give
a bare outline sufficient to explain the report of the
Committee, so far as regards the Chancellor, and the
proceedings founded upon it.

In 1864 an official inquiry had been instituted by
Lord Westbury into the truth of complaints with
regard to the administration of the Bankruptcy
Courts at Leeds and other large centres. The
result of the inquiry as to some of the Courts was,
as has been already stated, that large sums were
recovered from officials which had been improperly
retained. In the case of Leeds no pecuniary defal-
cations were discovered, but certain grave irregularities were reported, which the Registrar was called
upon to explain. His explanation was not deemed
satisfactory, and thereupon the Chief Registrar,
on behalf of the Lord Chancellor, wrote informing the Leeds Registrar that unless he promptly
applied to be allowed to retire he would be called
upon to show cause, in open Court, why he should
not be dismissed from office. The writer, as a
matter of kindness, as he afterwards said, but
without any authority from the Lord Chancellor,
officiously added the suggestion that the retire-

ment might be claimed on the ground of ill-health. This suggestion induced the Leeds Registrar to apply for permission to retire with a pension. He had for some time suffered from some failure of sight, and he obtained a medical certificate to that effect expressed in general terms. A petition stating the grounds of retirement, and the necessary affidavit in support of it, were sent with the certificate to the Chief Registrar, who afterwards confessed that he had himself prepared the petition.

The documents were laid before the Lord Chancellor, but there was a conflict of evidence as to whether his attention was directly called to the language of the certificate. He admitted that he ought in strictness to have read all the documents, but said that he could not have read the certificate, or he should not have allowed the petition to pass. He had felt very great embarrassment, because the charge against the Registrar was one which could not be dismissed without pronouncing a severe sentence. He was painfully struck, he said, with the great inconsistency of having directed the Registrar to show cause why he should not be dismissed, and then permitting him to resign with a pension. At the same time, unless he dismissed him, he had no alternative but to allow him to remain in his department. He thought the Registrar a bad public officer, and that it would be a gain to the public if he were permitted to resign; and having only those two alternatives before him,

he decided on allowing the resignation and signing
the order for a pension.   Upon this point the Committee expressed their opinion that 'the pension was
granted hastily and without due examination.' Such
haste and want of caution, they said, necessarily gave
rise to suspicion that a vacancy in the office was the
object sought, rather than justice to the officer or the
public.   They added : ' In this instance, however,
your Committee consider that no improper motives
are to be attributed to the Lord Chancellor.'

Upon the further heads of inquiry, viz. the circumstances under which a successor to the retiring
Registrar was appointed, the evidence given before
the Committee was in many respects contradictory.
It had been suggested that it disclosed the existence
of a corrupt bargain between certain parties, one of
whom was closely related to the Lord Chancellor, to
obtain the appointment by means of pecuniary transactions.   Into this part of the case it is not necessary
to enter, as the Committee expressed their conviction that any such arrangement was made without
Lord Westbury's knowledge.   After going at length
into the facts, they exonerated the Lord Chancellor
from all charge 'except that of haste and want
of caution' in granting the pension ; but they observed that the general impression created by the
circumstances was calculated to excite the gravest
suspicions, and they were of opinion that the inquiry
had been for that reason highly desirable for the
public interests.

As soon as the Report was published, Lord Westbury reiterated his wish to resign the Great Seal,
but again yielded to the advice of Lord Palmerston.
The following correspondence passed between
them :—

'*June* 26, 1865.

'My dear Lord—It would be a source of infinite consolation
to me if your Lordship would, on the occasion of any question
being asked in the House of Commons, say that my remaining in
office is with your approbation and at your desire—that I have
often expressed a wish to be allowed to resign, but that you have
overruled my opinion, and have told me that it was my duty to
remain in the public service. No one will then venture to say
that I remain from insensibility or from the love of office or its
emoluments.—Ever yours sincerely,   WESTBURY.'

'*June* 28, 1865.

'My dear Lord Westbury—I did not yesterday make the
statement which you wished me to make as to your having offered
to resign. George Grey and I thought it better that I should
not do so. Your opponents would not have set that offer down
to delicacy of feeling, but would have represented it as an admission of fault. They would have said *habemus confitentem
reum*, and such a statement if made at all should be delayed till
the storm of attack has blown over, and has left your fabric un-
hurt, as it certainly will.—Yours sincerely,

'PALMERSTON.'

If by resigning the attack could have been
avoided, Lord Westbury would have now insisted
on taking that step. Information was, however,
brought to him from a person of great weight with
the Opposition that, even if he resigned, they
would still press on a motion of censure. That
being so, he felt that he could not resign, as after

his resignation the motion would be a censure upon the Ministry.

On the 3d of July 1865 Mr. Ward Hunt, one of the leading members of the Opposition, moved a resolution of censure on the Lord Chancellor. The motion affirmed that the evidence taken in the Leeds Registry case disclosed that a great facility existed for obtaining public appointments by corrupt means; that such evidence, and also that taken in the Edmunds case, showed a laxity of practice and want of caution on the part of the Lord Chancellor in sanctioning the grant of retiring pensions to public officers over whose heads grave charges were impending, and in filling up the vacancies made by their retirement, whereby great encouragement had been given to corrupt practices; and that such laxity and want of caution, even in the absence of any improper motive, were, in the opinion of the House, highly reprehensible, and calculated to throw discredit on the administration of the high offices of State.

The notice of this motion brought up to town many members who had gone down to their constituencies in anticipation of the impending dissolution of Parliament. It was apparent that a vote of censure on a prominent member of the Cabinet in the very last week of the session would be a serious blow to the Government, and might have some influence on the elections.

In a speech of studied moderation Mr. Ward Hunt referred to the evidence at much length as supporting his charge against the Chancellor of 'supineness and carelessness' in not preventing the corruption which was going on around and below him. He said it 'was of the highest importance, not only that there should be purity in the exercise of the Lord Chancellor's high functions, but vigilance against corruption by his subordinates, because of the enormous amount of patronage placed in his hands. 'I am happy to say,' he added, 'that on this occasion I am not here to impute personal corruption to the Lord Chancellor; but I am here to impute to him that he has not shown that vigilance, that acuteness, and that anxiety for the public interest which his high station and the important duties attached to it imperatively demand.' While he acquitted the Chancellor of any corrupt motives, either in making the vacancy or in filling up the appointments, he said that he had given great occasion of scandal in the country, because people were led to think that places could be obtained by corrupt means. 'And I say that this state of things, this want of vigilance, this supineness, this indifference— I might almost say, this fatuous simplicity, if such words can be applied to such a man as the Lord Chancellor—I say that the unsuspiciousness that has enabled his subordinates and those around him to practise that corruption which, I admit, he himself is free from, is almost as bad for the country, although not for himself, as if he were personally guilty of this corruption.'

The Lord Advocate (Mr., now Lord, Moncreiff),
on behalf of the Government, opposed the resolution.
He had been put upon the Committee with Mr.,
afterwards Chief-Justice, Bovill, for the purpose
of examining witnesses, but without power to
take part in their deliberations or to vote. He
therefore claimed to be in a position to estimate
the evidence given at the inquiry at its true value.
He said that the imputations which had been made
against the Chancellor, but afterwards withdrawn,
made it difficult for the most impartial man to shake
himself free from the prejudices raised, and complained that the resolution suggested a great deal
which it did not express. He thought that the
House would have done well to be content with the
verdict of the Committee. The Lord Chancellor
was engaged in an arduous and thankless task, the
discharge of which was sure to be questioned, and
had found it his duty to reflect upon the conduct of
a great number of persons connected with bankruptcy
administration. 'The House should take care not
to be led by fine-drawn suspicions to weaken the
hands of a man who was thus addressing himself in
the public interest to a task of great difficulty, and
who was certain, if successful, to bring down upon
himself obloquy from the friends of all those against
whom he was proceeding.'

The Lord Advocate did not dispute the opinion
expressed by the Committee with regard to the Registrar's pension, though he thought the words rather

stronger than was necessary. They had seen not only in that, but also in the Edmunds case, how facile is the transition from the accusation of driving an innocent man out of office to the accusation of granting a guilty man a pension. Similar charges had been brought against many of the bankruptcy officials. Was it not, he asked, a fair matter for the Chancellor to consider whether he should proceed with an amount of severity towards individuals with which public opinion might not sympathise, and against which local opinion would unquestionably rebel? After an exhaustive review of the evidence, he expressed his conviction that the House would never agree to an indefinite motion of censure on a man so eminent for his abilities, who was an ornament to his profession, and in his public station had conferred great benefits on the country. He moved an amendment which declared that the House agreed with the Committee in acquitting the Lord Chancellor from all charge, except that of haste and want of caution in granting the pension to the Registrar, and was of opinion that some further check should be placed by law upon the grant of such pensions.

Of the other speakers, Mr. (now Sir John) Pope-Hennessy strongly attacked the Chancellor, and the Hon. George (now Mr. Justice) Denman defended him in a closely-reasoned speech, which was the more effective because, as he confessed, there was perhaps no man in the House who personally had less reason for doing so. The only occasion on which his public

duty had brought them into close relations was once
when Lord Westbury, then Attorney-General, had
told him that a certain claim which he advocated ought
not to be brought forward to trouble the House as
often as 'any young lawyer' could be found to take
it up.   Naturally, he said, a man who had been
struggling fifteen or sixteen years at the bar did not
like to be so described.   Mr. Denman analysed the
evidence with great care, and concluded a speech
which met with some interruption from the Opposition benches, by expressing his hope that the House
would not, by a party vote, insist upon driving from
office an illustrious judge and law reformer on
account of errors of judgment only such as many
others had committed.

It is probable that Mr. Ward Hunt's motion
would have been defeated if a division had taken
place upon it.   A fresh turn was, however, given to
the debate when the Right Hon. E. Pleydell-
Bouverie rose and intimated his intention, if Mr.
Ward Hunt's motion were negatived, of moving
a resolution, which, while it definitely acquitted
the Lord Chancellor of any personal corruption,
affirmed the existence of corrupt practices under
him, and conveyed the same censure as the original
motion.   His speech betrayed a bitter personal hostility towards Lord Westbury.   Amid loud cheers
from the Opposition he declared that he had no confidence in him.   His ability no one disputed.   But
what was the value of that ability unless it was

guided by sound discretion, and possessed by a man
in whom all could place confidence—a man who
would duly discharge those rare functions which
were committed to him for the good of his country.

Mr. Hunt at once allowed his resolution to be
negatived in favour of Mr. Bouverie's amendment.
This adroit manœuvre was completely successful.
Of the two members of the Select Committee who
addressed the House, Mr. Howes, the chairman,
approved of that amendment, and Mr. Hussey
Vivian opposed it, because he did not consider the
evidence in any way sufficient to cause him to give
a vote which would force the Lord Chancellor to
resign. The Attorney-General (Sir Roundell Palmer) delivered an earnest and admirable defence
of the Chancellor. He asked who had set the
Patent Office inquiry on foot? Who had discovered the gross abuses by which the public was
defrauded? Those abuses had been going on for
years, under several Governments, and it was
reserved for Lord Westbury to ferret them out,
remove the offender, and recover for the public a
very considerable sum of money. He had incurred
odium because he insisted on searching into the
bankruptcy abuses; he had corrected those abuses,
and punished, always mercifully, many offenders.
Sir R. Palmer declared that the Chancellor's disposal of his patronage had been characterised by an
anxious desire for the public benefit, without regard
to personal or party considerations. 'Looking,' he

said, in conclusion, 'to the shining merits of this great person, looking to his eminent and long public services, and to the total failure of the attempt which has been made to bring against him charges of a graver complexion and character, will not the House say—

> ' " Non ego paucis
> Offendar maculis, quas aut incuria fudit,
> Aut humana parum cavit natura,"

and refuse to concur in this unworthy motion ?'

After further speeches Lord Palmerston moved to adjourn the debate until the next day, on the ground that Mr. Bouverie's amendment had placed the matter in a new position, and they were not at that moment in a condition to determine how to deal with it. The fitness of the High Court of Parliament to undertake an impartial investigation into matters from which political considerations can hardly be detached has often been impugned ; certainly on this occasion some of the members, though occupying the position of quasi-judges, preserved scarcely the semblance of judicial calmness. The House was by this time in a state of unusual excitement, and the Prime Minister's proposal was met with loud cries of 'Oh, oh !' and 'Divide' from the Conservatives. Mr. Disraeli, whose rising was the signal for an outburst of cheers from his supporters, opposed it as having an air of mockery. He knew to a man the numbers on each side, and the probable result of an adjournment on the division list. The

result proved the correctness of his calculation. The
House divided upon the motion for adjournment, and
the numbers were : Ayes, 163 ; Noes, 177 ; giving a
majority of 14 against the Government. The announcement of the numbers was received with vehe-
ment cheering from the Opposition benches, again
and again renewed. Lord Palmerston accepted the
division as decisive upon the main question, and Mr.
Bouverie's motion was then put and agreed to. It
was as follows :—' That this House, having considered the Report of the Committee on the Leeds
Bankruptcy Court and the evidence given before
them, are of opinion that, while the evidence dis-
closes the existence of corrupt practices with reference to the appointment to the office of Registrar of
the Leeds Bankruptcy Court, they are satisfied that
no imputation can fairly be made against the Lord
Chancellor with regard to this appointment ; and
that such evidence, and also that taken before a
Committee of the Lords to inquire into the circumstances connected with the resignation of Mr.
Edmunds of the offices held by him, and laid before
this House, show a laxity of practice and a want of
caution with regard to the public interests, on the
part of the Lord Chancellor, in sanctioning the grant
of retiring pensions to public officers against whom
grave charges were pending, which, in the opinion of
this House, are calculated to discredit the administration of his great office.'

This vote of censure could of course have but

one result. Lord Palmerston wrote the same evening :—

'My dear Lord Westbury—I am grieved to say that we have been beat to-night in the House of Commons by 14. We were 163 to 177.

'The division was on my motion for adjourning the debate, but we were obliged to accept it as decisive as to Bouverie's amendment, on which, if we had divided, the majority against us would have been greater, as Ward Hunt's motion, which might have been construed as implying a charge of unworthy motives, was negatived without a division, the House having unanimously decided that the only charge maintained against you was that of too much laxity in the giving of pensions—certainly a very venial offence, though the Opposition and some on our side chose to make a mountain of it. However, I am afraid that after such a resolution adopted by the House of Commons, I can no longer urge you to abstain from carrying into effect your long-formed intention. The Cabinet will meet at my house to-morrow at one, and perhaps you will let me hear from you by that time unless you like to come here yourself at that hour.—Yours sincerely,   PALMERSTON.'

And Lord Granville, who had stood by Lord Westbury throughout with the utmost loyalty, wrote the next day :—

'My dear Chancellor—I will write to you as soon as I have seen Palmerston, but I cannot delay telling you how grieved and shocked I am, and how sure I am that there will be a reaction in public opinion from the violent note of last night. I was in the House of Commons last night and never saw anything less judicial. The Tory benches were crammed with M.P.'s from all parts of the kingdom, and even from abroad. They met the Cabinet statements with howls and laughter.

'Although our official connection may be severed for a time, it will not affect our personal friendship, or the feeling of regard with which I am, yours sincerely,   GRANVILLE.'

Lord Westbury instantly requested the Prime Minister to tender his resignation to the Queen. He said :—

'Matters have been brought to a bad end. . . . When and in what manner would your Lordship wish me to resign? To do so instantly is my desire, but I fear the form of proroguing Parliament and the language of the Commission will compel me to remain until Friday. On that day I hope to resign the Great Seal. I entreat your Lordship, as the last act of your affectionate friendship, to state to the House of Commons to-night that in the very beginning of these attacks upon me, at the commencement of the session, I entreated your permission to resign, because I felt that the holder of the Great Seal, even if innocent, ought not to be a person exposed to such attacks, and that I have remained in office wholly in obedience to your wish. I am sorry that my life is brought to such an ignominious end, but I shall ever retain the warmest personal attachment to your Lordship.'

Later in the same day he wrote again to say that he must not hold the Great Seal one moment longer than the exigencies of the public service imperatively required, and added :—

'Pray, my dear Lord, say a kind word of farewell for me to the Cabinet. I thank you all deeply for your uniform kindness. I regret deeply that I have given you so much trouble. I beg of you all to remember that in the outset I begged you to allow me to resign, and therefore I trust that my memory will not be subject to any reproach. And pray, my dear Lord, let it be known that my remaining in office until I have thus been driven from it has not been the result of my selfishness or my obstinacy. With kind farewells to all, and to you, my dear Lord, a thousand thanks for your unvarying kindness, I am, ever yours sincerely,

'WESTBURY.'

On the 4th of July his resignation was formally announced by Lord Granville in the one House and by Lord Palmerston in the other. Both Ministers expressed their satisfaction that the inquiry had resulted in an entire acquittal of the Chancellor of any corrupt motive, and explained how often he had previously expressed his wish to resign.

The feelings of his colleagues in parting with him were thus conveyed to him by Lord Palmerston :—

'I cannot adequately express the regret which I feel at the Government and the country being deprived of your valuable services. Your eminent ability and your energy in devising and executing improvements in everything connected with the law made you a most valuable member of the administration, but not on that account the less an object of opposition and political attack.'

By the advice of his friends, Lord Westbury made a short personal statement on quitting the woolsack. The Peers, it seems, expected that he would do so, and many had intimated their intention of attending to hear him. Lord Shaftesbury wrote :—

'It rejoices me much that you have determined to say a few words from the woolsack this evening.

'Half a dozen sentences, stated with calmness and dignity, will excite sympathy; a feeling having already begun that matters have been pushed too far.

'Do you remember a striking passage in one of Cicero's orations? He is rebuking a decree of the people : " Male judicavit populus, at judicavit ; *non debuit, sed potuit.*"

'I should, however, in this case, by sheer policy, be softer than him.

'May I suggest that you refer, with thankfulness, to the large law reforms you have been enabled to institute ; and that you give the country a promise to continue your exertions, as a private member of Parliament, on those and other important measures?'

Accordingly, on the 6th July, in a crowded House, amid the most profound silence, Lord Westbury rose and said :—

'My Lords—I have deemed it my duty, out of the deep respect I owe to your lordships, to attend here to-day that I may in person announce to you that I tendered the resignation of my office yesterday to Her Majesty, and that it has been by Her Majesty most graciously accepted. My lords, The step that I took yesterday only I should have taken months ago if I had followed the dictates of my own judgment, and acted on my own views alone; but I felt that I was not at liberty to do so. As a member of the Government I could not take such a step without the permission and sanction of the Government. As far as I was myself personally concerned, possessing, as I had the happiness to do, the friendship of the noble lord at the head of the Government, and of the members of the Cabinet, I laid aside my own feelings, being satisfied that my honour and my sense of duty would be safe if I followed their opinion rather than my own.

'My lords, I believe that the holder of the Great Seal ought never to be in the position of an accused person; and such unfortunately being the case, for my own part, I felt it due to the great office that I held that I should retire from it, and meet any accusation in the character of a private person. But my noble friend at the head of the Government combated that view, and I think with great justice. He said it would not do to admit this as a principle of political conduct, for the consequence would be that whoever brought up an accusation would at once succeed in driving the Lord Chancellor from office. But when the charges were first raised that were investigated by a Committee of your lordships, I did deem it my duty to press my resignation; and the answer which I then received, and to which I was obliged to assent, was that answer of my noble friend which I have just described to you. When the Committee was appointed in the House of Commons, I deemed it to be my duty, acting upon the same principle, once more to tender my resignation; but on this occasion also I deferred to the objections raised by the noble friend whom I have already mentioned. Again, when notice was given of the late motion in the House of Commons, I begged that that motion might be rendered unnecessary by my resignation being announced. But my noble friend thought it was still my duty to persevere; and accordingly, my lords, this resignation, earnestly as I wished it to be accepted, was postponed in the manner I described to you until yesterday.

'Let it not be for one moment supposed that I say this in order to set up my own opinion in opposition to the kind feeling which I experienced, and the judicious advice which I received, coming, as they did, from one whom I was bound to respect, and to whose authority I felt called upon to defer. I have made this statement, my lords, simply in the hope that you will believe, and that the public will believe, that I have not clung to office, much less that I have been influenced by any baser or more unworthy motive. With regard to the opinion which the House of Commons has pronounced, I do not presume to say a word. I am bound to accept the decision. I may, however, express the hope that after an interval of time calmer thoughts will prevail, and feelings more favourable to myself be entertained. I am thankful for the opportunity which my tenure of office has afforded me to propose and pass measures which have received the approbation of Parliament, and which, I believe, nay, I will venture to predict, will be productive of great benefit to the country. With these measures I hope my name will be associated. I regret deeply that a great measure which I had at heart—I refer to the formation of a digest of the whole law—I have been unable to inaugurate; for it was not until this session that the means were afforded by Parliament for that purpose. That great scheme, my lords, I bequeath to be prepared by my successor. As for the future, I can only venture to promise that it will be my anxious endeavour, in the character of a private member of your lordships' House, to promote and assist in the accomplishment of all those reforms and improvements in the administration of justice which I feel yet remain to be carried out. I may add, in reference to the appellate jurisdiction of your lordships' House, that I am happy to say it is left in a state which will, I think, be found to be satisfactory. There will not be at the close of the session a single judgment in arrear, save one in which the arguments, after occupying several days, were brought to a conclusion only the day before yesterday. In the Court of Chancery, I am glad to be able to inform your lordships, that I trust by the end of this sitting there will not remain any appeal unheard or any judgment undelivered. I mention these things simply to show that it has been my earnest desire, from the moment I assumed the seals of office, to devote all the energies I possessed, and all the industry of which I was capable, to the public service.

' My lords, It only remains for me to thank you, which I do most sincerely, for the kindness which I have uniformly received at your hands. It is very possible that by some word inadvertently used, some abruptness of manner, I may have given pain or exposed myself to your unfavourable opinion. If that be so, I beg of you to accept the sincere expression of my regret, while I indulge the hope that the circumstance may be erased from your memories. I have no more to say, my lords, except to thank you for the kindness with which you have listened to these observations.'

The conclusion of this address was received with cheering from all parts of the House, and its calm and dignified tone did much, as Lord Shaftesbury had anticipated, to produce a recoil in the popular feeling. The rushing tide of party spirit could not efface the recollection of great public services. It was now seen that Lord Westbury had not loved office too fondly, but the moment his honour received the first wound, he felt with Mercutio—' 'Tis not so deep as a well, nor so wide as a church-door ; but 'tis enough, 'twill serve.'[1]

[1] In reference to this address, Mr. W. P. Frith, in his *Reminiscences* (vol. i. p. 347), gives a story told him by the Speaker of the House of Commons, Denison, afterwards Lord

To his own children, who were then at Hackwood, he wrote: 'I have just sent in my resignation, which will be completed on Friday. Nothing could have been kinder than Lord P. and the Cabinet have been. Do not distress yourselves. I am quite tranquil.' The next day he wrote again: 'I am most thankful for the spirit with which you have met the suffering we have sustained.' And then, as if to assure his family of his calmness, if not indifference, he added that he hoped the men kept the woods and lawns at Hackwood in good order.

The effort on Lord Westbury's part to stifle resentment must have been a hard one, but it was successful. Writing to one of his daughters, he says :—

'I have had some difficulty in preserving a calm, serene demeanour mid these trials; but I have done so, and no one can charge me with any exhibition of violence or want of temper. The few parting words I addressed to the House of Lords have had a very good effect.

'The Peers came crowding round me to express their pain at our parting and their sympathy, and Lord Granville and others declared my short speech was the most dignified and graceful thing they had heard, so that you see I died like a Roman, with composure and decency. I feel as if a great load were off my shoulders.'

Ossington, which may be repeated here. Lord Ebury had brought into the House of Lords a Bill to effect certain changes in the Burial Service, which had been thrown out. 'The House was greatly moved [by Lord Westbury's speech], and as the Lord Chancellor was leaving it he met Lord Ebury and said to him: "My lord, you can now read the Burial Service over me, with any alteration you think proper."'

On the 6th of July Lord Westbury went to Windsor and resigned the Great Seal. 'The Queen,' he writes, 'very kind and marked in manner. Her words were: "I am very much grieved at the circumstances."' Lord Cranworth, then in his seventy-fifth year, for the second time resumed office, in accordance with the retiring Chancellor's express wish. On the same day Parliament was prorogued and then immediately dissolved. Before the new Parliament assembled Lord Palmerston died, and was succeeded by Lord Russell as Prime Minister.

Of the numerous letters of sympathy received by Lord Westbury on his retirement not a few came from persons who were total strangers to him. Most of them expressed the hope that he would not be induced by the recent attacks to retire altogether from public life, but would persevere in the reforms which he had advocated. Mr. B. W. Procter (Barry Cornwall), who was a very old friend, wrote :—

'I regret to be unable to come and ask for the honour of shaking hands with you. But I am so infirm and old that I now can travel only by the post. Pray, therefore, accept my tender of respect, and my expression of sorrow that you resign that troublesome office, when you have been the only one amongst many lawyers who have had the resolution to make great clearances in the old Law-gean stables.'

Though recent events showed Lord Westbury that he had, as he said, many enemies, they brought him the comforting assurance of much real friendship and sympathy. When the heat and excitement

which attended these occurrences had subsided,
many were of opinion that very severe justice had
been meted out to him.[1] But he himself made no
complaint of this, nor did he ever manifest the
slightest trace of resentment or vexation of spirit.
He had always thoroughly disliked public life, while
in some sense he despised it, and unquestionably he
felt an intense relief in his retirement.

[1] In a clever ' Imaginary Conversation ' between ' Lord Bacon '
and ' Lord Bethell,' this view was urged in *Punch* (15th July 1865)
with much force, and both the vote of censure and the composition of the majority were sharply criticised.

CHAPTER VII

1866-1868

AFTER quitting office Lord Westbury purchased an estate called Celle, at Pistoja, near Florence, with the intention of enjoying there the repose from an active life to which half a century of continuous labour had entitled him. To one of his daughters he writes: 'Bring some Italian books with you, as I am very busy with that language. Cato learnt Greek in his old age, which language was to the Romans what French is to us, and I am learning French and Italian. It is a great amusement.' But though he declared that 'half the number of years spent in the sunshine of Italy is equal to double the number of years of painful life spent in this gloomy isle,' he only visited Celle three times between the years 1865 and 1873.

It might have been supposed that his mind would have become soured by the premature closing of his

official career, but this does not appear to have been
the case. On this point the observations of his
daughter, the late Mrs. T. E. Abraham, may be
quoted :—

'It was a common error,' she writes, 'to suppose him to be
of a stern bitter nature. Those who knew him only as the keen
and sarcastic lawyer or orator were surprised at his simplicity and
tenderness in private life. His temper was often fiery, and
gave great offence to many ; but his anger was shortlived and
never retrospective, and if he ever felt he had been guilty of any
injustice he was the first to own it. It is true he could not "suffer
fools gladly"; of stupidity he was impatient, especially when
valuable time was wasted over matters that might have been
quickly settled ; but if led into any bitterness of repartee or
satirical remark, he would soon regret it, particularly in his later
years, and would often say so in talking over what had passed in
the home circle. Neither resentment nor envy had the smallest
place in his heart. Even at the trying time of his resignation,
when false motives and accusations were brought against him, he
never allowed himself to complain or speak with bitterness of
what had passed, only saying to his children, " Be tranquil ; time
sets these things right."'

In the spring of 1866 Lord Westbury returned
to his house in Lancaster Gate, and began to attend
to appeals in the House of Lords, and subsequently
in the Privy Council. Soon after he commenced,
probably for the first time in his life, to write a diary.
It bore the following preface :—

'*June* 8, 1866.—I intend (D.V.) from this day to keep a record
of my actions, pursuits, studies, and, if possible, of my thoughts,
feelings, and impressions, so as to effect what is the great object
and purpose of usefulness in such a diary—constant self-examina-
tion and attention to the employment and use of time during the
few years of life that may be still left to me. I am now very near

the completion of my sixty-sixth year, and am still in the possession
and enjoyment of more than an ordinary quantity (having regard
to my age) of health, energy, and strength. I have ample fortune,
notwithstanding recent losses. I have lost all ambition or desire
to take part in political disputes or controversies, or to join any
party, and my mind is therefore uninfluenced and undisturbed by
many of those desires and anxieties which commonly influence the
minds and act upon the conduct of men. I must, however, warn
those who may read these introductory remarks not to expect
either deep or learned disquisition, or philosophical speculation,
or sententious remark in that which will be written; for the
essence of a journal is to be a diary of common things and occurrences, and an easy transcript of mental impressions without effort
or premeditation. The chief benefit of a journal is to the writer
himself, and the loosest notes may serve to him as memoranda of
events and feelings which at a future time he may review with advantage. With this feeling the journalist writes without restraint
and without shame.'

The diary, started with such good intentions,
seems only to have been continued for a few weeks;
but a few extracts may be given to show the tenour
of the writer's life and opinions during that period :—

'*June* 8.—Attended the House of Lords. Heard an appeal
of Cardinal Cullen, who insisted that a sum of money bequeathed
to him on a secret trust for a charity was not subject to legacy
duty; but, in my opinion, the title of the charity was not a testamentary one. The charity was entitled *aliunde* the will by virtue
of the trust, and not by the bequest. . . .

'*June* 9.—Went a visit to Mr. Clifford at Magna Charta Island
on the Thames. To Windsor by railway. There Walter, I, and
Clifford rowed down the Thames to the island. Beautiful day,
and scenery very pleasing and interesting, but the uniform green
is monotonous, and I miss much the blue mountains and the bold
outlines of Italy.

'Fished with no success. Island very prettily laid out.

Lunched under the shade of a very old walnut tree, which tradition reports to have been planted at the time of the signature of Magna Charta, A.D. 1215, I think. . . .

'*June* 11.—Attended appeal in the House of Lords. Question of proof in bankruptcy on a covenant to pay premiums of insurance. The question arose under Act of 1849. It is removed by my Act of 1861. Sad exhibition of the uncertainty and imperfection of expression in the Act of 1849, and want of practical experience with bankruptcy law by the judges in many cases. Enactment insufficient to admit proof.

'Great defect exists in the bankrupt law with respect to liabilities on a contingency. Generally considered not to be proveable if incapable of valuation, and that liabilities to arise on moral contingencies are not proveable at all.

'News of Garibaldi having landed at Genoa, which destroys all hope of peace. My belief still is that there will not be war between Prussia and Austria, though Count Bismarck will certainly bring it about if possible. His aim seems to be to make Prussia the dominant power in Germany, and to make his own sovereign absolute by means of the army; and then, as he rules the king, he will become himself the Autocrat of all Germany. It is a desperate game, and will fail, after causing an immense amount of human suffering.

'*June* 12.—Attended House of Lords. Appeal on a Scotch entail. Miserable ingenuity. As soon as the Scotch are engaged in litigation, there is an entire absence of prudence, sound sense, and discretion. They are caught by the most wretched fallacies and subtleties.

'Garibaldi at Como. No hope of peace. Subscriptions for volunteers in Italy. The country gone mad with excitement, and the reaction will be dreadful.[1] . . .

'*June* 15.—Attended House of Lords on appeals. Difference of opinion between myself and Lord Chancellor[2] and Lord Chelms-

---

[1] The command of the corps was given to Garibaldi. War was declared against Austria by the King of Prussia on the 18th, and by the King of Italy on the 20th June.

[2] Lord Cranworth.

ford on the construction of agreement. As the case could not
be in any way a guide for others, gave up my own opinion to the
majority. The influence and weight of the judgments of the
Final Court of Appeal are much impaired whenever there is an
avowed difference of opinion among its members. In some
cases, however, it is necessary not to appear to concur in what
you believe to be an erroneous interpretation of the law. Dined
at the Bishop of Peterborough's. Lord Lyveden, Lord Justice
· Turner, Sir F. Heygate, and others. Lord L—— pressed me to
take an active part in the debates in the Lords.

'*June* 16.—War has begun. It will involve the redistribution
of Europe. The modern doctrine of nationalities is, that every
separate race and language ought to form an independent
organisation.

'*June* 16.—Rode in the Park. Went to a tea-party (morning) at
Fulham Palace. Had some conversation with Lord Wensleydale,
Lord Chief-Justice Erle, Dean Stanley, Dean Milman, and others,
including Bishop of London. Mr. Abel Smith came to see me
from Miss Burdett Coutts, touching the Colonial Bishops. It is
very difficult to make them understand the true position of the
Colonial Bishop in law, in consequence of the judgment which I
wrote, and the other members of the Privy Council agreed to, in
the case of *Colenso* v. *the Bishop of Cape Town*. Framed a short
declaratory Bill to be submitted to Parliament on the subject.

'*Monday*.—Attended the House of Lords on appeals.

'*Tuesday*.—I have foolishly neglected my journal for several
days, depending on memory to supply the record of each day,
and am very sensible of the great difference in the intensity and
force of the impressions which my mind now receives. They are
much weaker, not, I think, through any decay of intellectual
power, but from diminished interest and absence of anxiety producing less care about external things.

'*Friday*.—Attended the House of Lords on appeals. The
case one of some interest. The son of a man of some wealth
committed forgery. He forged his father's name to numerous
bills of exchange. They were held by a banker who, on discovery of the forgery, asked the father (in effect) whether he
would give a security for the amount of the bills to save his son

from prosecution. The father did so, receiving the bills of exchange, and afterwards filed a bill in Chancery to have the security delivered up as being fraudulently obtained. I considered it an illegal transaction. Not much research or philosophy in the arguments of counsel.

'The Ministry, being in a minority, resigned.[1] To Gladstone's unfitness as a leader the whole must be ascribed.

'*Thursday.*—Attended the House of Lords. Received evil news from Italy. The madness of the people for war is indescribable. "They furiously rage together, and imagine a vain thing." No doubt they are buoyed up and impelled by the Emperor of the French, who is resolved to make Italy his creature. No doubt it is agreed that if Austria be too strong for Russia and Italy, France is to make the balance even and secure Venetia to Italy, receiving as her reward Sardinia and perhaps Elba. My impression, however, is that the French will never quit Rome. She now calls her army there "an army of occupation."

'Dined at Lord Lyveden's. Had much conversation with Lady Airlie and with Lady Georgina, eldest daughter of Earl Russell. Lord and Lady Russell, Lord Chief-Justice Cockburn, Lord and Lady Houghton, and my old friend, Mrs. Dyce Sombre, now Mrs. Forester, were present.

'*Friday.*—Attended the House of Lords on appeals. Heard an appeal, which was the result of pure monomania in the appellant. Dined at Lord Houghton's. . . . Story, the American sculptor, was there.

'23.—Went down with my dear daughter G—— for the purpose of embarking in my yacht, the *Flirt*. She was lying in Portsmouth Harbour. . . . Sailed at eight in the evening; held on all night, which was beautiful; reached Portland Harbour about eleven. Did not anchor, but, as the weather was so fine, we on

'*Sunday*, 24, sailed back to the Needles, and anchored in

---

[1] The second reading of Lord Russell's Franchise Bill had been carried by the narrow majority of 5. In Committee an amendment which proposed to adopt rating, instead of rental, as the basis of the borough franchise was supported by the Conservatives and the 'Adullamite' party, and carried by 315 to 304.

Alum Bay, where we remained all night. This south-west extremity of the Isle of Wight bears manifest proof of the effects of the attrition of the rolling waves of the Atlantic, and yet there seems to be no wearing away of the Needles.

'*June* 24 *to June* 30.—During this week I have been guilty of negligence in not recording any events or impressions. A time of great excitement, and more wonderful events can hardly be imagined. On the Continent a foundation is now laid for a new constitution of Europe. It is plain that the Emperor of the French has arranged the whole affair in concert with the Prussian Minister, Count Bismarck, and the Italian Government.

'The energy and promptitude of the Prussians have been most remarkable ; the slowness and inaptitude of the Austrians most characteristic and traditionary. In ten days the Prussians have crushed the Austrian power. At home the resignation of the Liberal Ministry, which is the result of want of tact and of temper on the part of Lord Russell and Mr. Gladstone. Lord Derby has attempted a coalition, but having failed, has constituted a Government out of his own party. . . .

'*July* 2.—Attended the House of Lords. Judges present. Heard an appeal as to the right of the Lord Mayor's Court to issue the process of foreign attachment. Lord Chancellor Cranworth evidently failing in quickness of apprehension, for which I generally have found him remarkable. Mr. Justice Willes and Mr. Justice Blackburn the soundest and most useful lawyers among the judges. The case (*Mayor of London* v. *Cox*) exhibits in a remarkable degree the senselessness of our procedure at Common Law. If pleadings did no more than state facts proposed to be proved, the issues of fact or of law could be easily drawn out and settled for trial.'

Here the diary, or the only fragment of it which has been preserved, ends. Lord Westbury, to the end of his life, was characterised by a reluctance to put his thoughts on paper. Writing to his daughter, the late Mrs. Mansfield Parkyns, a few months before his death, he says :—

'I have delayed thanking you for your most delightful letter
until I could inform you of the arrival of that wonderful book,
which is to be the receptacle of all your dear father's wise thoughts
and valuable compositions. I will not forget your advice, and
will try to act upon it. But I am and have been so long in the
habit of speaking instead of writing, that I find composition a
painfully tedious process. As I speak, thoughts and words are
rapidly suggested, and the association is quick and lively; but
the slow, mechanical process of writing checks the train of
thought, and the ideas, not being rapidly taken down, lose their
associations and become dull and vapid, the chain being broken.
Hence I am always impatient of writing, and what I express
clearly in rapid utterance has no force or lucidity when written.
Perhaps you may have heard how much my spoken judgments
are preferred to the written ones.'

The status of the Church in the Colonies, particularly with respect to the powers of the Bishops,
continued to engage Lord Westbury's attention,
notwithstanding the unsparing attacks which had
been made upon him in connection with the
Colenso judgment. The questions provoked by
the decision remain, however, unsettled by any
such measure as he referred to in his diary, or in
the following letter :—

'My dear Bishop of Peterborough—I so seldom think it worth
while to examine the judicial proceedings in the Rolls Court, that
I did not rightly apprehend the question you put to me with
regard to Lord Romilly's judgment in the Colenso case. I understand it now from the extract read by Lord Cranworth last night.
I was not present, as I feel no disposition to take part in public
affairs, though I may be moved (if it be necessary) to say something on Lord Carnarvon's promised Bill. Lord R.'s position is
quite erroneous. Except, perhaps, in a Crown colony, or except
under the provisions of an Act of Parliament, it is *not* competent

to the Crown to assign a see to any colonial bishop in a colony
having an independent legislature.   Lord Romilly does not seem
rightly to apprehend the constitutional law and principles involved
in the cases of Long and the Bishop of Cape Town and Bishop
Colenso.   The real question (as I may explain) is whether it is
expedient to declare by Act of Parliament the Crown's supremacy
over colonial bishops and ministers, for the purpose of securing
uniformity of doctrine and discipline among colonial churches.
This would be the result of giving an appeal to the Queen in
Council.   To this there may probably be many and very grave
objections both here and in the colonies.   I have thought much
on the subject, and have somewhat changed my views on it.   The
colonial churches are now free and independent religious communities.   If you bind them all with the bond of submission to
the Queen's supremacy, you do *pro tanto* interfere with their
freedom, and you make them submissive to a tribunal, the composition of which many think very objectionable.   On the other
hand, if there be not this bond, there is the danger, almost the
certainty, of multiform variations and divergences in matters both
of doctrine and discipline.   Think well of these things before the
introduction of the promised Bill.   The opinions, or rather notions,
of men in the highest positions, both ecclesiastical and lay, on
this recondite and difficult subject appear to me to be somewhat
crude and vague.'

An ecclesiastical appeal in 1866[1] gave Lord
Westbury's clerical detractors another opportunity
of attacking him.   The case was a suit for 'per-
turbation' of an ancient pew, which was held as
appurtenant to Waddon Hall in Yorkshire, and had
been destroyed by the orders of the incumbent of
the parish.   The incumbent admitted the destruction, but pleaded that the church was not in law a
church, as it had never been reconsecrated since it

[1] *Parker* v. *Leach*, Law Reports, 1 Privy Council Appeal
Cases, 312.

was rebuilt in 1826, and that therefore the Court
had no jurisdiction.   It appearing, however, that
the church had been rebuilt on the same foundations, the Judicial Committee held that it required
no reconsecration.   In delivering the judgment in
the Privy Council Lord Westbury adverted to the
deplorable consequences which a contrary decision
would involve, not the least of which was that all
the marriages and other rites performed in the
church for nearly forty years would be rendered
illegal.   The report of the judgment in the newspapers was very incorrect, and the Bishop of Peterborough having asked for an explanation of it, Lord
Westbury writes :—

'I must explain it to you.   In the course of the argument
the preceding day, I had observed that in Roman Catholic times
dedication of a church to a saint, or to one of the two inferior,
that is, the second and third persons, of the Trinity, was part of
consecration.   Immediately some clergyman, eager to misrepresent, proclaimed that I had denied the doctrine of the Trinity,
so at the end of the judgment, in a few words, I said that to
prevent misrepresentation I had used the word "inferior" (which
was an incorrect expression) in the sense of denoting the secondly
and thirdly named persons, and not as implying anything contrary
to the creed that all were co-equal and co-eternal.   These few
words were all that I used.   With respect to the judgment, we
found that in many cases Dr. Lushington had advised the Bishop
of Canterbury that reconsecration was necessary, and that his
opinion was founded greatly on the old Roman Catholic doctrine
that where the Altar had been removed, reconsecration was
necessary.   We repudiated and overruled this doctrine.   I said
the Communion Table at which the feast of the Lord's Supper
was held did not in any manner correspond to the Altar of the
Roman Catholic Church where the sacrifice of the Mass was

offered.   There was no analogy, and the rule derived from the
removal of the Altar was not applicable to the removal of the
Communion Table.   That might well happen in the repair of
part of a Protestant Church without involving any necessity of
reconsecration.   We intimated a clear opinion that a church completely pulled down and built up anew on the *old foundations*
would not require reconsecration.   In such a case the area of
consecrated ground remains without addition.   On the case of
a church rebuilt and *enlarged so as to include a larger area*, we gave
no opinion.   The case before us we considered to be one of mere
reparation, without rebuilding or enlargement, and therefore clearly
not a case for new consecration.   The conduct of the clergyman
was scandalous.   As much interest appears to have been excited
by the judgment, which was oral and extempore, I will have the
shorthand writer's notes printed and send you a copy.'

Between 1866 and 1870 Lord Westbury delivered in the House of Lords several of those
admirable judgments which, in a short judicial
career, gained for him an enduring fame.   In cases
of domicil his marvellous power of dealing with
facts and applying to them settled principles more
than once found admirable scope.   Such cases depend on the inference which the law derives from
the circumstances of a man's birth and residence,
and it becomes necessary to look closely into the
history of a lifetime.   In the Udny case,[1] which was
a Scotch appeal to the House of Lords, Lord Westbury delivered a judgment which, as a clear and
concise exposition of legal principles, could hardly
be surpassed.   In a few sentences he contrasted the
political status of the citizen, involving the tie of

[1] *Udny* v. *Udny*, Law Reports, 2 Scotch Appeal Cases, 441.

natural allegiance, with the civil status of the individual, which depends on the domicil, and went on
to distinguish between the various kinds of domicil.

'It is a settled principle,' he said, 'that no man shall be
without a domicil, and to secure this result the law attributes to
every individual as soon as he is born the domicil of his father if
the child be legitimate, and the domicil of the mother if illegiti-
mate.   This has been called the domicil of origin, and is
involuntary.   Other domicils, including domicil by operation of
law, as on marriage, are domicils of choice.   For as soon as an
individual is *sui juris* it is competent to him to elect and assume
another domicil, the continuance of which depends upon his own
will and act.   When another domicil is put on, the domicil of
origin is for that purpose relinquished, and remains in abeyance
during the continuance of the domicil of choice ; but as the
domicil of origin is the creature of law, and independent of the
will of the party, it would be inconsistent with the principles on
which it is by law created and ascribed to suppose that it is
capable of being by the act of the party entirely obliterated and
extinguished.   It revives and exists whenever there is no other
domicil, and it does not require to be regained or reconstituted
animo et facto, in the manner which is necessary for the acquisition of a domicil of choice.'

On the death of Lord Kingsdown, Lord Westbury began to preside more frequently at the sittings
of the Judicial Committee of the Privy Council.
This led to correspondence with Mr. Henry Reeve,
then the Registrar, which was continued during the
remainder of Lord Westbury's life.   The latter part
of the subjoined letter affords a specimen of his
humour :—

'75 *Lancaster Gate, Oct.* 9, 1867.

'My dear Mr. Reeve—I write to condole with you on the loss
of our lamented friend Lord Kingsdown.

'I feel sure that the admirable biographical notice in the

Times came from your pen. It was a very just eulogy, and a very correct appreciation of poor Lord K.'s mind and character, and I concur with every word. I wish it had been possible to have given the history of his magnanimous conduct with respect to the late Sir R. Leigh's will, and to have referred to some of his noble acts of charity. I should like too to have noticed his bold opposition to the House of Commons when it went mad on the subject of actions for libel contained in blue-books which it ordered to be sold, and which conduct was the more to be admired because Peel partook of the mania. Perhaps he had a little too much of the *odi profanum vulgus et arceo*, but not for his own enjoyment. We shall not live to see him replaced.

'I must pass to another subject and confide to you a dreadful secret. My mind has sunk so low, perhaps from want of the long accustomed exercise, that I have fallen into a malady frequent with those who pass from much mental activity to sudden repose, and I believe that I am *always accompanied by a spirit from the unreal world.* "When I walk, I fear to turn my head, Because I know a frightful fiend, Doth close behind me tread." The apparition is not like the spectre of the Count d'Olivarez, nor like the gory head that sat on the table of the late Earl Grey ; it is a still more curious product of a disordered fancy. I see before me, behind me, and on each side perpetually, night and day, the spectral appearances of dishes of mutton chops and potatoes, and on each dish sits a tongue of fire constantly repeating, " Pay for me, pay for me, that I and you may rest in peace." To you as the greatest repository I know of all kinds of learning, sacred and profane, I entrust my disease. It cannot be cured but by your ordering to be sent to me a prescription in the shape of a bill for mutton chops. When I have paid it I shall defy the fiend and say, " Avaunt, let the earth hide thee," etc., and so being gone I'll be a man again. I thought I was strong enough to join battle with Beelzebub himself and to disprove his existence (objectively though *not subjectively*, for " *quisque suos patimur manes* "), but you see 'tis conscience that makes cowards of us all, and it has certainly given birth to my apparition. So pray send me the prescription, for without it " piacula nulla resolvent."—Yours sincerely, WESTBURY.'

Mr. Reeve's witty reply shows a proper appreciation of the joke, and explains the incident which
gave rise to it :—

'*Geneva, Oct.* 16, 1867.

'. . . I now approach with proper awe the frightful disclosure
contained in the second part of your letter.   My knowledge and
experience which extend, as you rightly suppose, to all the mysteries of the unseen world, at once enable me to recognise the
symptoms of your disorder.   You are the victim of one of the
worst of the powers of darkness, namely, the gridiron fiend.   That
was the power which consigned St. Lawrence in the earlier ages
of the Church to the pangs and glories of martyrdom.   Again, in
later times, the gridiron brandished by William Cobbett established
a moral reign of terrors in Britain.   And if Dr. Pusey had his
own way at this moment, we should probably see the Judicial
Committee stretched on gridirons in the Court of Christ Church.
Such is the influence of this terrible spirit.

'Yet when its powers are confined to the proper function of
cooking mutton chops, they are, as your Lordship knows, beneficent
and grateful.   I shall always remember the wisdom with which
you criticised the feeble efforts of our cook at Whitehall last
autumn.   It is true that the cook did, I believe, send in a small
bill for that very homely entertainment.   It amounted to very
little, and after due consultation with the authorities, we ordered
Lord Westbury's chops to be charged to the miscellaneous estimates
of the ensuing year, and paid for as one of the civil contingencies
out of the Consolidated Fund.   Possibly this course may not have
been strictly constitutional ; but I do not suppose that the attention
of Parliament has yet been called to the circumstance.   Should
it be absolutely necessary, in order to stay the persecution of the
gridiron fiend, I will inform you of the amount when I return to
England, which will be, I hope, about the 9th November.'

In fulfilment of his promise to assist as a private
member in the accomplishment of reforms which he
had advocated from the woolsack, Lord Westbury, on
the resignation of the late Government, generously

undertook, at Lord Cranworth's special request, to devote his attention to the further revision of the Statute Law. His Act of 1863 had extended to the statutes from the time of Magna Charta to the Revolution, and the previous (Lord Campbell's) Act of 1861 covered the period between 1770 and 1858. By these revisions 3000 Acts were disposed of; and all that was now needed was to continue the revision for the intermediate period.[1] In this manner 'the statutes at large' would be reduced from eighty-five volumes to six or seven; and Lord Westbury proposed to supplement the task by forming a complete classified index, which might be continued from year to year, as has since been done.

Sir Fitz-Roy Kelly, who had recently succeeded Sir Frederick Pollock as Chief Baron of the Exchequer, in his reply to Lord Westbury's congratulations on his appointment, refers to this undertaking:—

'Though removed from the stage upon which for a long time we played the same part, and whence afterwards I had to look up to you in a much higher sphere, I shall ever remember the days when we struggled and laboured on and forwards, *haud passibus æquis*, till you had reached the highest point to which either could aspire.

'One thing more: you have taken up with energy and your usual success a great work which I began ten years ago, the consolidation of the statutes. I have done with the legislature and legislation perhaps for ever. You remain, and may go on and complete and perfect this greatest of all law reforms. From a distance I can only offer you my good wishes, as I now do in that and all your undertakings.'

---

[1] This was accomplished by Lord Chelmsford in 1867.

About the same time a Royal Commission had been appointed ' to inquire into the expediency of a Digest of Law, and the best means of accomplishing that object, and of otherwise exhibiting, in a compendious and accessible form, the law as embodied in judicial decisions.' Lord Westbury was made one of the Commissioners,[1] and on the subsequent death of Lord Cranworth he became Chairman of the Commission.

This was his first return to any participation in public work, apart from judicial duties. He could, indeed, scarcely refuse his services in connection with a subject which he had made peculiarly his own. But from the time of his resignation he showed a marked preference for a life of comparative privacy and solitude. When residing in England, during the summer and autumn months, he passed his time in the country, renewing his acquaintance with favourite classics, or perusing some scientific treatise. ' My father made it a habit,' writes his youngest daughter, ' for me to read aloud to him for three or four hours in the day. Any one who was staying in the house and liked to join these readings was welcome to do so, and his remarks and explanations were very interesting. One or two books were read straight through, such as Buckle's *History of Civilisation*

---

[1] Among the Commissioners were Lord Hatherley, Lord Cairns, Sir James P. Wilde (Lord Penzance), Sir Erskine May (afterwards Lord Farnborough, Mr. Robert Lowe (Lord Sherbrooke), Sir R. Palmer (Lord Selborne), Mr. Justice Willes, and Mr. (now Lord) Thring.

and Lewes's *History of Philosophy;* but, as a rule,
he preferred to vary the readings, and sometimes it
was part of a play of Shakespeare or one of Bacon's
Essays, some pages from Lecky, or a chapter from
the Greek Testament, and so on.   He had a remarkable facility in extracting the pith of a book
in a very short time.   I have often seen him take
up some book of the day off the table, and, while
standing, turn it over for ten minutes or so, and in
this short time he would take in all its most salient
points, and in speaking about it afterwards you received the impression that he had read it from
beginning to end.'

As he advanced in life he seemed to find the
keener enjoyment in intellectual culture, and the
scholarly tastes which had characterised him through
life exerted their strongest influence.   His friend,
Mr. Frederic Harrison, has supplied the following
personal recollections which give prominence to
Lord Westbury's classical attainments, and convey
a just appreciation of his extraordinary powers.

' How Lord Westbury knew and loved his classics
was amongst my earliest school recollections.[1]   It
was by his advice that I was sent, as a small boy of
nine, to a schoolmaster whom he knew and valued

---

[1] 'He was one of my father's friends in youth.   After
leaving Oxford he rowed stroke in a six-oared boat on the Thames,
of which my father and uncle were members.   I always heard
him spoken of as a fine oar.   The intimacy between the young
men continued during life.'—F. H.

highly—Mr. Joseph King, of Maida Hill. Mr.
Bethell, as he then was, warmly supported the
method of Mr. King, one of the first to introduce the
results of modern German philology, which in 1840
was still in its infancy and little in vogue in schools.
We were taught to trace all words to their root or
crude form, to see in the inflexions mere variations of
a common type both in Greek and Latin, and to
explain the syntax of both languages by general
principles of logic, without rules in set words learned
by rote and not understood.

'From the first Mr. Bethell, absorbed in practice
as he was, would send for us youngsters from time to
time to try what we could do. Child as I was in those
days, I can remember how he would open *Homer*
or *Virgil*, and turning to some favourite passage
would show us how it should be done into English.
He would read it into English, very slowly, and
with great refinement of intonation, but always without stumbling or correcting a word. It seemed to
our ears like a recitation from a printed translation,
so carefully modulated was the phrase, and so
finished the expression. The stately and elaborate
form of speech, which strangers and the outside
world usually took for affectation, from habit seemed
to me to be entirely natural in him. How and
whence it began with him I know not. It was certainly the only mode of speech that I ever heard from
his lips. I never heard him utter, on any occasion
of surprise or excitement, a single broken phrase ;

his gift of absolutely exact expression seemed to be an involuntary act of instinct.

'All through my school life he would from time to time hear us boys turn a passage from the classics, with which he seemed glad to keep up his interest. Nor was his knowledge superficial. He would tackle a chorus in the *Choephori* or a dialogue of *Plato ;* and of course a boy at the top of the sixth form could easily judge if he was at home in it or not. I cannot undertake to say that his scholarship was faultless, for we did not, of course, question him, or choose our own passages, and he probably was not surpassed in his own age for the power of acquiring such knowledge as was needed for the purpose in hand. But my strong impression is, that throughout life he always remembered and enjoyed his classics.

'It was by his advice that I was sent to compete for a scholarship at Wadham, where his friend and old tutor, Dr. Symons, was then warden. And during my life at Oxford we sometimes had a talk about the books for the schools. He had much to say about the narrow and stereotyped list of authors which it was then the fashion to offer. In particular, he thought the range of ancient philosophy too small. The " Politeia," as he always called it, was a very meagre representative of the entire Platonic philosophy; and he once gave me a scheme of about a dozen dialogues which he declared would more fully do justice to the various sides of Plato's system. I have not retained the list; but he gave me the impression that

he was speaking with knowledge at first-hand, and
with real conviction and interest. I doubted, as I
doubt now, the wisdom of his advice.   For wide and
fruitful reading is perhaps a luxury for those who
have passed examinations.   At any rate I stuck to
my " Republic " and my college tutor's advice.   And
I read the more varied selection of dialogues in
mellower days, when *cruces* and " tips " were become
to me vanities as indifferent as football or " collec-
tions."

   ' Of his career at the bar and on the bench I saw and
knew no more than any junior barrister of my standing.
It was after his political career was over that I saw
him from time to time on the Royal Commission for
Digesting the Law, of which he was the chairman,
and I was secretary from 1869 until the winding up
of the Commission.   The great problem of consolidating the whole law of England, the fusion of law
and equity, and the practical codification of both in
a uniform plan, had long and deeply engaged Lord
Westbury's mind.   His intellect had an extraordinary
tendency to symmetry—a turn peculiarly rare in an
English public man, and almost unknown in an
English lawyer.   The various schemes for simplifying and organising the law which he continually put
forth in public and in private were, I think, due quite
as much to irresistible impulses of his mental constitution as they were to any ambition of public
achievement.   As a lawyer, his mind had indeed
something of the qualities of Lord Bacon's, both on

the stronger and on the weaker side. The restless desire to bring order out of disorder, to classify, group, and harmonise ideas, outstripped in both the knowledge of details and the stubborn reality of facts. It may be doubted if Lord Westbury had ever been sufficiently great a lawyer to succeed in the gigantic task of consolidating the whole range of English law. Probably at that period of his life such a task was wholly beyond the remaining powers he possessed. I think he early realised the fact that, under the conditions imposed on him, and with the materials which the Commission supplied, it would be impossible to do more than to furnish suggestions and specimens for the future, and to direct attention to the extraordinary difficulties of the task. Accepting this as inevitable, he applied himself to the work in hand with much freshness and versatility. He was then much past his highest powers of concentration and laborious application. But his ingenuity, wit, and felicity of brain had never been greater. I shall not easily forget the conversations which I used to have with him alone in his house of an evening,—the brilliant suggestions and novel schemes that he flung off, the inimitable phrases in which he summed up his idea of this or that contemporary, the irresistible pictures that he gave of his opponents, the visions of reform which he conceived, often ending in some eloquent and elaborate speech which he was about to make in the House of Lords, and which, alas! he never made.

'Such are some of my personal recollections of the one or two matters whereon I had extended and intimate relations with him. Of the advocate, politician, and man of the world I have no special knowledge, and have nothing to say—I willingly add that personally I have never found him anything but kindly, and indeed peculiarly indulgent. Indulgence he carried to a fault ; he was only too ready to avoid conflicts and to yield to the pressure of others, even against his better judgment. And many a difficulty was caused by his always finding it easier to say "Yes!" than to say "No!" His famous tendency to sarcasm was due, I always thought, not to any wish to wound or any ambition to display, but to an instinctive genius for clear-cut phrases, coupled with an habitual indifference to the opinion of others. In private and alone these phrases would flash from his brain, as if they were automatic and involuntary reflex acts, at times when there was nobody to wound or to dazzle. His brain seemed never to have known repose, and his lips never to have practised restraint.'

The Digest Commission lingered on for five years and then collapsed. This was due partly to the inherent difficulties of the subject, and partly to the want of precision in the terms of the reference to the Commission. The Commissioners had no definite scheme to work upon, and they were unable to agree upon any recommendation except that a digest was expedient, and that the work, based on a comprehensive plan, and with a uniform method, should at once be undertaken.   In a letter to Mr. Henry Reeve, written in the spring of 1870, Lord Westbury complained :—

'I am in despair as to the Digest Commission : *quot homines, tot sententiæ.*   I cannot get the simplest report agreed on as to future proceedings.   The νοῦς ἀρχιτεκτονικός is miserably wanting in the English mind.   In my despair I have offered the Government to undertake the entire control and superintendence of the work myself, with of course a proper staff of working men, not more than seven, and I think the Civil Code might be completed in three years.   There is no chance of the Government agreeing to my offer.'

Mr. Reeve's reply indicated the real cause of the hopeless failure of the Commission, and suggested the proper mode of procedure :—

'I am very glad you have made a proposal to the Government to direct the Digest of the Law.   But it appears to me that before anything is, or can be, actually done, it is necessary to shape out distinctly in writing what it is proposed to do.   And this can far more effectually be done by a single mind, duly qualified, than by any Commission.

'Permit me, therefore, to suggest that as there is, probably, no man amongst us so fit to make the building plan of the structure as yourself, you would do the country great service and yourself great honour, by drawing up a scheme or Institute (Organon ?) of the Law, which other men could more easily be found to fill up.

'This is a worthy subject for your meditations, and it recommends itself the more to the mind that it can be done *proprio motu,* and without consulting anybody.   Set to work upon it in the spirit in which Bacon applied himself to the "Novum Organum" and the "De Augmentis," and you may yet surpass

the achievements of an advocate and of a judge, for this would
be a gift to posterity.'

It is possible that if the task of planning a digest
of the case law had been entrusted to Lord Westbury alone on the same terms as Brodie, the eminent
conveyancer, undertook to draw the Fines and
Recoveries Bill—that not one word in his draft
should be altered—it might have been brought to a
successful issue. He had ideas on the subject which
seemed, to himself at least, clear and definite. To
review the whole of the reports, distinguishing cases
which ought not to be included in any new collection ; to classify the residue, after this elimination,
according to an analysis settled for the statute law ;
and then to state the rules and principles to be extracted from the reports so classified; these, it would
appear, were the main outlines of his scheme. But
Lord Westbury's age, rather than the reason assigned
in the following letter, forbade the hope that he
would undertake the formidable labour suggested by
his correspondent. He replied :—

' How shall I thank you for your inspiriting letter, which was
as the sound of the trumpet to the aged war-horse ? I fear my
contemporaries have taken a more accurate measurement of my
power, and that I shall never fulfil any such glorious destiny as
you hold before my eyes. It is true of many men that "possunt
quia posse videntur," and that they accomplish many things
simply because they are not fastidious ; I should never do
anything, simply because I should tear up one day what I had
written the preceding. It would be Penelope's web. Our
education is too æsthetical. Unless a cultivated taste be over-
powered by personal vanity, it is very difficult to complete any

composition. I can most truly say that I have never done anything, speaking or writing, of which I could say on the review,
mihi placido.

'We have a great difference of opinion in the members of
the Digest Commission. Many think that the work should be
handed over to two or three very able men (not Judges or *emeriti*
Chancellors) who should be well paid, and that to them, with a
staff of subordinates, all the work should be committed. Others
think that there should be added to this establishment some
presiding power, consisting of one, two, or three distinguished
Judges, to whom all questions should be referred, and whose
duty it would be to give an *imprimatur* to the work. So we
cannot agree on a recommendation to the Government. And
when we shall do so but little weight will attach to it.'

The Roman case law is said to have been
digested in three years, under the superintendence
of Justinian thirteen centuries ago, and in our own
times private enterprise has shown that, notwithstanding the chaotic state of English law, it is
possible to obtain a compilation of this kind. To
codify the law would be a far heavier task. A
systematic reconstruction and republication of the
whole body of the statute and case law, stamped
with the authority of direct parliamentary enactment, must be deemed essential to the completion
of a satisfactory code. 'There is no analogy,' wrote
Lord Westbury, 'between English law at the present
day and either French law at the era of the first
revolution or the Roman law at the era of Justinian.
The way in which codification has been conceived
and attempted in England is that of progressively
digesting the law into a scientific framework until

the result is attained that every legal rule is
somewhere or other expressed in a compendious
proposition.' The Commission of 1866 gave
a heavy discouragement to this particular pro-
ject of reform from which it has never since
recovered.

Two years elapsed from the time of his resignation before Lord Westbury's voice was again heard
in Parliament. In the summer of 1867 he began to
take part very sparingly in debate, supporting his
former colleagues in the House of Lords in their
opposition to the Government Reform Bill. Thenceforth, though he spoke occasionally on subjects of
law reform, he showed little inclination to return to
official life. 'I shall take no part in politics,' he
writes, 'for I am convinced that in point of happiness and comfort I could not by doing so improve
my own position or that of my children.' Another
letter, written early in the following year, expresses
the same resolve. 'Do not waste a thought on
politics. There is nothing to be found in that
area of selfishness and falsehood to give any real
pleasure. I never wish to enter it again. My
disinclination is so great that it actually produces
incapacity. No doubt there are great events
about to happen which will be the parents of
much good or evil.'

The following letters give some idea of his life at
this period, and show his continued interest in the
subjects which had long engaged his attention :—

'My dear Mr. Reeve—I thank you very much for sending me Mr. Justice Markby's letter. The question of the Colonial Bar, and the proper mode of supplying it, has long engaged my attention. That any Inn of Court should have admitted men to the Bar, on a shorter period of residence and with lower requirements than are demanded for English barristers, *but with a condition that they should not practise in Courts in England,* was an unwarranted proceeding and wholly *ultra vires.*

'On the other hand it is a very oppressive, although at present it may be a very useful thing, to say that the Colonial Bar shall consist of men who have been regularly called to the Bar in England, Scotland, or Ireland.

'This obligation cannot long continue. Colleges for the education of young men and for conferring degrees in Jurisprudence will soon be established in the Indian Presidencies and in Australia, and it will be absurd to impose upon its students the obligation of coming to the United Kingdom and residing for three years in London, Edinburgh, or Dublin. The absurdity is the greater because we have no established system of legal education. All my efforts have been baffled. In 1847 I prevailed on the Middle Temple to recognise the obligation of supplying the means of education to the students. Accordingly it founded a Professorship of Civil Law or Jurisprudence, that being the department in which, as it appeared to me, our young men stood in the greatest need of instruction. The other Inns of Court followed reluctantly, almost all the Judges at Law and in Equity opposing the measure. A Joint-Committee was appointed, of which I was Chairman. To that Committee I submitted a plan for forming the four Inns of Court into a legal University with power of conferring degrees, which should be required for admission to the Bar, and as a condition for holding any office in the Civil Service in India to which any judicial duties might be incident.

'But the proposal had no support. Lord St. Leonards, Lord Cranworth, Dr. Lushington, Mr. Baron Alderson, and Lords Justices Knight-Bruce and Turner being my most determined antagonists, and resisting to the last the minor scheme of competitive examination. It must be the work of the next generation. . . .

'Now for another subject. In my theological and anthropological studies I have often been much struck by that expression in Horace, "Genus Iapeti."[1] Do you know of any similar expression in any classic? The Japhetian race, 'Ιαπετὸς, occurs in Hesiod as one of the Titans (I write from memory); but I know of nothing equivalent or similar to this expression, which is plainly used by Horace as a distinctive appellation of all the European nations. I have few books here. Can you enlighten me? Is there anything to show a belief in the Greek or Roman writers that the posterity of Japhet colonised Europe? Horace uses the phrase as if it were well known. Is there anywhere any mention of Shem? As far as I know (little enough certainly) there is no trace of any tradition of a deluge in the Egyptian hieroglyphics, nor is there any mention of it in Herodotus. Whence was derived the Deucalion and Pyrrha fable? Excuse my ignorance and remember that for five and fifty years my mind has been spellbound within the narrow circle of the practice and administration of technical English law.—Yours sincerely,   WESTBURY.'

'Hinton St. George, Jan. 14, 1868.

'My dear Mr. Reeve—It will give me much pleasure if I can render any public service by presiding during the next sittings of the Judicial Committee. I did not make any offer to do so because I thought the Committee so strong by the addition of the two Lords Justices, Sir W. Erle and Sir R. Kindersley, that you would not require any outsider. Will you do me the favour to tell me what members of the Committee will sit with me? I hope my old associates, Williams, Colvile, and Peel will be of the number, as we get on so well together, and I esteem them highly. When I use the word "well," I mean pleasantly. There was not a single instance of difference of opinion during our sittings.

---

[1] 'Audax Iapeti genus
Ignem fraude mala gentibus intulit.'

          Bk. I., Ode iii. 27.

'Pray, if you can, give us a paper with some variety and not
wholly composed of dreary Indian Appeals, the hearing of which
always reminded me of the toil of Pharaoh's charioteers when
they drave heavily their wheelless chariots in the deep sands of
the Red Sea.

'Who is it that has dug so deep into the Talmud and written
that remarkable paper for which a century ago he would have
been the subject of a Writ *De Heretico Comburendo?* But to
return to the sheep of the Council. Would it be possible to have
the sittings begin on Tuesday instead of Monday? I have invited some friends to shoot on Saturday and stay till Monday,
but if it be necessary I must put off their visit. If you find it
necessary for me to come, pray send me the first six cases in the
paper. What with the weather and Fenianism, London cannot
have been a very agreeable abode this Christmas.—Yours sincerely,   W.'

The reference to the composition of the Judicial
Committee recalls the following story. The late
Sir William Erle, in reply to Lord Westbury, who
asked him why he did not attend the Judicial Committee of the Privy Council, said that he was old and
deaf and stupid. 'That is no sufficient excuse,'
returned Lord Westbury, 'for Chelmsford and I are
very old, Napier is very deaf, Colvile is very
stupid; but we four make an excellent tribunal.'

CHAPTER VIII

THE greatest of the 'great events' predicted by Lord Westbury was the contest on the question of the Disestablishment of the Irish Church. On the 23d March 1868 Mr. Gladstone moved his resolutions condemning the Establishment in general terms. The resolutions were carried by overwhelming majorities, and Mr. Disraeli advised a dissolution, that the question might be submitted to the constituencies.

The Suspensory Bill, which was the necessary sequel of these proceedings, passed with little modification through the House of Commons; but in the House of Lords, after one of the finest debates ever heard in that Assembly, it was rejected by a majority of 95. Lord Westbury entertained grave objections to any scheme of disestablishment which involved an interference with the Royal Supremacy. On this occasion, however, he voted in the minority with the

Government in support of the voluntary principle in the case of the Irish Church.

The general election, which took place in the autumn, sealed the fate of the Government. Mr. Disraeli immediately announced the resignation of his Ministry, and Mr. Gladstone formed an Administration pledged to the principles of disestablishment and disendowment. To the principle of universal disendowment Sir Roundell Palmer could not agree, and he renounced, in obedience to his conscientious scruples, his undeniable claims to the highest prize of his profession. Lord Cranworth had died in the previous summer, and the return of Lord Westbury to the woolsack was by many regarded as a likely event. Even the leading organ of the Conservatives spoke, without expressing any disapproval, of the probability of his reappointment. It was natural that his friends should desire it, but he himself constantly declared that he never entertained the slightest expectation of resuming office. ' I am *civiliter mortuus*,' he used to say, with absolute equanimity.

In the later months of this year he was asked to serve on the Commission appointed to report on the Scottish Law Courts and their practice and procedure, which sadly stood in need of reform. He assented, naturally expecting to find himself ranked in the Commission according to his right of precedence. Subsequently the Lord Advocate (Mr., afterwards Lord Gordon) wrote that it was proposed to make Lord Colonsay Chairman of the Commission, and asked whether that arrangement would be agreeable to Lord Westbury. This letter, through misdirection, was not received for several days ; but immediately it arrived Lord Westbury, not wishing to hurt any one's feelings, withdrew his name on the plea of ill-health. Meanwhile the Commission was issued, with Lord Colonsay's name at the head of it. This discourtesy drew forth an indignant protest from Lord Westbury :—

'After all the delay that has occurred,' he wrote to the Lord Advocate, 'since I first pressed on the Government the propriety of issuing this Commission, it was hardly too much to expect that you would have waited for my answer to your letter. You had no authority to place my name on the Commission in any order save according to my rank and right of precedence, which is the usual rule. I am sorry to have received this slight from *you*. I must beg you to strike my name out of the Commission, and to make it public that I decline to serve upon it.'

He seems to have supposed that there was an intention on the part of the Government that Lord Colonsay should regulate the inquiries of the Commission, whether he (Lord Westbury) assented or not. Except that Lord Colonsay was resident in Edinburgh when Parliament was not sitting, there was no apparent ground for departing from the proper order of precedence. 'It was impossible,' wrote Lord Westbury to his youngest son, 'to put up with such an affront, nor was it possible to expect any good from such a Commission.'

The two next letters, addressed to Mr. Reeve,

show the equanimity of the ex-Chancellor in his retirement, and the improbability that he would return to public life :—

'*Hinton St. George, July* 16, 1868.

'. . . The gorge rises at the thought of being fed on curry rice and chutnee sauce for three weeks. I shall certainly contract a disease of the liver. If you can send us occasionally to sea on an Admiralty case, it will certainly be a little relief. . . .

'The best advice that his friends can give Rolt is to resign. It is the only chance of long life. Let him not be afraid of ennui from idleness. He has great love of the country and country pursuits, and that is all-sufficient. Age cannot wither it nor custom stale its infinite variety. And it is so much better to be a looker-on than an actor in life. Aristotle, in the last chapter of his Nicomachean Ethics, sets himself to consider what can be the happiness of the gods, and he finds nothing in which he can put it but in contemplation. And it might be so, if it were still true— "And God saw (contemplated) all that he had made, and behold it was very good."

'I thought it was an 'Ebrew Jew that wrote the article entitled "Talmud." I have only read a few extracts. It is quite in keeping with the times that it should be in a Tory journal. The Conservatives have begun by being avowed reformers, and next they will be declared Freethinkers. This is the first step to their confession. Their great schoolmaster Dizzy gets his compatriot to publish this article. *Macte virtute pueri.* I am glad to hear from you that it is shallow, but novelty and originality now are nothing but the reproduction of forgotten things, and to speak seriously, I thought it seemed a thing likely to lead many to some form or other of Arian opinions. Dr. Johnson on his deathbed earnestly begged Sir Joshua to read without ceasing Dr. Samuel Clarke's Sermons, because they were the fullest on the subject of the Divinity of Christ and the Redemption. Was it known at that time that Clarke died an Arian, or was that fact subsequently ascertained?

'I am sorry to see in your handwriting traces of the Cheiragra.

My knowledge of physic leads me to send you the following prescription. Abstain from *all* wine except some good hock, and
that only during dinner. If any stimulus to the stomach be found
wanting, some old Irish whisky and water after dinner. Every
morning on waking drink a glass of the Carlsbad water. So
shall the *mala praxis* in the chymistry of the body be corrected
and healthy blood produced. And now having chattered about
law, theology, and medicine, I am, yours sincerely,   W.'

'*London, Nov.* 1868.

'My dear Mr. Reeve—These written judgments are a great
bore. I imagine (no doubt from vanity) that at the end of the
argument I could have pronounced *vivâ voce* a much more effective and convincing judgment than that which I have written.
The *vis animi* evaporates during the slow process of writing.
The conception fades, and the expression becomes feeble. What
we shall do with the other case of M——— I dread to think.
I wish we had knocked it off while the iron was hot, as we used
to do the running down cases. There is no chance of a decision
this side of Christmas.

'I have come up to town on some private matters, and
have not the least notion of mingling in any political matters.
In fact, I gave my people to understand so clearly last session
that I should reject with abhorrence any measure that embodied these two wicked things—1. Stripping the Irish Church
of its property to convert it to *secular* uses, which is robbery;
2. Destroying episcopacy in and the Queen's supremacy over the
Established Church in Ireland, which is a wanton, unnecessary,
and most mischievous act; that of course I could not expect any
communication from them. The weakness of the Government
in its legal staff in the House of Commons will be very great, but
the Opposition will be weaker. It cannot be expected that Palmer
will take a very active part in opposition. Then what lawyer
have they? But in the House of Lords I hope the principles of
English Law and of political expediency will be abundantly illustrated and explained, and shown to be in direct opposition to the
Government's destructive and revolutionary measure; and if this

be done, as the people of England are a law-loving and law-abiding people, there may be a great reaction in public feeling. And what will Wood be able to do against those opposed to him? What a Cabinet! Misery, says Trinculo, makes one acquainted with strange bedfellows. So it seems does unlooked-for prosperity. . . .

'I am very thankful that I have an opportunity of conversing in quiet with philosophers and poets at Hinton.—Yours sincerely,

'W.'

Mr. Reeve took the opposite view of the question as to the better mode of delivering judgments, which has long been in dispute among lawyers. He wrote :—

'In spite of your own preference for the "wild freshness of morning" and all the dewdrops hanging on the roses, I must be allowed to assure you, that in my poor judgment they are improved by this severe revision, and that the judicial style is, like Musidora, when "unadorned adorned the most."

'Of that style I think these judgments will be quoted hereafter as masterly specimens.'

Referring to the recent change of Government and the appointment of Lord Chancellor, Lord Westbury wrote to the same correspondent :—

'*Dec.* 3, 1868.

'I suppose London is full of excitement and surprise. I was forewarned of what was about to happen. I am sorry that we shall lose the Lord Chancellor,[1] for his place will not be easily supplied. Some verses from one of Seneca's tragedies exactly express my feeling, though I am not sure that I quote accurately—

'"Stet quicunque volet potens
    Aulae culmine lubrico :

---

[1] Lord Cairns.

> *Me* dulcis saturet quies.
>   Obscuro positus loco,
> Leni perfruar otio.
>   Nullis nota Quiritibus
> Aetas per tacitum fluat."

This temper is not of necessity but from will.'

'*Dec.* 6, 1868.

'. . . Of the three candidates, Romilly, Cockburn, and Wood, I think, on the whole, Wood is the best. But I fear he will break down under the accumulated labour.

' I made no secret last year to Granville and others that my mind did not run with total confiscation of Church property, or with the total destruction of episcopacy or the supremacy of the Crown. Therefore I neither have had, nor expected to have, any communication from my former Party. Who would have believed ten years ago that Gladstone and the High Churchman Wood were the fated instruments to destroy the Episcopal Church in Ireland ?

'The Psalmist says, " Put not your trust in princes," but I say, put no trust in any man, nor believe that he will retain to-morrow his dearest principles of to-day. There is but one rule, that given by Lord Stanley, " I will vote for anything that is proved to be expedient." A man who avows this will be always consistent in the theory of his principles of action, and really I see no other rule. But such fantastical tricks disturb even a contemplative beholder. I gave you some Latin verses in my last, and I will give you some English verses to compare (I think advantageously) with the celebrated "Suave Mari," etc.—

> ' " He that of such a height has built his mind,
>   And reared the dwelling of his thoughts so strong ;
> As neither hope nor fear can shake the frame
>   Of his resolved powers ; nor all the wind
> Of vanity or malice pierce to wrong
> His settled peace, or to disturb the same :
> What a fair seat hath he, from whence he may
> The boundless wastes and wilds of man survey !
> And with how free an eye doth he look down
> Upon these lower regions of turmoil

Where all storms of passion mainly beat
On flesh and blood."   (DANIEL).

'It is pleasanter to dwell amid these studies than to write dull opinions even in the Privy Council.—Believe me, yours sincerely,
                                                        'W.'

The new Cabinet was formed in December 1868, and Sir W. Page Wood, who had lately been appointed a Lord Justice, received the Great Seal. Apart from his other qualifications for the office, Lord Hatherley had, it appears, long advocated the measure which the Government was pledged to promote. Lord Westbury, on the other hand, disapproved of several important features of Mr. Gladstone's scheme. Some light is thrown on his views and his relations to the Ministry by the following reply to a letter he had addressed some months before to Mr. Gladstone :—

                                            '*May* 20, 1868.

'My dear Lord Westbury—I thank you very much both for the matter of your letter and for the kind terms in which it is conveyed.

'The operations of the Ecclesiastical Courts in Ireland are marvellously small, but that, of course, is no reason why they should not be provided for.

'I have been assured by my lawyers, if so I may presume to call them, that they are provided for by the Ecclesiastical Law; but I will take care, after learning your opinion as I have now learned it, that the matter is further considered.

'With respect to the Supremacy, the link of connection with the State was what in my own mind I last gave up long after I had embraced Disestablishment in all other respects.

'I do not know what might be done if the members of the Irish Church should show a general desire to be placed under

some especial power of review.   Unless they did so, I think we
who are stripping them of property and privilege could not ask
to leave them the restraints of Establishment alone.   And, as far
as I can judge, to ask it would break up our phalanx, which is
now pretty compact.

'The experience of Scotland and America, the only cases in
point, seems to show a very strong desire to keep in substantial
unity with the Church of England, and even to draw the bonds
closer when they had been relaxed.

'I presume that in some way the Irish Church must get her-
self organised on a voluntary basis, and, perhaps, when the affair
is well started, the Synod or Convocation might meet to consider
in what way this could be done.   I imagine it has been well
and effectively managed in Canada and some other colonies.—
Believe me, sincerely yours,   W. E. GLADSTONE.'

On this letter Lord Westbury, writing to his
son-in-law, Captain Cardew, subsequently made the
following observations :—

'Ever since my resignation of office, I have always manifested
towards my former colleagues the most friendly feelings and the
greatest readiness to afford them every possible assistance.   I
have not obtruded myself, because I thought it would be officious
and in bad taste, and in truth I did not consider that any services
of mine could be of much value.

'But when the resolutions on the Irish Church were passed,
and it was known that Roundell Palmer would not support the
Government, I wrote to Gladstone, and after pointing out the
difficulties that would attend the details of legislation on the
subject, I offered freely such aid as I could give in advising and
superintending the form and manner of legislating on the subject
and preparing the Bills for Parliament.   At the same time I
stated the grave difficulty that would arise from the abolition of
the Supremacy of the Crown, and that, in my opinion, that point
was unnecessary and inexpedient.   I pointedly added that nothing
I might do (if my offer was accepted) should be construed or
understood to impose on Gladstone the least obligation with

respect to myself, in the event of his being called on to form a new Ministry.

'It was a very serious offer, prompted solely by the desire to be of use.

'You remember Gladstone's answer. It touched on the difficulties I had pointed out (as we thought in a wild and unsatisfactory way), but it took no notice at all of my offer, not even thanking me for it, and it plainly evinced a desire not to have any further communication (you can show it to Otway, if he has any curiosity). Thus repulsed, what could I do? I disapproved of a very important part of the measure. I thought Gladstone, by adhering to it, was most unnecessarily running his head against a stone wall. The omission of it would not have impaired the efficiency of the measure, and it would have disarmed much opposition and removed much difficulty. Notwithstanding, I determined not to oppose my former colleagues and to vote for the Bill. When the debate was coming on, Lord Russell, in my presence, asked Lord Romilly to speak in favour of the Bill, but he made no request to me. Nor did Lord Granville. In fact, in every way I was made to feel that no participation or assistance on my part was required. Still I have shown no sulkiness or discontent, or in any way evinced the least disappointment. In fact I felt none. I should have been glad to have been of use; but finding no help was needed, I was equally content to remain without any interference. No one congratulated Lord Granville, the Duke of Argyll, the present Lord Chancellor, and the rest of the Government, with more sincerity than I did on Thursday last. I told Lord Granville: "I will support the Government in all things; but if they are resolved to convert Church property to purely secular uses, and to utterly abolish Episcopacy and the Supremacy of the Crown, I cannot for a moment follow them to such conclusions, which are most unlawful, unjust, and inexpedient."

'I have sometimes thought that perhaps the Queen might have entertained some personal objection, although her manner of parting with me was markedly kind, but —— assured me that the Queen always spoke of me with kindness, and, in fact, with much gracious feeling.

'This is a plain statement of the facts which have occurred. I have not the smallest feeling of regret or disappointment, much less of ill-will, in consequence of what has been done.

'The Government has not anywhere a more sincere well-wisher than myself, although my overtures have been slighted, and, in fact, wholly repulsed.'

That the Ex-Chancellor misinterpreted the feelings of his late colleagues towards him, or that the exigencies of the ministerial position speedily led to a conviction on their part that his services would be of greater value to them than he supposed, will appear from the sequel.

The promotion of Lord Hatherley to the woolsack created a vacancy in the post of Lord Justice in the Court of Appeal. It is evident from the following letter that Mr. Gladstone looked forward to a time when Lord Westbury might resume his former position, and that he was disposed to make arrangements likely to facilitate that event.

'*Dec.* 16, 1868.

'My dear Granville—I wish to lay before you my views, and to have the benefit of your opinion respecting the vacant office of Lord Justice.

'In days when the principles of administration were more strict than they now are, I think it would have been the admitted duty of the person charged with the appointment to ask himself whether there was any distinguished man of the legal profession, who had passed through great offices and was at present unemployed, and who might possibly be disposed to accept the vacant seat. In a word, to proceed on the principle applied in the case of Lord Lyndhurst : to do this, before entertaining any question of promotion ; and to leave it entirely to the person concerned to judge of all the nicer questions of personal rank and dignity, of which, in truth, he would be the only person competent to dispose.

'With these views, I must call to mind that there are now in the House of Lords two peers originally of the Equity Bar and still in their full vigour, who have held the office of Lord Chancellor: Lord Westbury and Lord Cairns. And the question for me appears to be this: if it is possible that Lord Westbury might be disposed to accept the Lord Justiceship, ought not the power of taking it to be given him?

'Doubtless it may be asked, Does the precedent of Lord Lyndhurst cover this case? and would he (Lord Westbury, not Lord Lyndhurst), if it does not, be inclined to enlarge it? But (as it seems to me) there is no consideration of public interest which allows me to close these questions. They are questions (so to speak) for the other side.

'Some men take as a friendly act and mark of regard what other men take in an opposite sense. If an offer of this kind were viewed *in malam partem* by any one, I could not help it. If it more justly deserves a better construction, this ought greatly to recommend it to the old colleagues of Lord Westbury. Lord Westbury suffered heavily in 1865. He became to a great extent a scapegoat. The vials of public virtue, a very acrid composition, were discharged upon him. In 1868 it has been my plain duty, at a great crisis, to overlook former official relations, and to ask myself one question only—all circumstances taken as they are, what combination, embracing the Chancellorship, would give most weight to a Government, which will need every service it can get? But, this being so, I ought, and we all ought, to be the more desirous to pay to Lord Westbury every just tribute in our power, whether as an old colleague, as a most distinguished lawyer, or as a most remarkable man.

'The upshot then of my thoughts is really this: that I ought, in the manner most acceptable to Lord Westbury, to find out whether an offer of the vacant Lord Justiceship would or would not be acceptable to him; and to ask you as leader of the Government in the House of Lords, and as the man qualified above all others to answer the question, whether you can help me in this important business.—Ever yours sincerely,

'W. E. GLADSTONE.

' Of course in any event this matter must remain strictly private until a later stage.

' I cannot but think the profession would think Lord W.'s acceptance a *high-minded* act.'

The precedent of Lord Lyndhurst cited by Mr. Gladstone was his appointment in 1830, when ex-Lord Chancellor, to the office of Chief Baron of the Exchequer. What Lord Westbury thought of it is shown by an extract from a letter to Mr. Reeve :—

' Gladstone tried to induce me to accept the Lord Justiceship by citing the example of Lord Lyndhurst. My answer was that Lord Lyndhurst would have done the country more service if he had attended the House of Lords on Appeals and saved *it* and the cause of justice from the reproaches that attach to Lord Brougham's presidency. This truth is strongly illustrated by Lord K.'s [Kingsdown] remarks in the case of Brookman *v.* Rothschild. And yet no one had courage to oppose Brougham's delinquency.'

In conveying this offer to Lord Westbury, Lord Granville wrote :—

' *Dec.* 18, 1868.

' My dear Lord Westbury—Your letter this morning gave me very great pleasure. It shows that you are aware of how sensible I am of your great and constant kindness to me.

' Gladstone sent me the enclosed letter the day before yesterday. I wished to feel my way as to broaching the subject to you. After your note, I feel sure that I may send it to you without any preface.

' I agree in the last sentence, and there are other reasons why the question may be worthy of your consideration.

' In fairness to Gladstone I must add that all he writes about you he has said to me in conversation more than once during the last ten days.—Yours sincerely,   GRANVILLE.'

An offer made in such cordial terms could not fail to be very gratifying to Lord Westbury and his

friends.   His refusal of it was based entirely on
considerations of the public interest; but, in truth,
he had little desire to recommence an active life.
' Have I not earned a right to repose ?' he wrote,
justifying the refusal to one of his daughters. ' " The
end and the reward of toil is rest." '   The letter by
which his refusal was conveyed drew from Lord
Granville the following reply :—

' My dear Lord Westbury—I send you, with Gladstone's glad
assent, his letter to me.   I have kept a copy to place with your
remarkable letter.   I cannot conceive anything better in tone
and feeling.

' Did you inherit, or did you acquire, the Dean Swift-like power
of always placing the right word in the right place ? '

Rest   and   repose   were,   however,   with   Lord
Westbury merely relative expressions, for his active
mind required graver and more exciting occupation
than could be supplied by the literary and country
pursuits which would have satisfied a man of less
extraordinary energy.   He assisted the Board of the
Brighton Railway in the early stages of the intricate
investigation into its resources—a very critical period
in the history of the Company.   Mr. R. L. Lopes,
one of the directors, afterwards bore public testimony
to the appreciation on the part of those connected
with the Company of Lord Westbury's ' searching,
exhaustive, yet delicate examination of the witnesses,
and his patience in the disentanglement of every
detail; his general courtesy ; his desire never to
place in prominence his own conspicuous talents ;

his generous recognition of any assistance his colleagues were able to impart.'   He also became
Chairman of the Foreign and Colonial Government
Trust, and subsequently of the General Committee
formed by the holders of Spanish bonds upon default
being made in payment of coupons, and was able
on more than one occasion, when their interests
were threatened, to render very material assistance.

Soon after his retirement from office he rented
from Earl Poulett the fine estate of Hinton St.
George, three miles from Crewkerne, in Somersetshire, which he retained until his death.   The estate
comprised some excellent preserves, and as long as
his physical powers enabled him, he continued to
derive much recreation from field sports, though he
was exercised in his mind by the depredations of
poachers, which he endeavoured to prevent by
ingenious arrangements of maroon lights and
spring wires.   In spite of all precautions, the
pheasantries were one night entered by thieves,
who stole all the tame birds, including eighty hens.
In the autumn of 1868 he writes to a friend com-
plaining, ' I cannot offer you very good shooting, for
the poachers rob me grievously, though I have a
little army of about twenty men nightly on the
watch.'   On more than one occasion an affray took
place between the keepers and poachers, and several
of Lord Westbury's letters at this period contain
minute instructions for the employment of watchers
to check these depredations.

'We have had a battle royal with the poachers,' he writes, 'and have carried off their spoils. I had directed G—— to watch. He had two men and his son. Tuesday night—Between four and five in the morning they heard men in the covert, and came down on them. The men were eight in number, and had just set a very long net by the covert side. G—— rushed at one man, who, putting his hand in his pocket, took out a handful of powdered quicklime, which he threw into G——'s face and nearly blinded him. The other men produced bludgeons and swore they would kill any man who touched them. However, they made off, and our men, pursuing, came upon two sacks containing seventy rabbits, which they captured, together with a beautiful lurcher, and they brought these *spolia opima* to the house yesterday afternoon.'

Sir Alexander Cockburn used sometimes to shoot at Hinton, when he and his host would tell anecdotes and poke fun at each other all day long. Once seated in the chimney-corner of a keeper's lodge, discussing a savoury 'hotpot' and mulled claret, they kept on capping each other's stories, and it was difficult to get them outside again to finish the coverts. Meanwhile the pheasants were running out like hares at the other end of the adjacent wood, and the head keeper was in a state bordering on frenzy at the fatal effect the delay would have on the bag, to say nothing of the falling off in the shooting of the sportsmen after so long an interval.

One day, when there was a 'shoot' in the home coverts, Sir A. Cockburn was of the party. The wood culminated in a steep 'sidling,' upon which two guns were posted to stop the game going

forward, while Lord Westbury and the Chief-
Justice remained below with the beaters. The
pheasants kept on rising at the top of the 'sidling,'
near the upper guns, rocketing back high above the
sportsmen in the lower ride. The Chief-Justice,
who was an indifferent shot, and much preferred the
luncheon, with its opportunities for some racy story-
telling, to the sport, did not notice any of the birds
until one of the upper guns dropped a cock pheasant
which came crashing down through the trees, nar-
rowly missing Sir Alexander's head. Greatly
startled, and supposing himself to be in peril, he
called out : 'Fire high! Hullo, there, fire high!' in
a state of some excitement. Whereupon Lord
Westbury said : 'Don't you be alarmed, Chief-
Justice ; you are quite safe. You are not as near
heaven as that bird was when it was shot, and I
am sadly afraid, after those sultry stories of yours,
that you never will be.'

Lord Westbury made an interesting but fruitless
attempt to introduce pheasants on to his estate in
Italy. No sooner, however, were the birds turned
down than the peasants of the neighbourhood, overcome by the instincts of sport to which so rare an
opportunity irresistibly appealed, mustered in force,
armed with scythes, rakes, flails, and other rustic
weapons, and held an irregular battue, in which the
whole of the game was ruthlessly exterminated.

CHAPTER IX

1869-1870

THE gravest peril of the Ministerial position during the early months of 1869 lay in the opposition threatened in the House of Lords to the Irish Church Bill. It was generally anticipated that the majority of the Peers would have the courage of their recently-expressed opinions and reject the Bill. On the other hand, many of the more moderate Conservatives considered that it was the clear duty of the majority, however strong their convictions, to yield to the opinion of the country, so decisively pronounced. The Government were, comparatively speaking, weak in debating power in the Upper House, and their difficulties were increased by the violent language of some of their supporters out of doors.

Before the Bill reached the House of Lords,

Lord Westbury gave emphatic expression to his disapproval of the introduction of the measure unless the land question was dealt with at the same time. Referring to the universal depression of spirit and depreciation of property which had followed the proposals of the Government, he showed that the demands on which the agitation in Ireland was founded were the demolition of the Church, fixity of tenure, and the uncontrolled dominion over the education of the people. He added prophetically : ' These three things are demanded by agitators in Ireland ; but there is a fourth card which they hold in their hand, to be played at their convenience, when the other tricks have been won, *and that is the repeal of the Union.'*

At length the Irish Church Bill, having passed triumphantly through the House of Commons, was presented on the 14th of June to the House of Lords. On the fourth and last night of the debate on the second reading, Lord Westbury, whose speech was looked forward to with great interest on account of his known dislike to the disendowment provisions, addressed the House. His opening observations, in which he attempted to define the limits of the constitutional right of the House of Lords to oppose the wishes of the people, have a more than passing interest. Though he expressed his conviction that the Bill was not only an evil in itself, but that if carried it would provoke still greater evils—

he denied that the logical conclusion to be drawn from that confession was that it became their duty to reject the Bill. Rather was it their duty, he said, as a matter of constitutional principle, to accept it for the purpose of amendment. The people at the hustings had a right to express their opinion that the Irish Church was a grave evil, but that did not in his opinion settle the question of the duty of Parliament.

‘ If the people have chosen to affirm that the Irish Church is an evil, it is not to be supposed—as many times it has been supposed in this debate—that the verdict of the hustings involves the acceptance either of this measure, or of the principle of disestablishment and disendowment. My lords, constitutionally, it involves nothing of the kind. Disestablishment and disendowment are conclusions which it peculiarly belongs to the wisdom of Parliament to accept or reject. They are modes undoubtedly of remedying the evil; but they are not within the power of the people to dictate,—they are entirely for you to determine. I agree with the right rev. prelate who spoke last (the Bishop of Lichfield) in many of his remarks, though I cannot agree with him in all the principles he laid down ; I fear that we must come back to the sterner realities of actual life. But when I am told that we must look to the verdict of the country as conclusive on the subjects of disestablishment and disendowment—words which I agree with the right rev. prelate are of very ugly coinage—I will say that I do not believe that there was one man in 20,000 who had the least conception of the proper meaning of these words.’

He argued that if the people again and again present an evil to be redressed, and you are aware

that they know what they want and understand the
subject, it is the duty of Parliament not to stand in
the way of the fulfilment of their desires.

'So, in like manner, with regard to the other House of Parliament. If they send up to you a measure once, twice, or three
times, according to its nature, well considered and seriously
required, you are not to stand between them and the object ; you
are bound to assume that what is so presented by the representatives of the people is in reality *vox populi*, when that *vox populi* is
properly expressed, not in clamorous tones, not when the people
imagine a vain thing, but speaking with an understanding mind.'

Lord Westbury proceeded to lay down the principle of the law with respect to the Church property,
insisting that the only distinction between private
and corporate property lay in the difference between
the characters of the holders.   Unless the Irish
Church could be treated as a delinquent corporation,
the State had no right to take away what it had
never given.   He repeated his objection that the
time was inopportune for the introduction of the
Bill, and again predicted that it would increase the
difficulties of the land question.

'It comes with no trace of generosity, because it will be
regarded everywhere as the mere offspring of fear—the mere
child of terror. You have embodied in this measure a great
statement. That statement is this—that the Irish Church is a
grave injustice, a wicked evil, and ought never to have been imposed upon the Irish people. So says the Irish peasant, and he
will also say this : "You came into our country with an army ;
you carried your Church in one hand, and fire and sword in the
other. You fastened your Church upon us ; you burnt our dwell-
ings ; you slew us in the field ; you murdered us on the scaffold ;
you confiscated our land, and gave it to an alien and a Protestant

proprietary. We rejoice at your penitence. You have taken 300
years to learn the dictates of religion and the rules of justice ; it
is a somewhat tardy application of them ; but better late than
never. We give you all credit for your sincerity and truth ; and
therefore, as you did us injustice then, which we will charitably
forgive, no doubt you will complete your work of penitence by
restoring to us the lands of which you have robbed us." Will you,
my lords, accept these principles of justice and of religion, but
say, " Thus far will we go and no further " ? Shall a man come
to me after knocking me down and picking my pocket, and while
telling me he is very sorry indeed for what he has done, say to
me, " I don't intend to return you your purse " ? My lords, it
is impossible to bring the mind of the Irish peasant to accept this
conclusion. Do you think he will be satisfied if I tell him, as a
lawyer, " Oh, there have been 300 years of possession. I am
sorry that we can't take away the land that was confiscated, but
we will take away the land of the Church." Will he not at once
say, " We will take the law into our own hands in order to carry
out the dictates of our reason ? The destruction of the Church is
the only good thing we have had from you ; you must do complete justice ; and that complete justice we are determined to
have." '

Lord Westbury went on to describe the authors
of the Bill, in the words of Burke, as 'admirable
architects of ruin.' He found in it nothing but ruin,
and feared it might be the herald of other measures
founded on the same principle. He avowed that he
had little love for the atomic theory, but the Bill,
the joint production of Her Majesty's Government
and the Liberation Society, appeared to him a
perfect realisation of the 'fortuitous concurrence of
intellectual atoms.' Adverting to the statement in
the preamble that it was expedient to satisfy, as far
as possible, upon principles of equality, the just and

equitable claims of the several religious denomina-
tions in Ireland to the property of the Church, he
declared that equal distribution was the only conclusion reconcilable with humanity, reason, and law.
Though his voice might be but 'as the voice of one
crying in the wilderness,' he urged that the property
should be dealt with upon a recognition of the
claims of Roman Catholics, Presbyterians, and Pro-
testants alike.   Let the loaves and fishes of the
Church be parcelled in due proportion among those
who laboured in the vineyard, as one common field
for all who ministered in it, whatever their opinions
and whatever their denomination.   In conclusion, he
said that the Bill, in relying on the voluntary principle,
proposed to remove the Church, which was founded
upon a rock, and to build it again upon the sand.
He agreed to the second reading, because it proposed, in the main, a great act of justice ; but there
was hardly any provision in it that he concurred in
except 'that just provision—that benevolent rule
—which by some accident had crept into the
preamble.'

The Lord Chancellor (Lord Hatherley) followed
Lord Westbury, and in his opening observations
ironically expressed his satisfaction that, after hearing the eloquent address of Lord Westbury, 'in which
he has denounced the motive of the Bill, in which he
has denounced the principle of the Bill, and in which
he has denounced nearly every clause in the Bill,'
there were still three points on which they were

agreed—the first of which was to support the second
reading.

The second reading was carried by a majority of
33. The next day Lord Westbury wrote to Captain
Cardew :—

'I voted for the Bill. The Ministers were not at all vexed
at my speech, but after it made me sit between Lord Granville
and Lord Clarendon for some time on the Treasury Bench—I
suppose to show the House they were not offended. I wish you
had seen the House during the debate—crammed to the utmost
—ladies three deep.

'I think it is the end of my political life in which I take no
pleasure. Did not get to bed till past four. How foolish for
the sake of a little vanity !'

Nevertheless the ex-Chancellor showed much
interest in the discussion and amendment of the Bill
during the subsequent stages, and took occasion
more than once to restate with much force his
objections to the application of the Church property
to secular uses. In the course of one of his speeches
he said :—

'There is a great controversy just now touching the conduct of
a long-departed saint, St. Ambrose, who is said to have been a
model of piety, and whether in applying the vessels of the Church
to secular uses he was guilty of sacrilege. What might be the
opinion respecting St. Ambrose in the days when he lived I do
not know; but all I can say is, with the modern ideas of property, that if St. Ambrose had been brought before me in a court
of equity, I should not have hesitated to pronounce him guilty of
a breach of trust, and to order him to refund the property he had
taken.'

On the third reading of the Bill Lord Westbury
again entreated the House to accomplish the objects

of peace, religious equality, and justice by distribut-
ing the surplus of the Church property in accordance
with the demands and necessities of the several
religious bodies in Ireland.   He lamented their
failure to guide the people to measures superior to
the feeling that declaimed against concurrent endowment, and pronounced it to be a sin to give anything to relieve the necessities and supply the wants
of Roman Catholic Christianity, although it was the
religion upon which nineteen-twentieths of the
Christian world depend for their salvation.   He
added :—

'And I, for one, cannot with any countenance send this Bill
down again to the Commons, ostensibly in the spirit in which it
was sent, as a message of peace and religious equality, with that
exceptional benefit given to the Protestant Episcopalian clergy,
unless it be supplemented, equipoised, and balanced by equal
benefits for the Roman Catholic and Presbyterian clergy. . . .
I entreat you, in the interests of your own measure, to lay aside all
notion about your having no right to pronounce an opinion in
favour of the Roman Catholic religion.   Why, you fling damnation
round Europe when you condemn the Roman Catholics, and
pronounce that great religion to be an error which you would sin
in giving anything to.'

It does not appear that any factious hostility towards the Government of which he had been a
member stimulated his opposition to the measure.
In reply to some such assurance Lord Granville
wrote :—

'I cannot tell you the pleasure the second part of your letter
gave me.   It can be no object of indifference to any Government
whether you support or oppose them, and if I may venture to

say so, your action in concurrence with the party whose principles you are known generally to admit to be yours, must be much more powerful than when you find yourself obliged to oppose them.

'For myself I can only say that our personal relations make it extremely annoying when we differ in public, and proportionately agreeable when we are acting in concert.'

Both in 1868 and 1869 Lord Westbury introduced a Bill to consolidate and amend the loose and uncertain enactments relating to the copyright in works of fine art. The existing law gave an imperfect protection to the authors of such works compared with that afforded by the laws of other countries. Lord Westbury's own Act of 1862 had established copyright in artistic productions for the life of the author and a period of seven years afterwards. He was now anxious to assimilate the law relating to works of fine art to the law of literary copyright. He said :—

'There is no better criterion of the progress of a nation in civilisation and intellectual culture than the respect and protection afforded by its laws to works of literature and art,—works which are the noblest possible addition to the wealth of a country, but the production of which is greatly dependent—in modern times at least—on the protection given to men of genius. Such works, moreover, as possessing the essential attributes of property, ought surely to enjoy the protection extended to other species of property. I can indeed imagine nothing which has a more complete title to be considered property than works of imagination, for they are the pure creation of the mind. Now I am sorry to say that, if laws are taken as a proof, these creations of mind are more valued and respected in other countries than in England ; for, whereas in this country works of art of a particular class enjoy protection for twenty-eight years, with a contingent extension of another seven years, that protection extends in France to fifty, in Germany to thirty, in Belgium to twenty, and in Spain to twenty-five years in excess of the author's life ; while in Italy it lasts for forty years, with a contingent extension of forty years longer. In England literature and art are protected in the most imperfect and grudging manner.'

Great difficulty attached to the requisite definitions of works of art, and though the Bill led to much interesting discussion, after being referred to a Select Committee, it made no further progress.

In the summer of 1869 the death of Lord Justice Selwyn created another vacancy in the Court of Appeal, and Mr. Gladstone again expressed his desire that Lord Westbury would accept the appointment. Lord Granville wrote on the 10th of September :—

'My dear Lord Westbury—I wrote to you about four weeks ago to the following effect :—

'I had just seen Gladstone, who talked to me of Selwyn's death. He had no doubt of your being the person he should prefer seeing as his successor, but although the fact of Selwyn being gone removed one of the objections you had raised, he felt that he had no right to worry you.

'I asked him to suspend the appointment, which he gladly did, till I had the opportunity of confidentially ascertaining your wishes.

'As I have had no answer, you may not have got my letter, or what is not unlikely, you may have thought it required no answer. If the latter is the case, please telegraph to me, "answer unnecessary."'

Through misdirection the first letter had not reached Lord Westbury. The renewal of the offer and the pressure of many friends made it more difficult to refuse a second time. In a letter to a member of his family with reference to it, he writes : 'Of course my own opinion is the same that it was last November, but I felt the kindness of men who, after my refusal and what has since passed in the House of Lords, still pressed on me the acceptance of certainly the most important office next to the Lord Chancellorship.' His friends again begged him to consent to take the office for a time, and he was therefore half driven from his own judgment. He plainly showed an increasing disposition to withdraw himself as much as possible from the world, and shrunk from what he termed 'the irksome sense of being compelled to discharge a certain duty.' He added, 'I trust nothing will come of it.'

It will be seen from the next letter that, though he did not absolutely refuse the offer, his reply was designed with the view to preclude his appointment :—

'*Hinton St. George, Sept.* 12, 1869.

'My dear Gladstone—Our excellent friend, Lord Granville, sent me a letter from Walmer, dated the 13th of August last, in which he very kindly hinted to me that you still retained a wish that I should accept the vacant office of Lord Justice of Appeals in the Court of Chancery. Before I consider whether it would be for the good of the public that I should accept the vacant office or not, allow me the liberty of stating .to you my opinion, that there is no necessity for filling up the office at all, and certainly not for the next three months.

'The Lords Justices were originally created as a pair of crutches for Lord Truro to enable him to walk as Lord Chancellor, but for some time past there has not been sufficient appellate business in the Court of Chancery to employ fully the Lords Justices and the Lord Chancellor. By a recent statute one of the Lords Justices may sit alone and perform all the functions originally given to the two. At the present time there is no considerable arrear, and as the Lord Chancellor will be enabled to sit without interruption through the months of November, December, and January, he and Lord Justice Giffard will be enabled to sweep the Appellate Court clean before the Lord Chancellor's attendance is required in the House of Lords. The arrangements recommended by the report of the Judicature Commission would involve the abolition of the Court of the Lords Justices. It is supposed that you will direct some great measure founded on that report to be brought into Parliament during the ensuing session; and if the appellate business in the Court of Chancery can, as I am convinced it may, be well disposed of by the Lord Chancellor and the Lord Justice Giffard, in the interval, until the fate of such future measure is ascertained, it would seem wrong to embarrass matters by the appointment of a new Lord Justice.

' If this view of the law does not appear to you to be the correct one, and that it is necessary that a new appointment should be made, I would consent, subject to two or three conditions, to accept the office for a time, if my doing so would relieve the Government from any embarrassment. I must frankly state to you that I know of no man either on the Bench in the Court of Chancery, or at the Bar, except Sir Roundell Palmer, who could, with perfect satisfaction, be appointed to the vacant office. But I must state, I hope without vanity, that I believe I am and shall be of more service to the public as an appellate judge in the House of Lords, and by occasional attendance at the Privy Council, than I possibly could be as a Lord Justice in the Court of Chancery. I adhere entirely to the reasons which through Lord Granville I had the honour of submitting to you in November[1] last, when you in so kind and gratifying a manner pressed on me the acceptance of the same office. I assure you the appellate tribunal in the House of Lords is of the greatest importance to the public, and that its present constitution is such that no portion of its strength ought to be taken away. It is my settled

---

[1] Note by Mr. Gladstone : 'December.—W. E. G.'

opinion that things will go on very well in the Court of Chancery under the Lord Chancellor and Lord Justice Giffard until the end of next January, and I would humbly advise you to postpone until that time all thought of filling up the vacancy.'

He wrote the next day to Lord Granville, explaining the cause of his silence, and giving his reasons for not accepting the office with great frankness :—

'My dear Lord Granville—How could you suppose it possible that I should neglect to answer a letter of yours, and one dictated by such a spirit of kindness? The fate of your letter is a strange one, and requires some investigation.   It was misdirected to me at Hackwood Park, Basingstoke, where I have not resided since 1865, four years and a half ago.   The postmaster at Basingstoke, instead of altering the address, sent it back to London, where it appears to have been opened, sealed up again, and directed to me at my town house, at which place it was delivered last Friday, and was forwarded to me by my servant on Saturday last. . . . Your second letter was posted at Walmer on the 10th, went to Sandwich on the 11th, remained somewhere or other on the 12th, and reached me this morning, on the 13th.   A letter from Deal to Somersetshire takes three whole days!   Pray ask Hartington to reform his postal arrangements.'

After repeating the substance of his letter to the Prime Minister, he continued :—

'I hope I express myself clearly.   If my acceptance of the office on the 5th of January next, for a time, will be any accommodation to the Government, I will take it.   Until then, *certainly*, no second Lord Justice is wanted.   I have not yet regained my usual health and strength, and I am afraid of undertaking to reside in London during the next November and December.

'I told Gladstone that I had but one object, namely, to consider how I could be of most utility to the public, and that I

believed my position, as one of the Law Lords in the House of
Peers, enabled me to render greater service than I could do as
Lord Justice.   Don't charge me with vanity if I venture to say to
you *confidentially* that I believe it would be much easier to find a
Lord Justice than it would be to find one to replace me as a
Judge of Appeals in the House of Lords.   I am not ashamed to
tell you, who will not misinterpret me, that the constitution of
the Appellate Tribunal is now so weak that it cannot bear to
have any part of its strength taken away.   Last session, from
various causes (and particularly because from private reasons I
could not sit on Miss Sheddon's case, which was, strangely,
allowed to occupy twenty-six days), I did not attend so much as
I desired, but next session I hope to be present every day.

   ' My own opinion is, that it is better to leave me where
I am ; but if you cannot prevail on Sir Roundell Palmer (whom
I should advise you to press to take it at once), then if you
suspend the appointment to January next, and at that time
find it necessary to fill up the vacancy, and are still of opinion
that I can be of service, I will take the office for a time.
This letter is not perfectly consistent with my letter to Gladstone
in one respect, viz.—I think, in my letter to him, I gave him
to understand that if an immediate appointment was absolutely
necessary, I would *at once* consent to take it ; but I now feel
that my weak health would not admit of my being in London
next November and December, and, therefore, I must in any
event postpone acceptance until January next.

   ' If you should agree to this, you *must not* be considered as
at all bound to me.   If, in the interval, you can prevail on Sir
Roundell Palmer, or make any other arrangement, you will re-
lease me, and I shall be the better pleased.   With every kind wish
and feeling of regard for yourself, I am, ever yours sincerely,

                                        ' WESTBURY.'

The course suggested by Lord Westbury was
adopted, and for some months the Lord Chancellor,
with the assistance of Lord Justice Giffard, was able
to keep down the appeals.   In the summer of 1870

the Lord Justice died, and Sir W. M. James succeeded him.

Lord Westbury was in his seventy-first year, and his health was declining. He was decidedly of opinion that aged men should not be appointed to judicial office, and that our judges continue on the Bench till too great an age. Shortly after the date of the last letter he gave expression to these views in the House of Lords. 'I believe,' he said, 'in America the age of retirement is sixty-six, and I doubt whether it is advisable that a judge should hold his office long after that age, for at an advanced period of life undoubtedly there is a loss of quickness of apprehension, a failure of memory, and an incapacity of continued attention.'

He had recently met with three accidents, by one of which he was seriously injured. When walking at Hinton by the side of a very deep ditch, the bank gave way, and he fell to the bottom on his head and back ; and shortly after he was thrown from a pony-cart when returning from shooting a home covert. He was driving a neighbour, Mr. Hoskyns, and in turning a sharp corner, while they were deep in conversation, the cart, which was loaded with game, guns, luncheon-baskets, etc., was upset. Lord Westbury fell on the top of his friend, and so escaped with little injury, but Mr. Hoskyns, also a heavy man, happened to have in his pocket some pin-fire cartridges, which ran into his thigh and inflicted some damage. Another misad-

venture had a more serious result. The sash of a
window, which Lord Westbury was opening, sud-
denly broke, and the window-frame fell with great
force on his head and neck, causing intense pain.
These accidents probably laid the seeds of the
disease which eventually proved fatal. Moreover,
the rigours of the English winter began to try him
severely. 'Every year,' he wrote, 'I feel less able
to bear our changing climate. I am painfully sensible
that I am growing very old, and that my strength
and spirits decay daily.'

He writes about this time to one of his
daughters :—

'It grieved me much to go out of town without seeing you.
I was obliged to go to escape from endless invitations to dinner.
I assure you I get quite misanthropical, as far as the world is
concerned, and if I can help it will not go to another party.

'Old men get garrulous, and talk more than they ought to do.
I am sensible of this infirmity, and am resolved not to give way
to it.'

Yet though he expressed a disinclination for
much social intercourse, to the end of his life he exhibited a pleasing pride in assuming the character of
a patriarch in his own home, and in this respect he
had a good deal of the ancient Eastern feeling. He
was never so completely happy as when surrounded
by troops of grandchildren, into whose little joys he
entered with a surprising interest. And he dis-
pensed much graceful hospitality under his own roof,
the charm of his conversation on social occasions,
when 'wit its honey lent without the sting,' making

him an admirable host.   Bishop Abraham gives a
pleasant description of one of such gatherings :—

'I think it was in the year 1870, soon after I
had returned from New Zealand, that I met a
distinguished party at Lord Westbury's house in
Lancaster Gate.   The company at dinner consisted,
amongst   others,   of   Archbishop,   now   Cardinal,
Manning, Lord Justice Giffard, Vice-Chancellor
Stuart, Mr. Roebuck, and Sir George Bowyer, and
the conversation, like the company, varied from legal
to clerical subjects, interspersed with general subjects of interest.   I remember that Lord Westbury
said he had been sitting in the Privy Council Court
of Appeal that day, and the case before the Court
was that of *Burgess* v. *The Dutch Church in the
Cape of Good Hope.*   The latter had removed the
Rev. Mr. Burgess from his cure of souls for denying
the personality of the Evil Spirit, and for asserting
that the doctrine was a mere survival of Paganism,
derived from Virgil's *Æneid*, vi. 743—

'" Quisque suos patimur manes,"

which the learned counsel translated as meaning,
"Every man has his own devil."   Lord Westbury
asked Archbishop Manning what he thought of
that translation.   The Archbishop cleverly turned
the question over to me, saying that he knew I had
been an Eton master, and was more "up" in such
points.   I, by way of keeping the ball rolling, said
that *manes* was not likely to mean "evil" spirits,

but "good," because *immanes* meant cruel. From
this the conversation turned to the more general
question of the natural conscience as seen amongst
the heathen, and it was very pleasant and instructive
to hear the Archbishop discourse on this, especially
so to me, because I had had large opportunities for
twenty years past of observing the varied degrees
of light in the hearts and minds of the natives of
New Zealand and the heathen of Melanesia, and I
told how Bishop Selwyn and Bishop Patteson
always assumed and appealed to this "Light, that
lighteth every man that cometh into the world."

'After dinner the conversation took another
turn, and a lively discussion ensued between Vice-
Chancellor Stuart and Mr. Roebuck, as representing
the Northern counties, and the Archbishop and
others as representing "the sluggish South." The
Vice-Chancellor and Mr. Roebuck told us some racy
stories of Yorkshire wit and humour; but the Archbishop closed the case with the following record of
his own experience when Rector of Lavington, in
Sussex. He said that he went to visit a poor old
parishioner, a widow between seventy and eighty
years of age, who had had nine or ten children, of
whom all but one daughter had gone out into the
world and left her. At last this daughter married,
and she was alone. The Archbishop said to her,
"Dame, you must feel it lonely now, after having had
so large a family."—"Yes, sir," she said; "I do feel
it lonesome. I have brought up a long family, and

now here I am living alone. And I misses 'em,
and I wants 'em ; but I misses 'em *more* than I
wants 'em." The Archbishop added, " I will trouble
you representatives of Northern wit to match that
fine distinction and analysis of feeling." Lord
Westbury and all of us awarded the palm to the
sluggish South.'

To the charm of Lord Westbury's conversational
powers all those who enjoyed his friendship bear the
strongest testimony. At times, when disposed to
descend from the transcendental regions of harangue,
in which he revelled, his playful fancy and witty
repartees or stories provoked his hearers to laughter ;
at other times by his pathetic earnestness he could
almost move them to tears. 'His conversation,'
wrote his eldest daughter, 'was delightful, and bore
the stamp of real genius. It was varied, animated, and
full of information, and even the youngest and most
ignorant could always understand what was said, his
language was so simple and lucid. In argument he
was irresistible. He had also the merit of being a
good listener, and was always pleased to talk with
any *homme de spécialité* and gain information, for,
like Lord Bacon, he did not disdain "to light his
own candle at the lamp of any other." In speaking
to young men one of his favourite topics of conversation was the love of independence, the duty and
comfort of making one's own fortune and relying on
one's self alone. Another theme was the delights
of learning in all its branches. He did not approve

of the ordinary public school system of education, maintaining that too much time was given to the acquisition of the dead languages, too little to modern tongues or general literature. Accordingly, he highly approved of the Scotch system of education, which aims at higher objects than mere learning. To the young he was always kind and encouraging, though he had perhaps but little reverence for the dreams of youth, and would occasionally show contempt for mere foolish babble. Still he never thought any one too young or insignificant to have an opinion of his own, and would listen patiently while it was being expressed, unless indeed it was set forth in an arrogant or conceited manner, in which case the unfortunate individual was soon extinguished by a few words of caustic ridicule.'

The late Mr. Edward Lear, in a letter to the Hon. Mrs. Adamson Parker, recalling some of his reminiscences of Lord Westbury, says :—

'My recollections of your father go back as far as fifty years ago, when you were at Littlehampton ; but I seem to remember him more distinctly at Lauderdale House, Highgate, Hackwood, and Hinton St. George ; at all of such places I used to receive unvarying kindnesses from him and your mother. . . . I used, when I came to England, most frequently to pass my Sundays at Hackwood, and generally accompanied your father, who rode a white pony, in rambles about Hackwood Park and the contiguous places ; and during these excursions I was always struck by the variety, the liveliness, and the instructiveness of his conversation.

'Lord Westbury, after he was Lord Chancellor, never became

the least changed in manner towards me, but was as glad to see me at his house as when he was simple Richard Bethell, and on my frequent visits to England I had only to propose a visit to Hackwood or Hinton St. George to be received with marked kindness. The *Books of Nonsense* I wrote from time to time greatly amused him, and when I made that absurd story for Slingsby's children, who went (or didn't go) round the world, it was wonderfully funny to hear the Chancellor read the whole aloud with a solemnity befitting the perusal of grave history. He also took great interest in my travels in Greece, Crete, Egypt, etc., and delighted in looking over my sketches and in asking me questions about the people, buildings, etc. Many of his witty replies or repartees have been ventilated by numerous persons in the habit of frequenting his society ; but I do not think such detached quotations give an idea of the general vivacity and interest of his conversation, nor do I imagine that those who merely saw him in public life had any idea of his playful affection for his children and numerous grandchildren, the latter of whom, to the number of twenty or thirty, would sometimes romp with him as if he were a boy, and would combine to form pictures which it is to be regretted could not be photographed on the spot.'

He held that too little attention was paid to con-stitutional peculiarities in educating young children. Referring to a boy who showed a want of *vis vitæ* he wrote : 'He is evidently of a very delicate frame, and in truth ought not to be confined to the school-room, but allowed to run wild for a twelvemonth, being taught orally, and his mind and imagination fed and enlarged by being read to from books of history, poetry, and fable. But then such a course would unfit him perhaps for the routine of a public school, where, however, I feel confident that many minds are extinguished or dimmed.'

Among the shortcomings of our educational system Lord Westbury gave prominence to the neglect of early instruction in the principles of art, and lamented that we sacrifice so much to utility and so little to beauty. In the course of a speech at one of the Royal Academy dinners he urged that we should be taught how to observe, how to discern that which is beautiful, for though the whole creation, both of nature and of art, is accommodated to the human eye, the eye must be educated to apprehend and appreciate that beauty. He added : ' Undoubtedly we deny ourselves much of the gratification we should enjoy for the want of that which I will call the worship of the beautiful. Unfortunately born beneath a leaden sky, too seldom irradiated and warmed by the light of the sun, we ought to compensate for that deficiency by some greater education of the mind in that which contributes more to happiness than a constant devotion to the ordinary demands of life.'

CHAPTER X

Marriage with Deceased Wife's Sister — International neutrality —
The French and war — Constitution of the Judicial Committee —
Remedial Act of 1871 — Collier appointment — Letters from the
Lord Chief-Justice — Motion of Censure — Lord Westbury's speech.

IN the session of 1870 the Bill to legalise marriage
with a deceased wife's sister was defeated in the
House of Lords by the narrow majority of four,
after a debate which revealed much difference of
opinion among the members of the Government on
the subject. Lord Westbury warmly supported the
measure, and lectured the bench of Bishops with
affected solemnity on an opposition founded, as he
said, on a too confident interpretation of the Levitical
law. 'Are we,' he asked, 'to take the responsibility of restraining marriage, which is a part of
man's natural independence, upon a critical interpretation of a passage in the Old Testament? Looking to the condition of our great towns and our
pauper population, we are not in a position to regard
ourselves as the special favourites of providence or
the chosen depositories of divine truth.' He en-

treated the prelates to approach the subject in a
humbler spirit—a spirit that would make them
inquire whether there might not be a doubt in the
correctness of the interpretation so positively enun-
ciated.

'Let them remember that the interpretation was one in which
the Roman Catholics did not join, which the great body of Pro-
testants on the Continent did not give their assent to, in which
the Wesleyans were not with them, in which the Independents
did not concur, which the Baptists altogether repudiated, and
which the Quaker lifted up his testimony against. Therefore
the opposition to these marriages was confined to themselves,
and to those who had been indoctrinated into it by an Act of
Parliament.'

The ex-Chancellor's views on the interpretation
of the disputed passage in Leviticus were, however,
expressed with little of the diffidence to which he
had exhorted their Lordships, and the Bishop of
Peterborough replied in a tone of delicate satire
which was highly effective, and amused both sides
of the House.

In the summer of this year he wrote to Mr.
Reeve, who had been created D.C.L. in the Commemoration at Oxford :—

' "O Vir doctissime et in Republicâ Literarum potentissime!"
so said or sang the Chancellor of the University of Oxford in
violation of all the traditions of the place, for Oxford never used
before the phrase *Republicâ Literarum,* which words and the
thing signified she has ever repudiated and abhorred, and to be
potentissimus in republicâ are jarring and incoherent things;
but let this hypercriticism pass, and when I see Mrs. Reeve I
shall tell her that the words were chosen with singular felicity, and

that they are not more remarkable for their truth and justice than they are for their elegant tautology.   But I will not say that you are a doctor *only honoris causá*, which are most emphatic words, and are cruelly made to accompany the dignity, for when translated they mean, " Oh, Doctor, do not presume to teach by virtue of this *semiplena graduatio*, for it is only *honoris causá*, or merely complimentary, and do not trust this title as evidence of skill or erudition in law, for they are sounding words that signify nothing."

' How easy it is for envy and malice to depreciate.   I hope Mrs. Reeve and your daughter were there, because it is something fit and able to give genuine pleasure, and if I had been there I would have answered with stentorian voice to the well-known question, " Placetne vobis domini doctores, placetne vobis magistri ?" "placet imo valde placet." . . .—Yours sincerely, and with deeper respect than ever,   WESTBURY.'

' I don't suppose you will now miss a single bird.'

Early in July 1870 Lord Westbury went abroad for the last time, spending a few days in Paris *en route*.   He wrote home :—

' Hearing that the Emperor wanted to see me I returned on Tuesday, expecting to pick up my luggage, but was unable to find any trace of it, and actually was kept at Paris in a state of misery until mid-day on Friday before I could regain it.   I could not go to the Tuileries, and the Emperor could wait for me no longer, and so my visit was a *coup manqué*. . . .

' The state of France is financially very bad.   War is universally expected.   Internal discontent will be greatly increased.   The harvest has failed, and all the vines in the Burgundy district have been completely destroyed.   There will be no wine this year.'

The policy of strict non-intervention followed by the Government during the early stages of the Franco-German War received his heartiest approval. He writes to Lord Granville on the subject of neutrality :—

'*Hinton St. George, Sept.* 19, 1870.

'I cannot refrain from writing a few lines to express the pleasure with which I have read your correspondence with Count Bernstorff. Your exposition of the law, both international and municipal, is most accurate ; your remarks on international obligation are very judicious, and the whole is expressed in language felicitous and pungent.

'" Benevolent neutrality " is an absurd contradiction in terms. It would be a breach of the spirit of neutrality if a neutral government (apart from acts) expressed in words a more favourable opinion of the rights or merits of the law of one belligerent than of the other ; and it would be a serious violation of neutrality if a neutral nation guided itself by any principle or rule of conduct (however just or meritorious in itself) which had not been previously recognised and sanctioned by international law—that is, by the usage of nations. I carry this so far as to hold that if a nation, intending to be neutral, should, on the eve of a war between two other nations, alter its own municipal law, so as to impose a duty or restraint on its own subjects in their dealings with the intending belligerents, which was beyond the obligations of international law, it would be a just subject of complaint by that belligerent whose advantages were diminished by such unexpected alteration. On this principle the Government were right in abstaining from introducing into the recent statute a prohibition of the sale and exportation of munitions of war.

'The power of prohibition given to the sovereign by the Customs' Act was an enactment for the benefit and protection of England *alone*. It never was intended to give the Crown the right of taking away any trade-right of an English subject, unless it was, on *English national grounds*, necessary so to do. No foreign nation can *require* this power to be exercised. The foreigner has no interest in it, and it ought not to be used for the purpose of supplementing international law.

'If there be a discretionary power, conferred by the municipal law of a country, which enables it to do more than international obligation requires, the exercise of such power is *purely discretionary*. But if, as between two belligerents, the exercise of such

power, after hostilities have commenced, would be productive of
benefit to the one and not to the other, the neutral country,
possessing the power, ought not to exercise it, unless the exercise
be demanded by its own personal and peculiar interests.   The
status quo ante bellum must be left unaltered.   I am sorry that
the rest and recreation which you and every member of the
Government have so amply earned by the labours of the session
are so rudely broken by the cares and anxieties consequent on
the frightful condition of France.' . . .

The following extract from a letter, written a
little later, to a member of his family, expresses, with
characteristic vigour, his view of the real cause of
the war.   He seems to have had in his mind
Voltaire's description of the Frenchman as a being
compounded of the tiger and the monkey :—

'I have been much amused by your letter, but you must not
suffer yourself to be excited by political events, of which you are
by no means a competent judge.   I regard the French in the
same light that I should a wild tiger, and I am thankful to any
one who will draw his teeth and cut his claws in the hope of
preventing his doing mischief.   The miseries of Europe that
have resulted from the mad ambition and love of what is called
military glory of the French people during the last two centuries
have been incessant.

'In self-defence, and not from any feeling of revenge, I would
now reduce the French nation to a condition of helplessness.
Their mean falsehood in now attempting to charge the war upon
the Emperor, whereas it was they who drove the Emperor into
war, is most cowardly and most contemptible.'

In another letter is a passage which shows how
strongly he felt on the subject : 'Dined at Milner
Gibson's yesterday and met that abominable Duc de
Gramont, whose speech lit up the present dreadful
war.'

In the last two or three years of his life Lord
Westbury used to leave London for the seaside as
soon as his judicial duties allowed him. The follow-
ing extracts are taken from letters written from
Ilfracombe to his friend, Mrs. Harvey of Ickwell
Bury :—

'How I commiserate your wretched, crowded, heated draw-
ing-rooms in town ; and that miserable interchange of hypocrisy
and affectation, which are the daily food of London society,
when on the beautiful cliffs here I look over the broad Atlantic !
And to think of sacrificing one's health for such hollow intercourse ! . . . May you have strength to endure the wretched
imprisonment in London, to which you will be for some time
longer doomed, and it is a cruel punishment. . . .

'I ran away from town partly because there was no more
judicial business in the House of Lords, and partly because I
desired to escape the debate on the Army Bill, for when I do
not agree with the Government I am unwilling openly to oppose
them. . . .

'The sea-coast here is very grand. I am on the sea, or
seated on the rocks all day. I go tired to bed at ten o'clock.'

While admitting that it was 'the life of a veget-
able, or at the best of a limpet on the rock,' he
expressed his perfect contentment, in the evening of
life, with these simple pleasures.

The death of Lord Kingsdown, who had long
devoted his remarkable powers gratuitously to
the public service, greatly weakened the Judicial
Committee of the Privy Council, and the heavy
arrears of unheard appeals, particularly those which
came from India, was in 1870 a very serious scandal.
The Lord Chancellor (Lord Hatherley) proposed

to create a new appellate tribunal in connection
with the High Court of Justice. The Court was
to consist of the Lord Chancellor, the Lord Chief-
Justice, four Justices of Appeal, four Lord Justices,
and an addition from time to time of three puisne
judges from the other Courts. The constitution of
the proposed Court gave great dissatisfaction. It was
felt to be of prime importance that the Committee
should consist of none but the highest judicial
authorities, if it was to provide an efficient check on
the local Courts of our colonies and dependencies
and continue to give satisfaction to suitors.

Pending the introduction of the Lord Chancellor's
measure, Lord Westbury moved for an Address to
Her Majesty praying that immediate provision
might be made for the more rapid despatch of business before the Judicial Committee. He pointed
out that there were materials for the occupation
of the Committee for more than three years,
and pressed the Government to create at once
additional Judges of Appeal and add them to
the Committee, which might, he suggested, be
divided into two sections, one of which should
devote itself exclusively to Indian business. On
the promise of the Lord Chancellor to give immediate attention to the matter, the motion was
withdrawn ; but the Bill which Lord Hatherley introduced met with such universal condemnation that
it was not allowed to face the House of Commons.
From a Government so deeply pledged to economy

a comprehensive scheme, involving suitable provision for the salaries of competent men, was not to be expected.

In June 1871 Lord Westbury again called public attention to the subject, which he characterised as a disgrace to the administration of justice. He condemned in forcible terms the niggardly and patchwork scheme by which it was proposed to deal with the imperative question of the appeals 'hung up' in the Privy Council. The promised reforms of the Lord Chancellor had, it appeared, been delayed on the ground of their expense. Lord Westbury ridiculed the parsimony of the Government, and suggested as a motto descriptive of their policy in reference to such reforms the words

> ' Quærenda pecunia primum est
> Virtus post nummos.'

He declared, in the most determined and explicit manner, that if he could not obtain from the Government that which they had promised him two years before, he would, like the widow in Scripture, resort to importunity, and if a Bill were not at once brought in he would move an address to the Crown and divide the House upon the question.

Moved by this pressure from Lord Westbury, who was supported by Lord Cairns and others, the Lord Chancellor forthwith introduced a Bill which gave Her Majesty power to nominate four judges as additional members of the Judicial Committee. Two of them were to be either judges or retired judges of the

Superior Courts of Westminster ; the other two were to be selected from those who had held judicial appointments in India.   In each case the salary was to be £5000, taking into account, in the case of *emeriti* judges, their retiring pensions. The Bill was accepted as a temporary makeshift, though several of the Law Lords expressed their opinion that there would be a difficulty in inducing acting judges to accept the appointments.   Obviously it was not intended that the selection should be made from the bar.

No sooner was the Act passed than there was found to be a difficulty, as many had anticipated, in getting the English judges to accept an appointment under it.   Three in succession declined, each on the ground that there was no provision for their staff. Thereupon   the   Attorney - General,   Sir   Robert Collier (afterwards Lord Monkswell), to prevent the appointment being ' hawked about,' declared his willingness to be appointed.   The Act, however, as has been said, provided that persons appointed as persons qualified to become paid members of the Judicial Committee must at the date of their appointment be, or have been, persons of judicial experience.   In order to give Sir Robert Collier a kind of brevet rank, he was made a judge of the Common Pleas, where he sat for a few days in the robes of his predecessor, and was then immediately appointed as a paid member of the Judicial Committee.

The appointment was received with a chorus
of reprobation as a high-handed evasion of
an Act of Parliament. The Lord Chief-Justice
of England (Sir A. Cockburn), as a judge and
a member of the Judicial Committee, recorded
his emphatic protest through the medium of a
friendly letter to the Prime Minister. He declared
that, the Legislature having settled the qualification
for the office, momentarily to invest a party, otherwise not qualified, with a qualifying office, not that
he should hold the latter, but merely be transferred to
the former, was nothing less than the manufacture of
a qualification not very dissimilar in character from
the manufacture of other qualifications to evade the
law. 'Forgive me, I pray you,' he added, 'if I ask
you to consider whether such a proceeding should
be resorted to in a matter intimately connected with
the administration of justice in its highest departments.' Chief-Justice Bovill took the same view, and
complained that no communication had been made
to him, as head of the Court of Common Pleas, with
respect to this and other recent appointments. To
these letters the Lord Chancellor and Mr. Gladstone
returned curt replies, declining to afford any explanation except in Parliament.

On the other hand, Mr. Justice Willes wrote to
the Lord Chancellor, giving his opinion that the
appointment was legal, as being within the terms of
the statute, and that 'evasion' of the law, by
appointing a fit man according to the law, was a

'sensational' expression. The letter contained a rather lively attack on the Lord Chief - Justice. None of the elements of a very pretty quarrel between some of the most eminent judicial and political personages were wanting.

No one questioned the high merits of Sir Robert Collier, but the feeling in the legal profession was almost unanimous in condemning the impropriety of the appointment. The popularity of Mr. Gladstone's Government was rapidly waning through a succession of blunders, of which the 'Collier Scandal' seemed to be one of the least justifiable. In the debate on the Address in February 1872, Mr. Disraeli, after declaring that during the preceding six months Her Majesty's Ministers might be said to have lived in a blaze of apology, observed that if they were desirous of showing that one of the transcendental privileges of a strong Government was to evade Acts of Parliament which they had themselves passed, that opportunity would soon be furnished them. The Opposition had resolved to challenge the appointment in both Houses, and many independent members avowed their readiness to support them. The *Times* reflected the general opinion in declaring that if the resolutions to be submitted to both Houses could be voted upon irrespectively of party alliances and of the grave duties the Ministry must remain in office to discharge, they would probably be carried in each House

against minorities consisting exclusively of Ministers.

Lord Cairns tried in vain to persuade Lord
Westbury to move the resolution in the House of
Lords :—

'You are,' he wrote, 'in a manner the *custos* of the Act of
last year, and you have made the subject of the Judicial Committee your own by the interest you have always taken in it.
The move would be much less a party one coming from you than
from me. Moreover, it is not a *personal* move against the
Chancellor or any one Minister. The Prime Minister and the
whole Cabinet, adhering to and justifying the appointment,
challenge us all either to submit to and admit its propriety, or
else to state our reasons against it. And we have the whole
press, on all sides, in our favour.'

A little later Sir Alexander Cockburn wrote to
Lord Westbury :—

'I am sincerely glad that the Collier affair—or, as our jesters
term it, the "Colliery Explosion," in which Chelmsford says a
Prime Minister and a Lord Chancellor have been "blown up"—is
likely to be brought before the House of Lords, which—and not
the House of Commons—is the right place for a discussion upon
it. The grievous impropriety of the appointment is greatly
aggravated by the insolent and defiant tone which the Government
affects to assume, and which is re-echoed by their immediate
friends. Mellor tells me he met the Solicitor-General at dinner
yesterday, who referred to the subject, and spoke of the charge
against the Government with the most supercilious contempt,
saying that the House of Commons had again and again sanctioned
the evasion of Acts of Parliament, especially in the matter of the
qualifications of members of Parliament. I don't think this sort
of defence will do in Parliament. It will only serve to heap coals
of fire on the heads of those who were parties to this transaction.

'I am surprised to hear that Lord Romilly takes the same
line, and boldly asserts that there is not even a *primâ facie* case

against the Government. Big James talks equally big, and, I am told, abuses me for having first raised the storm. Lord Chelmsford takes the same view that you and Lord Cairns do. So, in his inward mind, does also, to my knowledge, Lord ———— ; but whether his recent peerage may not put a padlock on his tongue is another matter.

'I understand the main defence of the Government will be that the Lord Chancellor could not get any of the judges, except Montague Smith, to consent to go to the Judicial Committee. But you may take it as a certain fact that he did not apply to any of them besides M. Smith, Baron Bramwell, and Mr. Justice Willes. I asked ———— the other day if he would have accepted if an offer had been made to him. He immediately answered, "Yes," but a little afterwards added, "At least I believe I should," and "I was very much mortified that no offer was made to me." You may therefore safely affirm that there is every reason to believe that ———— (who had been a law officer, and therefore was in a certain sense entitled to the preference) would have accepted if asked. But even if the Chancellor's assertion were true, the obvious answer is that Government should have waited till Parliament met, and then got the Act amended instead of setting the bad example of a palpable evasion of a statute—an evasion the more scandalous by reason of the clause in the Bill of the previous session making barristers of seventeen years' standing eligible, having been last year purposely omitted. As to this, I would recommend you to look at what was said by Collier, as the organ of the Government in the House of Commons in August last. You will find it in Hansard.

'I think you are quite right in declining to move the matter in the Lords. The question is one which, as a censure on the Ministry is involved, ought to be brought forward by an avowed member of the Opposition, and the most fitting person is unquestionably Lord Cairns. . . .

'Let me just add before I quit this subject that Lord Chelmsford tells me that while the Bill was in the House last year, he pointed out to the Lord Chancellor the difficulty which would arise in getting the judges to accept, owing to no provision being made for their clerks, and he urged upon him to adopt some

arrangement for getting over the difficulty.   Another £1000 a
year to each judge, which no one would have grudged, would have
prevented the present precious mess.   But the economical
Chancellor would not give it, and passed his Bill in spite of the
certain difficulty which must occur in carrying the Act into effect.'

In a further letter the Lord Chief-Justice thus
justified the action he had taken :—

' My dear Lord Westbury—On looking over the correspondence
between the Lord Chancellor and my brother Chief-Justice, I
observe that the former talks a great deal about my having " condemned the Government unheard and without waiting for their
explanation." Nothing can be more untrue.   I simply warned
the Government against the course they were about to take,
desiring them to record my protest if they refused to give ear to
my remonstrance ; and the only answer I received was a very curt
reply from the Premier, and a very uncivil and contemptuous one
from the Chancellor.

' If therefore the learned Lord should touch the same string
to-morrow evening, may I ask you to set me right with the House ?

' After the treatment I received from the Prime Minister and
the Lord Chancellor, I do not think I can be properly blamed
for publishing the correspondence, especially when Mr. James and
other supporters of the Government were going about charging
me with having written in derogatory terms of Collier.

' What a simpleton that prince of legal coxcombs has made of
himself in his silly letter to the Lord Chancellor !   He really
deserves castigation for writing such egregious nonsense.

' I hear Lord Cairns will certainly be in his place to-morrow
night, and it is expected there will be an animated debate.

' I was told to-day that it was intended by the Government
that the Lord Chancellor was to hang back, so as, if possible, to
have the last word in the debate.   But this would be monstrous,
as the explanation of the Government ought to come as early,
not as late, as possible.   So I hope, amongst you, you will contrive
to force his hand.

' I trust to your speech, which will be the most telling one in
the debate.'

Lord Westbury was at first reluctant to take part in the debate. The misunderstanding that had arisen with regard to the Alabama Claims and the construction of the Washington Treaty was universally admitted to be a matter of the utmost gravity, and he had no desire to add to the difficulties of the situation or help to bring about the fall of the Ministry or a dissolution at such a crisis. The Lord Chief-Justice again wrote to him :—

'My dear Lord Westbury—I am sorry to hear you are likely to take no part in the debate to-night.

'Your views on the subject are well known. The Lord Chancellor himself has made no secret of them. The profession and the public will naturally expect that you should speak out on a matter on which no man can be more competent to form a judgment and guide opinion. And I conceive that the House of Lords has a right to expect it too.

'Take my word for it, your silence will have a very bad effect, and I fear that anything but a pleasant construction will be put upon it. To be the first mover in the affair was one thing, to be wholly silent is another.

'Believe me, those who advise you to take no part may be good friends to the Government—they are not so to you. And I shall regret your silence as much on your account as on that of the public.

'At all events, may I ask you to put Lord Cairns in possession of the facts I told you as to the Lord Chancellor having applied only to two of the judges—Willes and Bramwell—while ———, if applied to, would doubtless have accepted.

'Pray forgive me for presuming to give you advice ; but a man, even of your great powers, is not always the best judge of his own case.'

On the 15th of February 1872, in a House dressed for a grand debate, Earl Stanhope moved a resolution which expressed regret at the course taken in carrying out the recent Act, and declared that 'the elevation of Sir Robert Collier to the bench for the purpose only of giving him a colourable qualification to be a paid member of the Judicial Committee, and his immediate transfer to the Judicial Committee accordingly, were acts at variance with the spirit and intention of the statute, and of evil example in the exercise of judicial patronage.' Lord Stanhope, in moving his resolution, went so far as to charge the Lord Chancellor, the head of the law, with having counselled a deliberate evasion of the law, and the Prime Minister with having twisted to his own purpose the express words of an Act of Parliament passed by his own administration. Lord Portman, as an independent member of the House, moved an amendment that the House found no just cause for censure on the conduct of the Government in the recent appointment. In his view, if the proceeding could not be altogether justified, it was at least excusable. There had been no evil motive in it, and what had been done was the best that could be done in all the circumstances of the case.

The Marquis of Salisbury followed with a strong censure on the Government for the general exercise of their patronage. Appointments of this kind, he said, were not likely to increase the reverence which people felt for the administration of the law, or to reflect honour upon the constitution of the highest judicial tribunal of the realm. On behalf of the

Government the Duke of Argyll attacked Sir
Alexander Cockburn with great acrimony for writing
a letter which he described as 'a letter of railing
accusation.' It was not, he said, a letter from the
Lord Chief-Justice of England ; it was a letter purely
and simply from Sir Alexander Cockburn ; and what
was more, from Sir A. Cockburn in a state of considerable irritation and effervescence. It possessed
no judicial authority, though there was now and
then a little spot of clear water amongst the foam
and bubbles of wrath and indignation. When a
judge descended from the bench, and entered the
arena of personal or political debate, he had no
right to claim the sanctity of the ermine and the
immunities of the Bench.

This speech brought up Lord Westbury, who
warmly defended the Lord Chief-Justice. He had
listened, he said, with pain to the attack just made,
and anything more unjust and indecent he had never
heard, and trusted he never should hear again. He
little envied the taste and feeling of a man who
thought he could support a bad cause by such
declamation. He pointed out that the letter was a
private letter addressed to the Prime Minister by
one who had been for years his friend, entreating
him not to take a step which would be visited
with general reprobation. He (Lord Westbury)
did not desire a greater amount of censure to be
passed than would be passed if one of the decrees of
the Lord Chancellor pronounced in Chancery were

brought up to that House and reversed on appeal. There had been, in his opinion, an error of judgment committed, but no more. The complaint was this—that if, in a matter of civil right, the Chancellor had done what he had done in the bestowal of a great judicial office, the act would have been impeached as a fraudulent exercise of a power. It was not technically an evasion of the statute, but the misuse of the power was a fraud on the statute. The manner in which the fraud was perpetrated seemed, he observed, to be this—

'The Chancellor, in effect, said to Mr. Gladstone : "We have both agreed that he (Sir R. Collier) shall be appointed to the Judicial Committee, and I will put him into the Common Pleas, not that he may be a *bonâ fide* or a permanent judge, but that he may be qualified for the Committee." Thus he is appointed first and qualified afterwards. A sham judge is put on the Judicial Committee. It is quite odd to see how the agents in this joint transaction proceed. The Lord Chancellor says : "I have made him a judge of the Common Pleas, which is quite right and within my power ;" and the Prime Minister says : "I have made him a member of the Judicial Committee, which is quite right and within my power." But, and I put it as a problem for the dialectic subtlety of the Prime Minister, these two right acts make an insufferable wrong. There lies the fraud and the misuse of the statute.'

Lord Westbury sarcastically observed that he thought the Lord Chancellor had good grounds of complaint against Mr. Justice Willes for the part he had taken in the controversy. The opportunity of indulging a propensity for satirical observations at the judge's expense was too good to be resisted, so he went on to say :—

'Mr. Justice Willes came voluntarily to the aid of the noble and learned lord in a letter which unhappily shows that, though his experience as a judge in Courts of Common Law may be great, he is standing on a plain below the level of the higher regions of justice, and knows nothing at all of those higher maxims of equity by which the common law is controlled, and by which such a transaction as this ought to be judged. I do not make it a matter of grave complaint against Mr. Justice Willes that such is the case. It seems, however, to illustrate the infirmity of our institutions, which admit of our having two kinds of justice—the one in the Courts of Law of a lower and more degraded order, and the other in the Courts of Equity of a more exalted and sublimer character. I must express my regret that the Lord Chancellor should have received this letter; but as he has received it, I would advise him, whenever he brings in a Bill I long for, which shall have my most sincere attention, for the establishment of a great Court of Appeal and the fusion of Law and Equity, he should cite as an illustration of the need of a fusion Mr. Justice Willes. I would also suggest to my honourable and learned friend (Sir Roundell Palmer) that he might quote this letter as proof of the necessity of instituting a better system of legal education.'

Was the parsimony of the Chancellor of the Exchequer, he asked, to be held a sufficient justification for the Lord Chancellor's breaking the law ? Time was when the Chancellor would have vindicated his right of determining what was required for the due administration of justice ; and if he had knocked in vain at the door of the Chancellor of the Exchequer, he would have gone to the Cabinet and said to them : 'This must be done ! . . . I will not be driven, even with the approbation of the Prime Minister, into the evasion of a statute and the fraudulent use of an enactment, in order that I may get by a by-way that which I ought to do openly, directly, and in full conformity with the ordinary course of justice.' He concluded with the words :—

'For my part, though I fear I may have been betrayed by the language of the noble Duke into the use of stronger words than I intended, yet I will add my own personal feeling and earnest hope that the Lord Chancellor will succeed in satisfying your lordships that we are in error in condemning this proceeding, for nothing would please me more than that his great reputation should not be tarnished by any act which you may regard as open to censure.'

The Lord Chancellor, in a very elaborate speech, successfully defended his own conduct, while he attempted to vindicate the interpretation of the Act upon which he and Mr. Gladstone had acted. No one, indeed, having any knowledge of Lord Hatherley could possibly have charged him with an unworthy intention. He said he could not accept the interpretation of the motion offered him in such mellifluous terms by Lord Westbury. Referring to the comparison of Lord Stanhope's motion to a motion to reverse a decree, the Lord Chancellor retorted that it was not usual on reversing a decree to add a declaration of censure. The motion was as clearly a party manœuvre as ever came before Parliament. An adverse vote would not, he declared, affect him in the least ; but it might deeply affect the administration of justice in making it difficult for judges to accept office if, instead of being liable to be displaced only by a vote of both Houses, they might be branded by the vote of one branch of the Legis-

lature as having been the medium of a fraud in
distorting an Act of Parliament for their own
purposes.

The estimation in which the Lord Chancellor
was held in the House, quite as much as considerations of the probable effect of an adverse vote, turned
the scale in favour of the Government. After
speeches from Lord Cairns and Lord Granville, the
motion was negatived by the majority of a single
vote. A similar motion of censure in the House of
Commons was defeated by a majority of 27.

The Duke of Argyll's strong personal observations gave bitter offence to the Lord Chief-Justice,
and he declared that unless they were immediately
withdrawn there must be a cessation of all cordial
relations between himself and the Government,
which would so impair his status and personal weight
that he should feel it his duty to resign the office of
Arbitrator and Representative of England at the
Geneva Convention. Through the friendly inter-
vention of Lord Westbury the difference was
adjusted by the Duke of Argyll expressing his
regret in the House of Lords for any words used
in the debate which might have justly seemed
personally offensive to the Lord Chief-Justice.

CHAPTER XI

EARLY in the session of 1872, Lord Westbury made an interesting speech in calling attention to defects which still characterised the appellate jurisdiction of the House of Lords. It will be remembered that in 1855, when Solicitor-General, he had pointed out the evils of the existing system with a frankness which gave bitter offence to Lord Campbell and other Law Lords. The graver scandals had since been removed by the personal efforts of successive Chancellors; but the consideration of appeals was, and still is, conducted in a somewhat haphazard fashion; the sittings were dependent on the Parliamentary session and the voluntary and uncertain attendance of the legal Peers, and were frequently interrupted by the political duties of the Lord Chancellor.

In commenting upon these inconveniences Lord Westbury gave an amusing picture of the much worse position half a century before : 'A greater state of decency,' he said, 'prevails in these days. In Lord Eldon's time, when the Lord Chancellor attended to hear the Appeals, he occasionally found himself alone ; and inasmuch as three Peers were required to make a House, the officers of the House were sometimes obliged to catch a Bishop and invite him to act as dummy ; a lay Peer was sometimes pressed into the service, and the Lord Chancellor, gravely assisted by these two mutes, administered justice in a final manner.'

He advocated the consolidation of their Lordships' tribunal and the Judicial Committee of the Privy Council into one Supreme Court of Appeal, which would include the *élite* of the judges of the other Courts. He thought that if such a Court were carefully constituted, and made easily accessible and economical, sitting throughout the year, with its door open for the admission of every appellate suitor, one appeal would in general suffice for it. It was to the interest of the State to stop litigation after reasonable facilities had been afforded for obtaining justice. If a supreme tribunal could be constituted, which was entitled to unqualified approval as a Court of Appeal for the whole Empire, then, he said, their Lordships might, as honest men, part with their appellate jurisdiction.

With respect to the Judicial Committee, he would

gladly hail any measure that would eliminate the Bishops, who now formed a portion of that tribunal in ecclesiastical cases, because he believed that nothing would more tend than their exclusion to promote the peace of the Church.

The Bills introduced by Lord Hatherley from the woolsack in 1871 and 1872 for the establishment of a Supreme Court of Appeal were patchwork measures, of which Lord Westbury was reluctant to express the opinions he entertained through the fear that his doing so would be attributed to personal disappointment. He therefore contented himself with urging the hopeless nature of any attempt to reconstitute this Court until the jurisdiction of the inferior Courts had been considered and remodelled in accordance with the recommendations of the Judicature Commission.

He was strongly of opinion that the facilities for appealing were too great. As for Scottish appeals, he declared that their frequency would be insupportable but for the self-love of the people, which led them to attribute perfection to all their institutions. In introducing a Bill of his own to put restrictions upon the right of appealing to the House of Lords, he gave some remarkable statistics to illustrate the peculiar love of the Scottish people for litigation, in which they may almost be said to rival the natives of India. He showed that during the past four years the number of Scottish appeals had exceeded those from the English and Irish Courts

together.   Many of these appeals were of the most
trifling and vexatious description, on matters of no
greater importance than those which are daily decided
in our County Courts.   In one case the subject of the
dispute was of the value of 5s. ; but it went through
the whole range of the Scotch Courts, and finally
came before the House of Lords, the last appeal
involving a cost of £700 or £800.   In another case
the owner of a sheep sought compensation from the
owner of a dog for injury caused to the sheep by the
dog.   The owner of the dog contended that his
animal was sufficiently harmless and inoffensive, and
that the sheep must have been at fault.   The litigants
ultimately came to the House of Lords, where they
expended at least £800 over a sheep, whose carcass
could have been purchased for 40s.

Lord Westbury proposed to fix a pecuniary limit,
below which, subject to certain exceptions, it should
not be competent to appeal.   He further proposed that
where a judgment of any Court of first instance in the
United Kingdom had been affirmed on appeal, there
should be no further appeal to the House of Lords
without leave.   The effect of this, he pointed out,
would be to relieve the Law Lords of a great deal of
trumpery litigation, and enable them to assist the
Judicial Committee of the Privy Council in the decision
of important cases, while it would prevent the losing
party from revenging himself upon his adversary by
carrying his case to the last Court of Appeal.   'It
has been said,' he observed, 'that law is a luxury:

but as a luxury it should be restrained by sumptuary laws—by laws judiciously founded on considerations of the public good and general expedience.' The Bill, which was introduced more to call attention to the subject than with the expectation of passing it, merely obtained a second reading.

Several of Lord Westbury's speeches in the same session had reference to the important negotiations with the United States on the subject of the *Alabama* Claims. The whole controversy is too recent to require more than a passing reference. It will be remembered that the Treaty of Washington, concluded in 1871 for the purpose of settling these differences, laid down certain rules which, in the opinion of many of the most eminent legal authorities, among them Lord Westbury, impliedly admitted the 'Indirect Claims' put forward by the States—claims for losses which were alleged to have resulted from the prolongation of the war, the increased rates of insurance, the transfer to the British flag of the American mercantile marine, and other similar items of constructive damage. The text of the Treaty left its interpretation open to considerable doubt and question; and Lord Westbury bluntly declared that three boys of ten years old might have succeeded in making a more intelligible one.

The American Government at first insisted on going before the Arbitrators with these claims, and it was plain that the Treaty contained no explicit stipulation to exclude them. It seemed only too probable that unless forcible pressure was put upon them, the British Government would act on the supposition that these claims were excluded by the limits of the reference, and drift into an arbitration in which their validity would be admitted. Nor was it by any means clear, having regard to the miscellaneous composition of the tribunal, that the Arbitrators could be trusted to reject the claims on the ground of their intrinsic absurdity. The persons nominated by Switzerland and Brazil did not, it appeared, understand a word of English, which was the common language of the contending parties, and the language in which every document to be consulted was written. Such a proceeding had no parallel in history or in law.

Before the session commenced, Lord Westbury wrote several letters to Lord Granville, in which he repeatedly pressed the necessity of a more decided course of action. Although he had at that time practically withdrawn from political life, he felt the greatest anxiety with respect to the Arbitration at Geneva. In his view the Treaty, coupled with our apologies, was an abject capitulation which had encouraged the Americans to revive extravagant demands after they had agreed to abandon them. He was reminded, he said, of Brennus throwing his heavy sword into the scale when the Romans were bringing out gold to buy his retreat from Rome.

He wrote to Mr. Reeve upon the same subject :—

'Since writing to you and about three weeks ago, so soon as I heard of the American case, I began a series of letters to Lord Granville, strongly advising that a strong and firm protest should be *at once* presented to the American Government, with a notice that unless this portion of the claims was withdrawn England would not proceed with the Arbitration. I did not obtain from Lord Granville any reason to hope that a course so bold and straightforward would be adopted, but from the articles in the *Times* of the last three days I hope the Ministry will be courageous enough to attempt thus to remove the consequences of their former carelessness and unskilfulness. How Americans must laugh at us. It is mortifying to the last degree.

'I think the cup of the Ministry is full. . . .

'If the American matter does not end well, which of course it cannot do until after much bluster, there will be a severe panic in the City. In truth, we have not from the protocols any equitable case to reduce or restrict the reference.

'There is nothing in the published documents that should forbid the United States bringing forward these claims. Our real case is that the Americans must have seen from the conduct of our Commissioners that they did not suppose any such claims were intended to be made, but that they were so stupid and careless as not to see that the words of the Treaty did not exclude them. In short, our equity is that we were fools, and the Americans did not come to the aid of our stupidity. It is humiliating.'

The following letter from Sir Alexander Cockburn expresses with much frankness the views which he shared with Lord Westbury on the subject :—

'My dear Lord Westbury—Lord Granville is to a certain extent right, but his answer to you is by no means satisfactory on the whole. The Treaty, as I read it, certainly does not admit of any claim on the part of the American Government against this country in respect of the alleged premature recognition of the Southern States as belligerents, and the pretended prolongation of the war by reason of that recognition. But it does leave the question open whether, in addition to liability for the damage done by the *Alabama* and other vessels to specific ships and cargoes, this country is to be held responsible to the American nation and Government for the more remote and consequential damage done to American commerce through the destruction of their mercantile marine?

'Now it is quite certain that our negotiators did not intend to submit the latter head of claim to arbitration. But, unfortunately, instead of taking the precaution of expressly defining the limits of the inquiry, they have left the terms of the Treaty quite large enough to embrace any claim, however preposterous and remote, on the part of the American Government as well as of individuals, which bold and unscrupulous politicians may have the effrontery to put forward. It was, as it seems to me, the extreme of imprudence to trust to the good faith or honour of the people they were dealing with. It is true, as Lord Granville says, that the matter is subject to the control of the arbitrators, who may refuse to entertain the largest claim. But here is the rub! What if they do not so refuse? What security have we that they will? What confidence can we have in men of whom we know nothing, or, at all events, so very little? What security have we that they may not be tampered with in the long interval which is to elapse before the decision is to be given? Of course one feels great delicacy in suggesting anything of this kind, but where *millions* are involved, no risk should be incurred which could possibly be avoided. The system of our negotiators in dealing with our transatlantic cousins—of "making things pleasant," as the railway potentate used to express it, and then hugging themselves in the agreeable belief that they have achieved a great success and are entitled to great rewards—is one that is not likely to secure the interest or the honour of Great Britain.

'I quite agree that the Government, on these monstrous claims being preferred, should have at once brought the American Government to book—have declared that they had never intended to allow so large a scope to the arbitration—that the claims were inconsistent with what was understood in the verbal negotiations which had taken place; and that, unless the United States Government would consent at once to withdraw from such pretensions, the Treaty must be considered as at an end. A meeting of the Cabinet was held, I know, the day before yesterday on the subject of the *Alabama* claims, at which the law officers were summoned to attend. I have not heard what decision was come to. But I hope, if the Government mean to let things take their course without doing anything, Parliament will take up the matter and protect the interests of the country.'

During the early part of the session Lord Westbury joined in several damaging attacks upon the Government in connection with the Treaty, which drew from Lord Granville a letter of remonstrance, in which he said : 'It is the fate of man (in public life) to be attacked. But I trust you great lawyers in the Lords do not intend to put arms of (more or less) precision into the hands of the Americans.' At last even Lord Granville lost patience and challenged Lord Westbury in the House of Lords to bring forward his opinions in the shape of a deliberate vote of censure.

Though Lord Westbury was not prepared to take up the challenge, his strong representations found an echo in the resolution moved by Earl Russell to suspend the proceedings before the Arbitrators until the objectionable claims had been withdrawn. This resolution, which was treated by the Government as a motion of want of confidence, gave rise to an important debate. Lord Westbury, while opposing the resolution on the ground of its unnecessary embarrassment to the Government in the settlement of the difficulty, made observations on their conduct throughout the negotiations, which

the Earl of Rosebery, who followed him, happily
referred to as 'those precious balms with which the
noble and learned Lord is accustomed to break the
head of Her Majesty's Government.'

For the principle of arbitration Lord Westbury
expressed little regard, but he laid much stress on
the grave responsibility of putting off to an indefinite
period the settlement of the question just as they
had arrived at something certain; 'for,' he said, 'up
to the present time we have had a series of under-
standings in which nothing has been understood,—a
series of explanations in which nothing has been
explained.'

'Now, is this a time when, consistently with honour, reason,
and profit, we can smash the original Treaty? I have no love for
the introduction of uncalled-for novelties. I have no love for the
authority on which the Treaty was founded. I have no love for
the manner of proceeding which is pointed out in it. Remember,
however, that it proceeded from yourselves. It is a twelvemonth
since you received it. You received it with general acclamations.
It has been hailed as inaugurating a new era in jurisprudence and
in the mode of disposing of the quarrels of nations. Do you
think you can now turn round and say you have found out that
the Treaty is unwise, and that you will adopt a by-mode of annul-
ling it, and escaping the fulfilment of our obligations? I, for
one, am not prepared to go so far. A time may come when we
shall have to criticise the making of this Treaty; but it is at
present, and has been for twelve months, an accomplished fact
between the two nations, and I think it is a foundation on which
we may build, so as to conduct what remains to be done to a
profitable issue.'

The debate was adjourned from the 6th to the
8th of June, and satisfactory assurances, with respect

to the withdrawal of the indirect claims, having been received during the interval from the United States Minister, the motion was withdrawn. This was the very last appearance of Lord Westbury in Parliament.

In the autumn of 1872 Lord Westbury undertook his last public duty under the authority of an Act passed to settle the affairs of the notorious European Assurance Society. The Society had enjoyed the advantage of State recognition, Parliament having authorised its guarantee to be taken as security from persons employed in public offices, and the result was to give the public a confidence in its stability which was quite undeserved. While in a state of hopeless insolvency the European purchased the business of various Assurance Companies, some of which had already absorbed other smaller associations, subject in each case to the liabilities of the amalgamated Companies, and with an indemnity against all claims current at the time of purchase. The European had a capital of one million divided into 400,000 shares, of which upwards of 300,000 had been subscribed. After struggling on for several years the Society became a total wreck, and in 1872 it was ordered to be wound up.

No fewer than forty Companies were, through amalgamation, involved in the failure, and the enormous number of policyholders, shareholders, contributories, and general creditors, who were

interested in the assets or liabilities of the several
Companies made it impossible to wind up the
European Society in the ordinary course of
liquidation. Complicated questions arose touching
the position of the Society with respect to the
amalgamated Companies, and the position of these
Companies *inter se*, and the shareholders of such as
were solvent were threatened with the loss of a
large portion of their claims. It was thought too
that it might be expedient, either that the Society
should be reconstructed, or that its business should
be transferred to another Company, neither of which
schemes could be carried out without the assent of
all the creditors of the several Companies.

In these circumstances some special arrangement became necessary, and application was made
to Lord Westbury to undertake the office of
Arbitrator in the same way as Lord Cairns had
already done in the case of the Albert Society.[1]
Lord Westbury was very reluctant to accept the
appointment, but he ultimately yielded to the advice

---

[1] Lord Westbury had himself been so unfortunate as to become involved in the great losses inflicted by the failure of the
Albert Society, through having bought, twenty years before, some
shares in a Company which was afterwards amalgamated with the
Albert. 'I had quite forgotten the matter, which was then a
very trifling one,' he wrote ; 'but the other day I found a letter on
my breakfast-table, informing me that I should probably be made
liable for eight thousand pounds. It is the most unpleasant
part of my acquaintance with Chancery.' Though he was not
eventually called upon to pay as much as he feared, the loss
was considerable.

of Lord Cairns, to whose opinion at this time he attached more weight than to that of any one else. He disapproved of the makeshift principle of providing for such cases by exceptional legislation. ' This Arbitration,' he said, ' is an anomaly ; it is only to be justified by its necessity ; and its necessity is a great reproach to the judicial institutions of the country.' An Act was passed in July 1872, after some opposition from those who objected to the principle of arbitration, and from others who disapproved of an ex-Lord Chancellor sitting as Arbitrator, by which Lord Westbury was appointed Arbitrator, and invested with the fullest discretionary jurisdiction to determine all questions and settle the affairs of the Society and the several absorbed Companies as effectually as might have been done by an Act of Parliament.[1]

Apart from personal considerations, the undertaking was a very formidable one. ' There seems,' Lord Westbury wrote while the Bill was passing through Parliament, ' to be a great deal of malignity and ill-will in the matter, which, I fear, will make the task of Arbitrator a very disagreeable one. . . . For myself, I dread the labour of the judicial inquiry.'

The labour was indeed immense, but having undertaken the duty with which Parliament entrusted him, he addressed himself to it with extraordinary

---

[1] The Act provided that the Arbitrator should receive a sum of 3500 guineas as his remuneration.

vigour and success.   Among the many difficult
questions to be determined, the   most   important
were those of the liability of contributories and
'novation,' or, as Lord Westbury preferred to call
it, the substitution of a new contract in lieu and
discharge of the old.   These are questions which
have too little general interest to warrant a detailed
notice ; but any reference to Lord Westbury's
labours may appear incomplete which made no mention of the general rules which he laid down in the
Arbitration.   He took a somewhat broader view than
Lord Cairns of the principle of novation,—a view
which was more favourable to the policyholders, both of
the European and the amalgamated Companies, and
was considered to ensure more substantial justice.

'It becomes necessary,' he said, 'to prevent the rights of
men being defeated by innocent or equivocal acts being tortured
into evidence of intentions and conclusions directly opposite to
what they themselves held and what they intended to act upon.
When, therefore, I find a case in which by unequivocal acts a
man has accepted a new Company which had the power to contract with him in lieu of the old Company with which he contracted,
I shall give effect to the new contract ; but to raise that new
contract, there must be on the part of the new Company a power
to make it ; there must be on the part of the policyholder a
knowledge of the Company's right so to contract with him, and
there must be conduct on the part of the policyholder, when it is
an incomplete contract, or where there is no evidence in writing,
that unmistakably shows he intended to accept a new contract
and discharge the old.'

In many respects the Arbitration was a very
painful office. The failure of the European involved

the ruin of hundreds of poor widows and orphans who looked to the policies which had been provided for them as their only means of subsistence. The letters received from these unfortunate persons were of the most heartrending nature, and Lord Westbury often, during the progress of the Arbitration, privately expressed his bitter regret that those who were responsible for such widespread misery could not be brought to justice.

On the 25th of January 1873 Lord Westbury was married to Miss Eleanor Margaret Tennant, third daughter of the late Mr. Henry Tennant of Cadoxton, in Glamorganshire. Mr. Tennant, a bencher of Gray's Inn, had been a friend of Lord Westbury when both were practising at the Bar. After their father's death, the Misses Tennant became involved in a Chancery suit, with respect to which they sought the advice of Lord Westbury. With his usual kindness, he devoted much time and attention to the case, and the incident naturally led to the establishment of friendly relations between the two families, which resulted in Lord Westbury's second marriage.

During the early months of this year he was looking forward to greatly improved sport at Hinton in the following season, and making more extensive preparations than before with that object. His letters to his youngest son, who supervised these matters, were full of the minutest directions as to the breeding and preserving of hares and pheasants,

and of his hopes and fears relative to the prospects
of the anticipated sport.   Though his walking
powers had now much diminished, his love of
country pursuits continued unabated.   He could no
longer go through a day's partridge shooting, but
contented himself with a quiet walk for an hour or
two at a time, watching the dogs work while another
gun and a keeper beat the fields round him.   Still in
the principal shootings of the home-coverts he was
able to stay out for the whole day with his party,
keen even to the last shot.   And he continued to
take the liveliest interest in his farming operations,
driving round daily in a pony-carriage to see the
live-stock and give instructions as to cultivation of
the land and similar matters.

With failing health he began to manifest an even
greater disinclination than before to residence in
London, though he still retained his house there.
' I wish,' he wrote to his youngest son, ' you could
find a nice house mid the mountains, with some good
fishing in a river or lake.   Town was most oppressive
before I left.'   To another correspondent he declared :
' A London season is a coarse, exhausting, non-
intellectual life.   It is nothing but a repetition of
the same scenes, meeting the same faces, having to
listen to the same insipid conversation, until, I am
sure, if you would confess the truth, you feel the
very fulness of satiety.'

Towards the end of February, on his return
from Worthing, the sittings in the Arbitration were

resumed, and so rapidly did he dispose of the
cases prepared for his decision, that he began to
complain that he could not get enough work. And
yet, even at that time, he seemed quite unfit for such
an exertion, and soon the sittings had to be sus-
pended in consequence of his increasing indisposi-
tion. It was the beginning of the end. For several
months past he had suffered at intervals from pains
in the head and neck, and they now became uninter-
mittent. On the 18th of March he writes : ' I am
still a sad invalid, suffering from rheumatic pains in
the region of the left hip and neuralgia at the back
of the head. It was impossible for me to get to the
House of Lords. . . . The Bill is for an excellent
object, but it will be defeated by its own cumbrous
and ill-chosen machinery. I am glad I was spared
the task of proving this. Now, of course, for this
year the Bill is buried. How absurd is the succession of events in life.'

The Bill referred to was the colossal measure
introduced by the Lord Chancellor, Lord Selborne,
for the establishment of the Supreme Court of Judicature and the improvement of the constitution of
the Courts of Appeal. With admirable skill and
boldness Lord Selborne proposed to remodel the
entire jurisdiction ; but though Lord Westbury
approved of the principle and main features of the
scheme, he concurred with Lord Cairns in some
serious objections to its machinery and details. It
was, indeed, in its leading outline, little more than

the first report of the Judicature Commission, for
which Lord Cairns was largely responsible. But
both Lord Westbury and Lord Cairns differed from
Lord Selborne *toto cœlo* as to the way in which the
Bill treated the Court of Chancery—making it subordinate to the Queen's Bench Division, and thus
destroying the dignity, prestige, and power of the
Great Court; while, to complete its degradation, as
they considered, the Lord Chancellor, in place of
being head of the Court of Chancery, was to be a
mere unit in the Court of Appeal. In enforcing
their objections they were supported by the unanimous voice of the Equity bar, which represented that
the Bill, as drawn, endangered the very existence of
Equity jurisprudence.

Lord Westbury was extremely anxious to take
part in the discussions on it, and even to serve on
the Select Committee to which, mainly in deference
to his strong representations, and in the hope that
the Peers might have the benefit of his advice, the
Bill was referred. But the acute nature of his illness very soon precluded his leaving the house, or
even walking across the room without assistance.
'If I spoke in the House,' he wrote to Lord Cairns,
'I could not hope to express what I have to say in
less than an hour. I fear I should break down in
less than a quarter of the time.' The Bill ultimately
passed, with some considerable amendment in the
direction desired by Lord Westbury; but he who
had for thirty years expressed his earnest desire to

pull down the middle wall of partition between law and equity did not live to see the fusion accomplished.

His illness arose not from neuralgia, as had been supposed, but from a deep-seated inflammation of the external coating of three or four of the upper vertebræ of the neck, and it involved the most painful treatment. Notwithstanding the great suffering and exhaustion caused by this disorder, Lord Westbury, with characteristic fortitude, insisted on resuming the sittings in the Arbitration, and they were appointed to be held at his residence at Lancaster Gate. His grandson, the Rev. Thomas Palmer Abraham, then acting as his secretary, gives the following account of the indomitable spirit displayed in this last performance of a public duty :—

'On the last occasion that he held a court in his European Arbitration he was a dying man.

'For some days before it he had been suffering agonies of pain, which never left him until he became unconscious a day or two before his death. His medical attendants begged of him not to hold the court, and no one who knew what he was suffering thought that he could possibly carry it through. However, he scouted the idea of putting it off, and from the time that he came downstairs into the dining-room, where the sitting was held, until the close, he did not utter a single groan. The only way in which he could endure the pain was by my holding a bag of ice to the top of his spine, which I had to keep constantly renewing. I suppose that I, who knew him so well, was the only person in the room who had any idea how intensely he was suffering. The doctors, after his death, having made an examination, declared that the pain must have been agonising.

'All through the Arbitration his rapid grasp of the facts and points of each case, and his pithy judgments, had been the theme of general admiration ; yet in this his last sitting he literally surpassed himself.

'I remember, amongst others, Mr. Montague Cookson, Q.C., expressing to me his great pleasure and astonishment at the extraordinary power and clearness displayed by Lord Westbury on this occasion. He said too, if I remember rightly, that although he had been present at almost every sitting of the Arbitration, he had never heard Lord Westbury dispose of the difficult points brought before him with such wonderful ease, precision, and clearness. But the severity of such a trial of nerve and brain must have hastened the end ; and that was the last public business that he ever undertook.'

On the occasion referred to Lord Westbury affirmed with his customary clearness and vigour the principles upon which the transfer of shares to irresponsible persons with the intention of escaping future liability ought to be regarded : ' I do not care a rush,' he said, 'whether the Directors did their duty or not.' The only question in his opinion was whether the transfer was a *bonâ-fide* transaction. He denounced with unsparing severity the nefarious devices to which shareholders are apt to resort as soon as a Company gets into low water. In many of the cases transfers had been made to persons who had received a consideration for the transfer of shares instead of paying one, and whose designations were purposely misleading. Thus a transferee, described as a 'gentleman,' was in fact a blind pauper ; and a farm-labourer and a working collier had been dignified by the titles of 'sheep-farmer' and 'colliery

superintendent.'   All such transactions were treated
as illusory.

'Observe,' said Lord Westbury, 'how these Companies have
been filled with rotten, bankrupt people; how the unfortunate
creditors who trusted them and trusted the conduct of the
Directors have been betrayed,—the Company breaks up, and they
find a number of men of straw, that have been brought into the
Company in this way, who are unable to fulfil their engagements.
And that originates in the neglect of judges to watch over these
transactions, and to hold out strongly that they will undo everything that is not consistent with the purest reasons for transferring the shares, and the belief of the transferor that the man he
puts in his shoes will be as competent and able as he himself is,
or more so—will be fully competent to discharge the obligations
of his situation.'

At this last sitting a very old man had to be
examined as a witness, and there was some difficulty
in following and laying hold of his evidence.   Yet
the Arbitrator showed no trace of impatience.
'Nothing,' says Mr. Napier Higgins, Q.C., 'could
exceed his courtesy and kindness—indeed, I might
say, good temper.'   Throughout the Arbitration,
sitting as quasi-judge, Lord Westbury unbent a
little, and was full of sly humour.   He went back as
much as possible to the Roman law, and had always
an apt quotation from Justinian when settling the
rival claims of the 'mass of afflicted companies,' as
he called them; but the principles he asserted met
with very general acceptance.   A letter written by
Mr. Montague Cookson, now Mr. Cookson-Crackan-
thorpe, Q.C., to one of the daily papers[1] shortly after,

[1] The *Times*, 21st July 1873.

pays such a just and forcible tribute to the judicial
qualities which Lord Westbury displayed in the
Arbitration, that an extract may be given from it :—

'No one who habitually practised before him while he pre-
sided over the late sittings in Victoria Street is likely to forget
how that masterly intellect penetrated, as by instinct, into the
marrow of the difficult questions presented to it, and extricated
principles from a labyrinth of facts that might well have confused
a less vigorous brain. Although, as between the creditors and
the shareholders, the victory was more often with the former,
both classes alike, with rare exceptions, felt that their cases had
been thoroughly sifted, and that the decision had proceeded on
long-established rules, which were only the embodiment of common
sense. If, as often happened, the tediousness of the argument
was relieved by a flash of satire or a touch of the dramatic art,
the interposition was never rude, nor the irony offensive. His
patience as a listener was remarkable, even when suffering, as he
evidently was at times, from considerable physical pain ; and by this
simple expedient he was frequently able to get through the work
of the day long before the day was finished. But although
patient, he was not at all disposed to let those who pleaded before him have it all their own way, and he more than once
deprecated in his usual pungent language the habit practised by
some judges of concealing what is passing in their minds until
they are called upon to deliver judgment. As Arbitrator he
was not bound by the authority of cases, but he always deferred
to those cited, if relevant, without permitting himself to be led
away by false analogies or setting too much store on book-learn-
ing as such. The strong impression of extraordinary judicial
aptitude that he created during his recent labours was due, in
short, to his possessing four characteristics in a high degree,—
rapidity of apprehension, logical acumen, lucidity of exposition,
and (last but not least) uniform courtesy of manner. These are
great qualities, and when combined make any man's public life
memorable ; when found in a judge of first instance, they help
to bring about spontaneously that which the present session has
striven to accomplish by legislation ; namely, despatch of business,

simplification of the current law, and satisfaction of the general body of suitors.'[1]

Early in July it had become painfully evident, from the nature of Lord Westbury's sufferings, that no permanent relief could be expected, and the daily reports of his condition pointed to new and increasing complications which would probably end in suffusion of the brain. Yet his mind remained calm and unsubdued. A few days before his death, the Archbishop of Canterbury, who was his personal friend, visited him, and found his intellect and mind as clear and composed as ever. On leaving, he remarked on this to Miss Bethell, adding, ' I have not spoken to your father of his rapidly approaching end ; there is no need. Although we have not mentioned the subject, I can see how fully he is prepared for it.'

The doctors in attendance were filled with wonder and admiration at the clearness and power of his mind, which no pain or weakness seemed able to obscure or diminish. Only two or three days before his death he engaged in a long conversation with Sir William Gull and Sir James Paget on political and other topics, and among them that of euthanasia. Lord Westbury himself introduced the subject, but rather, so it seemed, as if intending to examine those who were with him than wishing to give his own opinions. His questions were as clear, definite, and pointed as possible, and he made at least one strik-

---

[1] Mr. Napier Higgins and Mr. Montague Cookson appeared in all the cases for the official liquidators.

ing quotation in commenting on what was said. Sir James Paget had observed that he always felt that as we can never tell which portion of any man's life may be most important to himself or others, so it could not be right that we should for any purpose shorten it. 'Ah, then,' said the dying man, 'you would hold by the trooper's epitaph—

> ' " Betwixt the stirrup and the ground,
>   Mercy I ask't, mercy I found." ' [1]

Through a long period of extreme suffering he displayed the greatest composure, fortitude, and resignation. 'I am content,' he said more than once, 'to suffer ten times the pain, and be thankful, *most* thankful.' He had not concealed from himself or those around him the hopelessness of recovery, though the end, by reason of his great constitutional strength, seemed slow in coming. On the 14th of July he began to dictate a farewell letter to his sister-in-law, Mrs. Harvey of Ickwell Bury: 'The much expected and much desired message,' he said, 'has arrived at last, and it has relieved my

---

[1] The epitaph, of which the above is part, is given in Camden's *Remains*, with the following preface: 'A gentleman, falling off his horse, brake his neck, which suddain hap gave occasion of much speech of his former life, and some in this judging world judged the worst. In which respect a good friend made this good epitaph, remembering that of St. Augustine, *Misericordia Domini inter pontem et fontem*—

> ' " My friend judge not me,
>   Thou seest I judge not thee :
>   Betwixt the stirrup and the ground,
>   Mercy I ask't, mercy I found." '

mind from great anxiety, though why it has been so long delayed——' Here weakness overcame him, and he could not finish the sentence. Two or three days after he sank into a state of insensibility, from which he partially rallied now and then sufficiently to recognise by a word or look Lady Westbury or those of his family who were around him. The end came rapidly at last, and on Sunday morning, the 20th of July, just as the dawn was breaking, he passed away without a struggle ; so peacefully, indeed, at the last that those who were present scarcely knew when the breathing ceased.

Only a few hours before, Bishop Wilberforce, through a fall from his horse, met with a sudden death. By one of those striking coincidences which most forcibly impress the mind in human affairs, the two great men, the divine and the lawyer, so widely different, and yet so alike in the possession of the intellectual gifts which distinguished them from their fellow-men, passed together into the unseen world—' where beyond these voices there is peace.'

'In those few hours,' said Dean Stanley, in the sermon preached by him in Westminster Abbey on the following Sunday, 'there had come the tidings that the angel of death hath summoned two of the foremost men from the high places of our country. One in the decline of years, the other in the prime of vigour ; but both in the fulness of their faculties ; both ornaments of the great professions to which

they were devoted ; both beloved by their friends
and dreaded by their foes ; each conspicuous for the
sharp weapons of war with which they had often
encountered each the other ; each conscious of the
other's strength ; each bearing before the world and
into the presence of their Judge that mingled and
mysterious tissue of human nature which He alone,
who trieth the heart and reins, can unravel with
absolute and unerring truth. " In their deaths they
were not divided." [1]

On the 24th of July the mortal remains of Lord
Westbury were quietly laid in the family vault at
the Great Northern Cemetery at New Southgate,
where his first wife was interred. He had recently
entered on his seventy-fourth year.

In the House of Lords a fitting tribute to the
memory of the two peers, who had been among the
most distinguished ornaments of that assembly, was
duly rendered. After Lord Granville had briefly expressed his sense of the loss sustained by the House
and country, the Lord Chancellor (Lord Selborne)
said :—

'In respect of Lord Westbury I should be sorry to lose the
opportunity of saying a very few words. I think he was a man of
as brilliant natural powers as any man he has left behind him. He
was also a man who, from his activity and industry in the application of those powers, had acquired a very great breadth of view

---

[1] The Dean's text was taken from the first lesson, appointed
for the day of Lord Westbury's death : 'How are the mighty
fallen in the midst of the battle! How are the mighty fallen,
and the weapons of war perished !' (2 Sam. i. 25, 27).

with regard to the science of jurisprudence, to which his life was devoted. He had all the qualities of an eminent judge. Personally, I have to say that from the earliest part of my professional career I was indebted to him for notice and kindness, when I was young and obscure, and when notice and kindness from such a person were most valuable. I was also indebted to him when he became Lord Chancellor for my first introduction to the public service ; and I was indebted to him for uniform confidence and consideration during the whole time of our official connection. I was no unconcerned—I will not call myself spectator, as I was in some sense an actor—in the Parliamentary struggles connected with his retirement from office ; and never had I the smallest doubt, for a single moment, as to his personal purity or as to his freedom from anything inconsistent with high, public, and private honour, in regard to those transactions as to which he was thought by some to have failed in vigilance—no doubt or misgiving of the kind ever crossed my mind ; and I could not but feel pained—more than I have ever yet up to this moment been able to express—that it was considered necessary to visit him with censure, which, so far as any public ground for it was then brought forward, was due, in my judgment, not to him but to others. Since that time he has performed, in a dignified and most useful manner, his part in the judicial and other proceedings in your Lordships' House ; nor did he ever show any feeling of resentment against those who had thought it their duty to oppose him. During the whole of this session I have deeply lamented the absence of that assistance which he could have given with regard to the great measure relating to our judicature, which has passed through your Lordships' House. I regretted his absence the more because I had reason to believe that there were some points of importance on which his opinion was not entirely the same as my own. He was frank and kind in his communications with me ; and his views, I need not say, were carefully considered ; but his absence from your Lordships' House, especially with regard to the discussions on that Bill, was a great public loss ; and the fact that we shall never again have that assistance will, I am sure, be most deeply regretted by all of your Lordships as well as by myself.'

Lord Cairns next eulogised the memory of the friend with whom, he said, he had been for so many years in the closest contact and intimacy, in the following words :—

'I recollect when I, yet a young man, entered the profession of the law, Lord Westbury was in the full blaze of his career at the Bar, and I remember—as my noble and learned friend in the woolsack does—the kindness I received from him then, when kindness was most valuable. I remember with gratitude and gladness the unvarying manner in which that kindness was ever after extended to me. I say this because in the contemplation of the great talents of Lord Westbury, remembering the splendour of his judicial career, recollecting the power which he brought to bear in the performance of his duties as a judge, and remarking also on those proofs of intellect which all of your Lordships must have noticed, we are apt to depreciate what I, at least, dwell upon with greater pleasure ; namely, the goodness of heart which lay below those more splendid qualities,—a goodness of heart which I am glad my noble and learned friend on the woolsack has alluded to in terms which I gladly endorse.'

Lord Hatherley added a few words, to which the high-minded character of the speaker gave peculiar force. He said :—

'As one who was often subjected to considerable criticism in this House on the part of Lord Westbury, I am sincerely glad to bear my testimony in addition to that of my noble and learned friends to his kindliness of heart. He evinced extreme kindliness towards myself during my occupancy of the woolsack, and I think it only due to his memory to say that in the course of those inquiries which led to his retirement from office I never understood that there was any stain on his personal honour. Whatever want of diligence there might have been on his part in reference to transactions in which other persons were concerned, that was not in my judgment, nor in that of others, any reason for imputing a want of personal honour to Lord Westbury himself.'

The same day, in a letter to the leading journal,
the late Sir Lawrence Peel summed up in a pithy
sketch some of the more notable characteristics of
his late colleague and friend :—

'. . . He was a man of wit, and a witty tongue often wags
and offends when there is no malice at the heart. It was so
with him. His nature was the reverse of malignant. He
treasured up no enmities and soon forgave. His knowledge was
ample and varied, rather than exact or profound. His intellect
was of the highest. I have listened often with admiration to his
marvellous displays of judicial eloquence, akin, and in no way
inferior, to those for which Lord Lyndhurst was renowned,
wherein everything was in its due place, every fact narrated in
its due order of time, and with its due degree of importance
assigned to it ; no words wasted ; every word the proper word,
and none too fine for the occasion ; every real difference in things
expressed by a due distinction of language, no argument unnoticed,
and no difficulty evaded. Such was he at the Council table,
where my knowledge of him was formed.

' He was "friendly and just to me," never arrogant nor unwilling to hear, kindly in his nature ; and if he did not take heed
enough not to offend with his tongue, it was because his witty
mind gave that "chartered libertine " its spring, and not because
"a heart of gall " diffused its bitterness unconcerned.

' Let us cherish tender thoughts towards all, while, in no spirit
of undue admiration for the great intellects of the earth, we implore
charity towards those whose eloquent tongues are mute.'

These are generous words of sympathy and
appreciation, but perhaps the best tribute of all will
be found in the simple sentence written by Lady
Forester to Lord Westbury's widow : 'A great
one has passed away : gigantic intellect, with a heart
as tender as a child's.'

CHAPTER XII

In the foregoing pages the story of Lord West-bury's life has been left, as far as was possible, to tell itself, and to suggest, if it did not explain, the leading features of a character which contained so many apparent contradictions that an accurate estimate cannot easily be formed. Without attempting to give a psychological criticism, a few general observations may be added, rather by way of summary than of portrait, by which, with the aid of the further recollections contributed by eminent contemporaries, the impressions produced by a perusal of the history of the life may be supplemented.

It cannot, certainly, be said of Lord Westbury, as he himself remarked of one of his successors on the woolsack, that 'the monotony of his character was unbroken by a single vice.' The world in

general may be excused for not striking the fair
balance between the merits and failings of one who
neither ostentatiously exhibited his better qualities nor
sought to conceal his defects.   But it may be claimed
that the faults and weaknesses of Lord Westbury
were in reality more than counterbalanced by a
goodness of heart, to which those who had the best
opportunities of judging have borne such forcible
testimony.   He was disliked because he was mis-
understood. Many who had formed prejudices against
him through some exaggerated representation of his
hauteur and bitterness, found these impressions melt
away when they came to know him personally.
'Why, how delightful and charming he is—how kind
in manner!   I always heard he was so different!'
were expressions often repeated to his friends.

The part that he took in promoting the Divorce
Bill first drew down upon him the odium of many
whose orthodoxy was stronger than their charity.
Soon after Lord Campbell was appointed Chancellor,
Sir Richard Bethell (as he then was), in the course of
a railway journey, overheard two passengers in the
same carriage discussing the appointment.   One of
them expressed surprise that the Attorney-General
had not been chosen.   'Oh,' said the other, a lady,
'that will never happen!   The Lord Chancellor is
keeper of the Queen's conscience ; and how could
such a post be given to an atheist like Sir Richard
Bethell ?'

With regard to the acerbity of speech for which

he attained a notoriety that has undeniably prejudiced his claims to favourable remembrance, it
may be observed that his sarcasms, inexcusable as
they might sometimes appear, were spoken usually
in quick irritation at pretentiousness or stupidity ;
they were not written down deliberately, in calmer
moments, like those of many eminent men, including
some of the highest dignitaries of the Church, whose
memoirs have lately been given to the world. Lord
Westbury never descended to coarse invective or
railing accusation. The too caustic wit that made
so many enemies sprang from no root of bitterness
in the heart. He was singularly free from personal
envy or malevolence. 'His hatred of all small
gossip,' writes a friend, 'and how he suppressed it
in his own family, and always checked it in his own
presence, are facts of which I have the clearest
remembrance.' Ever ready to give others their
due, he abhorred the carping criticism and ill-
natured aspersion in which 'the malice of inferiority'
finds its vent. Any expression of this kind strongly
moved him. He had no tolerance whatever for
those whom he styled the ragpickers of society.

At the same time he was characterised by an
extreme sensibility and a certain epicureanism of
the modern type, which seemed out of harmony
with his other qualities. He displayed wonderful
credulity in the matter of any appeal which was not
directed to his intellect. His sympathies and his
vanity were alike easily touched. There was

none of that hardening of the heart which might have been looked for in a man whose intellectual part seemed to assert such absolute predominance. In his later years he went unwillingly to any representation of a distressing character. On seeing Fechter in *Othello* his feelings were so overcome that he retired to the back of the box, and said afterwards that he must never be asked to see a tragedy again. Though he detested cant in every form, 'the still sad music of humanity' found a ready response in his breast. Some of his failings and the great reverse of his life were really to be traced to want of moral courage where his family affection was involved.

With respect to Lord Westbury's extraordinary intellectual gifts, little need be added to what has been already said. In spite of his wide and varied knowledge of all kinds of subjects,—and it may be truly affirmed that no branch of knowledge was either too profound or too trivial to engage his attention and interest,—the structure of his intellect was rather scientific and speculative than practical, or, in its widest sense, political. It has been said of him that he cared for little beyond law and the classics. The law, as it then found exposition in the Courts of Equity, no doubt afforded a congenial area for such a mind. Yet, even in a professional view, there was nothing commonplace about him, and he never sank into a mere lawyer or pedant.

It was Lord Eldon's opinion that a lawyer could

hardly be both learned in his profession and accomplished in political science. The careers of Lords Brougham, Lyndhurst, and Cairns have proved in later times that this rule admits of brilliant exceptions. In Lord Westbury's case, though his mental bent and training were almost wholly technical, the power and breadth of his mind enabled him to defy the limitations which impose themselves on less superior energies. Free from ambition in the popular sense, his intellectual capacity, coupled with the habit of always working up to his highest standard and a consummate self-confidence, gave him pre-eminence in the political world, whenever he chose to assert it. He convinced men by appeals to their sober judgment rather than to considerations of expedience or sentiment. His was an acutely judicial mind, whose cool, intrepid logic, unmoved by prejudice or passion, found appropriate utterance in the clearest diction. It was this rare combination of exactness in thought and speech which gave him his peculiar distinction.

Mr. Gladstone, whose own powers of thought and expression entitle him to speak *ex cathedrâ* on the subject, singles out these attributes for especial recognition :—

'It was subtlety of thought,' he writes, 'accompanied with a power of expressing the most subtle shades of thought, in clear, forcible, and luminous language, which always struck me most among the gifts of Lord Westbury. In this extraordinary power he seemed to me to have but one rival among all the men, lawyers and non-lawyers, of his age. I may be wrong, but the two men whom, in my own mind, I bracketed together were Lord Westbury and Cardinal Newman.

'That I do not pass beyond this single remark will not surprise you when I say that, though I have sat in Cabinet with between sixty and seventy colleagues (if my memory serves me right), there are hardly six of them whose characters I could undertake to sketch in any tolerable satisfactory manner.'

As an advocate he was by common consent unequalled for general excellence by any practitioner in the Equity Courts during the present century, and his success in Parliament as a law officer was scarcely less complete. To his forensic and senatorial powers the following recollections supplied by Lord Moncreiff, the Lord Justice - Clerk of Scotland, afford additional emphatic testimony :—

'My friendship with the late Lord Westbury dates from the year 1853, when we were members of Lord Aberdeen's Government. I had for some years before that time a personal acquaintance with him, arising out of professional engagements in appeals from Scotland at the bar of the House of Lords, and was well aware of his high reputation.

'These Scottish appeals furnish some test of the grasp and versatility of English barristers who are engaged in them; for they have then to deal with terms with which they are not familiar, and sometimes with legal principles which the law of England does not acknowledge. I never met with any member of the English Bar who more completely stood that test, or who more thoroughly succeeded in identifying himself for the time with the surroundings of a different system. I will not say that now and again a good-natured but pungent gibe might not escape him in private, at the expense of Scottish law, or even of his Scottish colleague; but without detracting in the least from his accurate appreciation of the principle involved, or entire loyalty to the cause of his client.

'I had many opportunities, after our House of Commons' intimacy had commenced, of estimating his powers as an advocate. On the whole, I think he combined more varied excellence in every department of the profession than any other I have known in my time. Supremely rapid in apprehension, and wielding with ease and security the principles and precedents which with most are the study of a life, he never allowed quickness to do duty for assiduity. He united, with unusual completeness, intuition and industry.

'He was not, however, a mere lawyer, but one whose mind was stored with a wide range of extensive and varied erudition. His conversation, instructive in itself, left the impression of a reserve of knowledge still undisplayed. He was never

taken at a disadvantage, whatever the theme might
be; and he often lighted up what seemed an
exhausted topic by some fresh and unexpected
source of illustration.

'Of course I can only estimate his professional
eminence from my Scottish point of view; and his
brilliant and unbroken success render it superfluous
to say more on this head.   But I came into closer
relations with him through our political and parliamentary experiences.   He was Solicitor - General
under Lord Aberdeen's Government in 1853, while
I held the office of Lord Advocate.   From that
time forward, for more than eight consecutive
years, we occupied the same bench in the House
of Commons, for the most part as members of
Government, and our companionship was only
severed in 1861 by Sir Richard Bethell's elevation
to the woolsack.

'I look back with unmixed pleasure to my
intercourse with him during that period.   There
is no better opportunity for estimating a man's
character than belonging to the same party, and
meeting him on the same bench in the House of
Commons for eight years together.   Where tastes
are congenial, there is a freemasonry, a spirit of
good fellowship about the position, apart from office,
and apart even from party.   You may politically
abhor, as you are bound to do, the man who sits
opposite to you, and divide earnestly against him;
but when it comes to seeing him there night after

night, for eight years, he becomes, insensibly, part
of your life.   And thus, in the end, come many fast
friendships, made up of materials apparently discordant.   Much more is this so, when the comrades
are also united by community of opinion and official
responsibility.   As it was, I early formed a strong
attachment to Sir Richard Bethell, which ripened
into a lasting friendship.   He had, as every one
knew, peculiarities of manner which detracted from
his general popularity ; but after short acquaintance,
these entirely vanished from my appreciation of him.
I think I saw the man as he really was ; and I came
to find that notwithstanding his caustic manner, and,
when he chose, his acrimonious style (and no one
had a greater command of the contemptuous), he
was essentially a good-natured, warm-hearted man,
who would take an interest in a friend, and liked to
take trouble for him—a quality not so common as it
might be.   When I came to know him well in his
hours of relaxation and leisure, two things in particular struck me in his conversation : the immense
range and accuracy of his knowledge, and the soft-
ness and gentleness of his heart.   As to the first,
his early history and academic distinctions gave
promise of it.   I can understand that success
achieved so early might have fostered self-confidence and self-esteem ; but it indicated also unusual
powers in the acquisition of knowledge, in all its
branches, which he in after life wielded with such
power.   As to the gentleness of his heart, I believe,

it was one main ingredient in his complex character; and that much of his roughness and acerbity was assumed to cover the stirrings of a kindliness which he could not smother, and would not and perhaps ought not to obey. It is not an uncommon phase.

'In the House of Commons, Sir Richard Bethell, whether as Solicitor-General, or as Attorney-General, as he became in 1856, was a tower of strength to the Treasury Bench. He was a dangerous antagonist to fence with, and repelled with ease assaults of that kind, generally with loss to the assailant. It has been said that his elocution, slow and accentuated, was not suited to the House of Commons; but even the critics could not choose but listen. It was so distinct, so clear, a chain so deftly linked, that whether his audience liked it or no, the meaning he wished to convey was fixed on their memory. When he did open his vials of reproof, the drops came out so deliberately, so smoothly, so untinged by passion, that the pangs of the sufferer were intolerably prolonged.

'He did not often take part in the general debates of the House of Commons unless the subject of them fell within his official province; but when he did, he never failed to make an impression. I have in my mind three instances in particular which very favourably illustrated his powers of debate.

'The first of these was the part which he took on the Succession Duty Bill in 1853, while Mr.

Gladstone was Chancellor of the Exchequer in Lord Aberdeen's Administration. Sir Richard Bethell, then Solicitor-General, had entrusted to his hands the task of carrying this Bill through Committee: a duty which he discharged with the most brilliant success. The subject was a very abstruse one, not familiar to ordinary frequenters of the highways of the law, and required for its elucidation the accuracy of a mathematician, the skill of an actuary, as well as the attainments of a jurist. I well remember the admiration, not unmixed with envy in my case, which his masterly grasp of the subject produced on my mind and on the audience which remained to listen to his treatment of a subject sufficiently uninviting in itself. The ease with which he handled the perplexing details of a theme so unusual, left behind an impression of power I have never forgotten.

'The second occasion was four years afterwards, in 1857. The Crimean War had come and gone, Lord Palmerston was Prime Minister, and Mr. Gladstone, for the time, was out of office. The subject in discussion was the English Divorce Bill, of which Sir Richard Bethell had charge in Committee, and of which Mr. Gladstone was a strong opponent. The discussion produced what may without impropriety be called an intellectual duel between Mr. Gladstone and the Attorney-General; and certainly no single combat could have been more exciting or more interesting. It went on for many nights, many legal and social questions being raised on the clauses of the Bill. One night is specially present to my recollection, when Mr. Gladstone made one of the ablest speeches I ever heard from him on the influence of Christianity on the position of women. The wealth and profusion of illustration which he called to his aid commanded the applause of the House. But the Attorney-General was quite equal to the emergency. The audience knew Gladstone's varied attainments, but I doubt if they expected so much versatility from his adversary. As it was—for I heard them both—it was hard to say on which side the advantage lay. A more brilliant passage-of-arms was probably never witnessed in the House.

'The third occasion which I associate with Sir Richard Bethell's name as a debater was the dis-̓ cussion and division on the war with China in July 1857. After a debate which lasted for four nights, the Government of Lord Palmerston was left in a minority on the division, and a dissolution followed. The incident itself, and the causes which led to it, have so utterly vanished from public memory, that it is needless to recall the rights or wrongs of Sir John Bowring and the Chinese lorcha. But at the time the controversy was hot, for the existence of the Government depended on it. The Attorney-General delivered a masterly speech on the second night, which riveted the attention and commanded the applause of the House. The House was not convinced, but the country was, and sent Lord Palmerston a large majority in reply.

'These are only detached instances in a long career of incessant labour and intellectual exertion. I select them because they are typical of oratorical power, and because I was personally present at the fray, and can attest the effect produced. It is more than thirty years since; but the times were full of interest, and it is pleasant to look back to them.

'From March of the next year until the end of 1859 the party were out of office; and although still in Parliament, we did not meet so frequently. In the end of 1859, however, on another change of Government, we resumed our old relations, which terminated, as far as the House of Commons was concerned, by the elevation of Sir Richard Bethell to the woolsack in 1861.

'Our friendship continued, although I missed him sadly from his former haunts. Engrossed as he was, he was never too much so to listen with ready sympathy, and aid with his advice, when I sought his counsel in difficulty. What I look back to, however, with most pleasure were the occasions when the "nationalities," as we called them, were represented under his hospitable roof of Hackwood, on sundry Saturdays to Mondays. It was on these expeditions, of which there were several, that I saw him "in his happier hour." His conversation was simply charming—varied and lively, giving the impression also of a solid background of attainment and of matured thought. These days remain in my memory as bright recollections of the past.

'I need not prolong this slight tribute to the memory of a friend for whom I had a great personal regard, and to whom I am indebted for many acts of kindness. Clouds came before the end, and the Chancellor found himself, from no fault of his own, enveloped by filaments he could not break. That he was entirely untouched by the imputations originally made against him admits of no doubt. It was thought by some that he was not so careful as he should have been to suspect evil where no signs of it were visible, and this formed the ground of the resolution which was ultimately carried in the House of Commons by a majority of 14 votes. From the position in which I stood as a member of the Committee, I had unusual opportunities of forming an opinion; and having read over again the proceedings, I retain the conclusion I expressed in the House of Commons, and which was affirmed by the votes of 163 members of the House, who formed the minority, that in respect of the matters charged against him there was no ground to justify the resolution. But a doubt was sufficient to decide his course of action; and his dignified and manly retirement was worthy of his position and his career.'

Of the painful passage in the life to which Lord

Moncreiff refers enough has been said.   The hope
to which Lord Westbury himself gave such graceful
expression in his farewell speech from the woolsack,
that after an interval calmer thoughts would prevail
and feelings more favourable to himself be entertained, may now be realised.   It has been truly said
that too frequently a solitary misfortune is so
severely visited upon the memory of a public man
as to outweigh and bury in oblivion the fruitful
services of a lifetime.   It may at least be claimed
that the magnanimity with which Lord Westbury
bore the heaviest trial which could be laid on one
who was still in the plenitude of his powers, deserved
the respect of even those who had thought it their
duty to visit him with censure.

On his judicial ability almost unqualified com-
mendation may be bestowed.   We must go back
to Lord Lyndhurst for a superior in the qualities
which command pre-eminence on the bench.   In
knowledge of equity he was perhaps inferior to
Lord Cottenham ; in painstaking assiduity he could
not be compared with Lord Eldon ; but for acuteness of judicial faculty and the fearless elucidation of
legal principles his reputation is unsurpassed.   The
striking passage in the *Orator* of Cicero,[1] which
was a favourite quotation of his, describing the

---

[1] Quid tam difficile quam in plurimorum controversiis dijudi-
candis ab omnibus diligi?   Consequeris tamen ut eos ipsos quos
contra statuas, æquos placatosque dimittas ; itaque officis, ut, cum
gratiæ causâ nihil facias, omnia tamen sint grata quæ facis.

judge who sent away even unsuccessful suitors
contented, suggested rules of conduct which he
habitually observed on the bench.

' He was a remarkable man,' writes Lord
Selborne, 'not unlike, in abilities and character,
and in natural kindliness and generosity too (though
obscured by some defects, due perhaps to the
circumstances of his early life), to Lord Thurlow ;
and he has left behind him a greater reputation,
as a lawyer, than almost any of his contemporaries,
though among them some (as Sir James Knight
Bruce) were equally brilliant, and others (as Sir
George Turner) were more learned and more
accurate.'

But it is in connection with legal reform that
Lord Westbury's fame is best assured. As to the
value of particular amendments which he completed
or proposed, opinions will reasonably differ. The
intense earnestness of his desire to simplify 'the
lawless science of the law, that codeless myriad of
precedent, that wilderness of single instances,'
cannot, however, be denied. He was for ever
harping on the difficulty of extracting pure law
from the precedents by which our modern decisions
are guided. 'Originally,' he declared, 'it was a
barren plain ; now a dense and tangled forest.
What may be deemed analogous no human mind
can foresee or predict—*Cæcis erramus in undis.*' As
for the statute law, it will be admitted that for
the comparative order to which it has been reduced

we are principally indebted to Lord Westbury. The confusion — *rudis indigestaque moles* — which he denounced so persistently has given place under repeated revisions to a systematic compilation of enactments which retain their force. There remains, however, that which he declared was the greatest evil of the whole system—the modification, and in some cases the direct contravention of the statute law by judicial decisions,—an evil which his short tenure of the Chancellorship gave him little opportunity to remedy.

His merit as a law reformer lay quite as much in drawing attention by his lucid exposition to the evils of an existing system, and in urging comprehensive views of the need and practicability of legislation, as in presenting the measures by which, during the ten years of his official position, he sought to effect reforms. Seldom is a public man permitted to complete the great work of which he has been the originator. Lord Westbury gradually, though unwillingly, submitted to the inevitable conclusion that he must content himself with having commenced reforms, and leave a future generation to complete them. Of all reforms those connected with purely legal matters are the most difficult to effect. The prejudices of ignorance and self-interest exhibit greater tenacity on technical subjects which do not appeal to the popular intelligence or sentiment. And the financial difficulties which impede so many legislative proposals are less easily superable when the weight of public opinion does not support a Minister's demand on the Treasury.

He gave, however, an impulse to law reform at a time when it was especially needed, and when the subject was less popular than it afterwards became, and he exhibited courage and foresight in accomplishing changes which other men would have liked but did not dare to attempt. Essentially a civilian, he boldly advocated the application to everyday life of the principles of the civil law, making use of all kinds of pressure to bring about reforms in that direction. He would have everything reduced to written rules, so as to make obligations certain. To break down the barrier of precedent and establish a rigid system of abstract rules to which fresh cases might be referred as they arose, without appealing to the past, was his unceasing desire.

The exactions of a public life of extraordinary labour left little opportunity for literary composition; and though he wrote with grace and vigour, his tongue was always readier than his pen. But his wide acquaintance, constantly renewed and extended, with the masterpieces of the old-world literature, and the best productions of modern writers, gave him a remarkably well-stored mind, and his powers of memory enabled him to make good use of his varied knowledge. His recollection of classical passages was especially noticeable. On one occasion, when the late Sir Henry Holland, for whom he had a great admiration, and in whose society he took much

pleasure, was dining at Lancaster Gate, Lord Westbury referred to the quotation on the title-page of
his guest's published *Recollections*.   Sir Henry,
taken unawares, tried to avoid a direct answer, and
at last, amid general laughter, had to confess that
he could not at the moment recall his own quotation.
But he pressed Lord Westbury to repeat it, which
he did.   It was, ' *hoc est vivere bis, vita posse priore
frui* '—a maxim which applied equally to both.

Though a first - rate classical scholar, he was,
in the colloquial command of modern languages,
like most of his countrymen, as he often lamented,
somewhat deficient.   But he read several languages
with ease, and his grammatical knowledge was
extensive and accurate.   He delighted in music
of all kinds, and for a season or two had his own
box at the opera.   But though fond of theatricals,
he seldom went to a theatre.

The durability of the impressions left by his
early training was a strongly-marked characteristic.
He loved to revisit the scenes and recall the memories
of his boyhood.   In accordance with his written wish
a tablet was after his death placed in the ante-chapel
at Wadham, recording the principal events of his
life, and stating that he dated all his prosperity from
the event of his having become a scholar of the
College.

Another marked feature was his unfailing delight
in a country life.   The older he grew the more
pleasure did he derive from it.   Though fate had

ordained for him a career of incessant action, he
seemed as if he would have preferred a life of contemplation and comparative solitude. He avoided,
as far as possible, 'the crowd, the hum, the shock of
men.' He cared little for society beyond that of his
own circle of relations and friends. It was an effort
to him to dine out. He often declared that an
evening's reading with his own children, or strolling
in the gardens or by the seashore, was worth more
to him than all the pleasures of society. ' I repeople
my mind with Nature,' he used to say. He was
perfectly happy when sitting with a party of children
fishing from a punt or from the bank, with a volume
of Wordsworth or Southey in his pocket to be read
between the bites.

He revelled in the character of a country gentleman, and had quite a Cincinnatus-like interest in
farming. When Solicitor-General, he took from
the Prince Consort a small place called King's Ride
at Sunninghill, the chief attraction of which was the
possession of some adjoining land available for farm
purposes, and he never after lost his pleasure in
agricultural pursuits. Many of his letters, evidently
written during the hearing of appeals in the House
of Lords, are entirely occupied with specific instructions as to the breeding and rearing of horses, cattle,
and pigs, haymaking and dairy operations. There
is scarcely a home-letter that does not contain
inquiries as to the coming crops, the stock, and the
state of the game on the various beats, or sug-

gestions as to the best mode of keeping down the
rabbits, or preventing the ravages of vermin.   He
frequently discusses the qualifications and duties of
keepers, and the points of dogs.   In the treatment
of every kind of equine or canine complaint he considered himself αὐτάρκης.   He would even vaccinate
with his own hand successive litters of puppies for
distemper.

A few words may be added as to his personal
habits.   They were very simple.   He was extremely
moderate in the use of stimulants, and did not indulge
in tobacco till he was more than sixty, when he
became very fond of smoking cigarettes, from which
he thought he derived some benefit.   He was much
in favour of gymnastic exercises, and was in the
habit of using dumb-bells both before and after a
cold morning bath.   Late in life, his stout, strong
figure, florid complexion, and white hair, gave him
the hale appearance of one whose whole attention
was devoted to outdoor pursuits.   In his love of
rowing, swimming, shooting, and every kind of
sport, he was a thorough Englishman.   At one time
he took up archery, and made good scores when in
practice.   A game of billiards was his favourite
indoor amusement.

He used to accuse himself, especially in his last
two or three years, of idleness, but the record of the
life is a sufficient denial of the charge.   Relying too
much on a strength which he had never spared, he
continued to devote himself to the public service

long after the period when he might fairly have claimed immunity from active work.

During the later period of comparative leisure, in the summer term, 'cum formosissimus annus,' Lord Westbury paid several visits to Oxford, where he was the guest of the Master of Balliol. His youngest son, Walter, had received his University education at Balliol College. Some account of these visits has been given by the Master in the following letter, addressed, at her request, to Mrs. Adamson Parker, who accompanied her father on his expeditions to Oxford. Professor Jowett's letter supplies also an interesting sketch, which will form an appropriate ending to this biography.

'Dear Mrs. Parker—You ask me to tell you what I remember of Lord Westbury. As you are aware, it was only during the last three or four years of his life that I had the pleasure of knowing him, but during that time I saw a good deal of him. Each summer he paid me a short visit at Oxford, and I used to visit him at Hinton in the winter. Those visits, at one of which I met the late Mr. Bagehot, are among the pleasantest recollections of my life. Your father was most gracious and attentive to his guests; he never appeared to greater advantage than in his own house.

'First in my remembrances of him comes a great act of kindness which he sought to do me at a time when I was personally unknown to him. This

arose out of the long-forgotten troubles of the Greek
Professorship. It was difficult to find an endowment for the Chair. He was at that time Lord
Chancellor, and he proposed to meet the difficulty
by annexing to the Professorship a canonry in the
Chancellor's gift. He introduced a Bill into the
House of Lords having this object. The Bill was
rejected, rightly in my judgment, because it would
have limited the appointment to a clergyman. But
I shall always feel grateful for this singular act of
kindness, which was unsolicited by me ; neither at
the time nor afterwards had I any communication
with him on the subject.

'I made his acquaintance some years later on
the occasion of a dinner which was given by my old
friends and pupils in 1871 at the Albion Tavern to
celebrate my election as Master of Balliol. To this
dinner he expressed a wish to come. The late
Dean Stanley was in the chair. The speech which
your father made on that occasion, in returning
thanks for the distinguished strangers, will never be
forgotten by those who heard it. There were no
reporters present, and I fear that I can only give
from memory a very imperfect idea of it. The
grave and earnest and pathetic tones of the speaker
are still ringing in my ears. But this seriousness,
which was never laid aside, was only the veil of as
much fun and mischief as could well be concentrated
in a speech of twenty minutes' duration. He began
by disclaiming the honour which had fallen upon so

unworthy an individual, at a moment's notice, of replying on behalf of such eminent persons. He proceeded to rally the Dean of Westminster and myself on the advantages which he would have enjoyed in early life had he had the good fortune to be the pupil of either of us. "How much better and wiser a man he would have been, how many errors he would have escaped, how different would have been his retrospect of life. In his own days the University was like a great ship, left high and dry upon the shore, which marked the place where the waters of knowledge had once flowed. But now, by the efforts of his two distinguished friends, the stream had attained a level, *lower indeed, but not much lower*, than in other places." He then proceeded to make hits at some of the principal persons who were present. He referred to a noble lord, a late colleague of his, who had been engaged in reforming the army. "He will have a hundred regiments and a hundred thousand men in fighting order by the end of the year—*as he says*." There was "another noble lord, a votary of the Muses, who had passed his life in their sweet companionship. He had laughed and sorrowed with them, he had sported with them by the Castalian spring, he had done everything but *bathe* with them." He gave similar sketches of some others. There was no trace of a smile on the speaker's own face, which preserved a sort of impassive sadness throughout, while laughter was "shaking the sides" of the whole company. The scene was such as would have made Mrs. Quickly say, " Lord ! how he keeps his countenance !" He left the table after repeating to me a Greek epigram attributed to Plato and addressed by him to his beloved Aster, in which the writer, punning on the name, expresses a wish that he too might be a star and look down from heaven on his friend.

'Another occasion on which Lord Westbury similarly distinguished himself was a dinner-party at Balliol College, where he met his old friend Mr. Christie, the celebrated conveyancer. There were present also the Dean of Westminster and Lady Augusta Stanley, Professor Bonamy Price, Professor Palgrave, Professor and Mrs. Campbell, and several others whose names I have forgotten. Mr. Christie had been a member of Balliol, and his memory of Oxford went back farther than any person's living at that time. He liked to speak of Bishop Parsons, a former Master, whom he had then known, and to whom he attributed the first success of the College ; and of the generous and noble character of Sir William Hamilton, who, together with J. G. Lockhart, had been his youthful contemporary. The two old friends soon began to poke fun at one another from opposite sides of the dinner-table. After dinner Lord Westbury, in a deep voice and in his most impressive manner, recited some noble stanzas of *Childe Harold* (21st to 24th of the 4th Canto), commencing—

'" Existence may be borne, and the deep root
   Of life and sufferance make its firm abode
   In bare and desolated bosoms : mute
   The camel labours with the heaviest load,
   And the wolf dies in silence,—not bestow'd
   In vain should such example be ; if they,
   Things of ignoble or of savage mood,
   Endure and shrink not, we of nobler clay
May temper it to bear,—it is but for a day."

And then, addressing the company, he asked
triumphantly what passage could compare with this
in any living poet, or rather in one living poet, to
whom he showed his dislike by giving his name a
feminine termination. I think that the challenge
might have been taken up, but none of us had ready
in our memories the passage to be compared. He
then proceeded to discourse on some eminent legal
persons not now living. There was a celebrated
judge who had gained a rather unenviable reputation
for his love of legal technicalities ; of him he said,
"Alexander the coppersmith did us much evil."
There was another eminent lawyer, whom he eulogised, not for his law but for his domestic virtues.
His attachment to his wife was beyond all
praise. I must not tell to which of the judges he
applied the line of Virgil, "Qui Bavium non odit,
amet tua carmina, Maevi." And so the evening
passed in great hilarity and enjoyment. It is impossible, fourteen years afterwards, to remember the
greater part of what was said—the pauses, the tones
of voice, the light hits passed from one to another,

the fun, sometimes fast and furious, elude the attempt to describe them. The recollection of that evening has remained in the memory of several of those who were present. The next morning at breakfast Lord Westbury expressed his approval of the excellent conversation which we had had on the preceding evening (in which, indeed, he himself had borne the greater part). He was reminded of a parallel passage in Boswell's *Life of Johnson*, where Boswell says, " I found him very proud of his conversational prowess."—"Sir," he said, "we had a good talk last night." Boswell—"Yes, sir; you tossed and gored several people."

'His visits to Oxford were a great pleasure to us, and I believe they were pleasant to himself, for they reminded him of the days of his youth, which he was fond of describing. He came up to Oxford in a jacket, and at the age of fourteen gained a scholarship at Wadham College. The anxious father asked the College tutor (the late Dr. Symons) what he could do for him. The answer was, " I think that we must first of all get him a tail-coat." After he was nineteen, as he told me with an honest pride, he had never cost his father anything. He was very kind in encouraging undergraduates who were going to the Bar. A wicked piece of advice, coming from him with an especial weight, which he inculcated on them was, "never to give in to a judge." He would get a knot of them round him and tell them that his own success in life had been

entirely due to the happy manner in which he
had construed a passage of Pindar in the Oxford
schools. He had thus attracted the attention of
the examiner, Dr. Gilbert, afterwards the Principal
of Brasenose, who insisted on his being employed
as junior counsel in a great Brasenose suit. The
senior counsel engaged were in favour of compromise, which he resisted, and won the suit. He was
never afterwards in want of a brief. I asked him
who was the best judge before whom he had pleaded,
and he said without hesitation Lord Lyndhurst.
Of the counsel who had pleaded before himself he
especially commended Sir Horace Davey, who, he
said, "in an argument is as clear as crystal." He
was a good scholar, and fond of drawing illustrations
from the classics. Polybius was a favourite author
with him, and he delighted to expatiate on him.
I remember his explaining at dinner, with great
lucidity and I think correctly, a difficult passage of
Thucydides. There is a chorus of Sophocles in
which a simple maiden watches the contest between
Hercules and the Centaur, and when the struggle
is over leaves her father's house and meekly follows
the conqueror, like "the lonely heifer." This tale,
adorned with various illustrations, he converted into
an allegory of a struggle between two great railway
companies for his own poor services, he, like the
simple maiden, meekly following and blindly obeying
the behests of one or other of the giants.

  'He had a singular talent for improvisation,

which he sometimes practised, not with any interested object, but simply to amuse himself and others. I made a passing allusion to a celebrated phrase invented by him, which may almost be said to have become a part of the language—" What you are pleased, sir, to call your mind." The expression is believed to have been originally used by him to a solicitor, who, after hearing Lord Westbury's opinion, ventured to say that " he had turned the matter over in his mind, and thought that something might be said on the other side ;" to which he replied, " Then, sir, you will turn it over once more in what you are *pleased to call* your mind." He assured me that this was one of the wicked inventions which the world had devised against himself, and which "had done him so much harm." The fact was that the "poor fellow was really mad ;" and in proof of this he narrated a circumstantial tale which he appeared to have invented on the spur of the moment. He would not allow himself to be credited with one of the best things which he ever said. It seemed to me that he did not intend this story to be taken seriously, and I have been told by one who had questioned him on the subject that he had really forgotten the origin of the famous phrase. But I am not certain of this, for his mind was so plastic, and he represented things to himself and others in so graphic a manner, that he may not have known at the moment whether he was feigning or not.

'I had many interesting conversations with him

at Hinton. On one occasion he gave me, in the most lucid language, an account of the growth of the English Law Courts. He had a great dislike of the pedantic school of lawyers ; these were the class of men who "had done us much evil." He was one of those who would have made common sense predominate over law. But though averse to the practice of legal subtleties, he had an extremely subtle intellect himself; and his greatness as a lawyer has been acknowledged by some of the most eminent of them. The late Sir George Jessel, who did full justice to his legal power, described him to me as "a man of genius who had gone to the Bar."

' He was not at all irreligious or free-thinking in his conversation, as has been sometimes supposed. He told me that until theological questions came before the Courts he had believed what was ordinarily believed by members of the Church of England. But when he began to examine for himself, he was surprised to find how slender was the foundation of many statements which were confidently propounded by theologians. I remember his giving an admirable discourse one morning at breakfast on the possibility of a rational religion. He was not always quite in good humour with the Church of England. On another occasion he said, " You cut off the head of one beast, the Church of Rome, and immediately the head of another beast, the Church of England, makes its appearance." A High Church young lady, who was sitting at the other end of the breakfast-table, gave a scream of horror at this rather unceremonious language. He said to her placidly, " I am speaking, my dear, the language of prophecy."

'The gentleness and apparent unconsciousness with which he uttered his most satirical sayings gave them a peculiar flavour. The verse of Scripture might have been applied to him, " His words are smoother than butter, yet be they very swords." They were like the precious balms that break the head. He seemed to study how to express himself in such a manner as would draw attention to the substance only of what he was saying. This was his way of rendering his words effective. The clearness and precision of his language were remarkable ; it was a lesson in elocution to converse with him. Like Dr. Johnson, he always studied to say everything as well as he could. There is a story of an electioneering agent who, when they were going about canvassing, complimented him on his gift of saying the right thing in the best manner, and he replied, " The reason is that from my earliest youth I have always endeavoured to frame my language on the model of the Old Testament." Numerous anecdotes about him have gone the round of society, some of them genuine, others mere parodies which grew in the hands of the teller, for he had many imitators and was much talked about, and his manner and the tones of his voice were so distinct that they easily

lent themselves to mimicry. He was a most amusing companion, always ready for conversation in
society, delighting in humorous sallies, and never
without an answer to any one who attacked him.
His memory was extraordinary ; on one occasion at
an Oxford Commemoration he heard a recitation of
the Prize Poems, and afterwards, meeting casually
the youthful author of the Latin verse composition,
he astonished him by reciting a considerable number
of his verses, which he praised as being the best in
the poem.

' I do not pretend to have fathomed his rather
inscrutable character ; he seemed to be made up of
opposite qualities. He would say the bitterest
things, and yet to some of his friends he appeared
to be one of the kindest of men. His rasping
tongue aroused many enmities, and the witty
attacks which he made on others were sometimes
revenged by attacks of another kind directed
against himself. One who knew him more than
seventy years ago has told me that he had in
early life the same sedate and imposing manner
which was characteristic of him in later years. He
had always cultivated self-control ; it was the mask
of a too great sensitiveness and weakness which he
perceived in his own character. Notwithstanding
his great experience of life, he was childishly
ignorant of human nature. There were some other
traits which were not easily explained in him. He
was very industrious himself, and a great enemy to

idleness in others ; but he was wanting in force of character and continuous purpose. It would sometimes seem as if the troubles of his childhood and early life, which he fancifully exaggerated, had weighed too deeply on his mind, and that he determined from the first to be master of himself and of the world. The public neither liked nor understood him, and the temper of his mind led him to defy rather than to conciliate them. Upon those of his contemporaries who knew him well he left the impression that he was a great man, who, leading a mixed and rather troubled life, and in spite of some waywardness and vanity, nevertheless rendered many eminent services to his country.—I remain, dear Mrs. Parker, yours very truly,   B. JOWETT.'

No one who has given impartial consideration to the history of Lord Westbury's career will, it is believed, dissent from the conclusion, as to the value of his public services, which is expressed in the last sentence of this letter. The work and influence of Lord Westbury remain, and have secured for his name an honourable pre-eminence in the annals of our law.

INDEX